# DAUGHTERS OF DARKNESS

## Sally Spencer

**SEVERN
HOUSE**

First world edition published 2020
in Great Britain and the USA by
SEVERN HOUSE PUBLISHERS LTD of
Eardley House, 4 Uxbridge Street, London W8 7SY.
Trade paperback edition first published
in Great Britain and the USA 2021 by
Severn House, an imprint of Canongate Books Ltd,
14 High Street, Edinburgh EH1 1TE.

British Library Cataloguing in Publication Data
A CIP catalogue record for this title is available from the British Library.


ISBN-13: 978-0-7278-8949-2 (cased)
ISBN-13: 978-1-78029-716-3 (trade paper)
ISBN-13: 978-1-4483-0437-0 (e-book)

Typeset by Palimpsest Book Production Ltd.,
Falkirk, Stirlingshire, Scotland.

# DAUGHTERS OF DARKNESS

# PROLOGUE

*13th April, 1972*

S he had never imagined there were such things as buses with only one deck, but that was what this one had.

And that wasn't the only way in which it was strange – the entrance was in totally the wrong place, too. On London's big red double-deckers, it was at the back, which was just where you'd expect it to be, but this green single-decker had a door at the front. It was very disconcerting to discover that even such an ordinary thing as a bus could be so different from the ones she was used to, but she'd come this far, and she was not about to lose her nerve now.

She climbed the steps of the bus, and – avoiding looking at the driver – turned left once she reached the top.

'Oy!' the driver called after her. 'Just a minute! Where do you think you're going?'

She felt her heart sink. She had been so very, very careful – had taken as many precautions as she could – and yet *they* were on to her almost as soon as she'd got off the train.

Well, they would not take her back without a struggle. She would bite and kick and gouge. She would not stop even if they started beating her with clubs – even if they brought in the dreaded electric shock machine – because she was not going to be turned back now.

'I said, where do you think you're going?' the driver repeated.

Perhaps she could bluff it out, she decided.

'I'm going to take a seat further down the bus,' she said.

'Oh no, you're not – leastways, you're not until you've paid your fare,' the driver countered.

'I will pay my fare,' she said, with all the icy dignity she could summon. 'I have every intention of paying my fare. But I will not give it to you – I will pay the conductor.'

The driver chuckled, as if he'd suddenly realized she was not the problem that he'd thought she was going to be.

'You'll pay the conductor, will you?' he asked. 'Well, sweetheart, it's a long time since we've had conductors working on the country routes. A long time! Where have you been living for the last ten years? In a cave, was it?'

No, she thought, not in a cave.

In something far worse!

And for much longer than ten years!

'So I pay you, do I?' she asked, trying to sound as if she'd just understood that she'd made a silly mistake, but really did want to be co-operative.

'Now you're catching on,' the driver agreed.

She returned to the front of the bus, and took out the purse they'd given to her to make her feel normal.

'How much is it?' she asked.

'That all depends on where you're going,' the driver told her.

For a second, she went into a complete panic, as she realized she had forgotten what the nice man on the railway station had told her. Then, mercifully, it came back to her.

'It's a place called Crocksworth Manor,' she said.

'You know how to get there, do you?' the driver asked, and when it became obvious she had no idea what he was talking about, he added, 'I mean, when you get off the bus?'

She thought about lying, in case admitting her ignorance sounded suspicious, but if she didn't admit it she wouldn't know where to go, so she said, 'I'm not really very sure.'

'Then you're lucky to have me as your driver, because I was brought up near there,' he said, and he sounded quite friendly now. 'Most of the other drivers wouldn't have a clue where it was.'

She didn't know what to say. She had no idea how to deal with people like this bus driver.

Fortunately, he didn't seem to require her to speak.

'It will involve you doing some walking, because the manor isn't on the bus route,' he said. 'There's not even a bus stop anywhere close to the main gate, but I think that, seeing as it's you, and we've become such good friends' – he winked at her – 'we can make an unauthorized stop.'

'Thank you,' she said.

'Think nothing of it,' the driver said, 'but you're still going to need to pay your fare.'

'Of course,' she replied, fumbling in the purse.

She took a seat halfway down the bus, and examined the change the driver had given her. When she'd set out that morning, she'd thought she had enough money to last for days – possibly even weeks – but everything so far had turned out to be much more expensive than she'd ever imagined it would be, and she was almost out of cash already.

The bus left Oxford and was soon deep in the countryside. It passed through small villages where a post office and a pub were the sum total of the facilities, and for much of the time the bus and its passengers were surrounded by fields.

She was a town girl who had never been into the countryside before – not even once – and it was as strange to her as another planet might have been to most other people. It frightened her because she did not know the rules – did not understand how it worked – and such information was vital to someone about to do something as important as she was.

Suddenly and unexpectedly, the bus stopped in the middle of this alien landscape.

'Here we are then, love,' the driver called back to her.

'What? I'm not sure what you mean.'

'You still want to go to Crocksworth Manor, don't you?'

'Yes.'

'Well, this is as close as I get,' the driver explained. 'Do you see that gate by the side of the lane?'

'Yes.'

'You go through that and keep walking for about three quarters of a mile. You can't miss it – because there's nothing else there.'

The lane was little more than a track – a rutted clay canyon between two tall hedgerows – and walking down it frightened her, as almost everything that had happened that day had frightened her.

But it did not deter her – not for a second – because this was the most important thing she had ever done – or ever would do.

She thought of all those years that had been stolen from her – wasted years, when she'd been barely alive. She could not get any of them back, whatever she did now, but at least it might be possible to get a little satisfaction – to see a little justice done.

She could see the manor house looming up in the distance. The roof seemed to have a vast collection of chimney pots, and at each end of that roof there was a large dormer window.

'It's like a chateau,' she said with awe.

She'd never seen a chateau in real life, of course, but once – and only once – she'd been to the cinema, and she'd seen one then.

The film had been called *The Scarlet Pimpernel*, and she'd gone with Mrs Clarke, a neighbour, who'd seen, first-hand, the kind of wretched life she lived, and had taken pity on her.

The film was set at the time of the French Revolution, and was about an English gentleman called Sir Percy Blakeney, who went across the Channel to rescue French aristocrats from the revolutionaries.

She had sat there in the darkness and watched as the noblemen and noblewomen were led up the steps to the guillotine, while the mob below them howled. She knew that you were supposed to be on the side of the aristocrats, but she just wasn't, and as the wicked blade came down to separate their heads from their bodies, it was all she could do to stop herself applauding.

Why shouldn't they be executed? she had asked herself. They owned nearly everything, but they had still tried to take from the poor what little *they* had – and what was happening to them now, they had brought on themselves.

She had almost reached the manor. She wished she had brought a knife with her in case she needed it, but that didn't really matter, because if a sharp blade was required, she was sure she would find one inside.

# PART ONE
## Monday 27th October, 1975

# ONE

I am sitting in my office on the upper story of a two-storey building at the unfashionable end of the Iffley Road, awaiting the arrival of a potential client. Over the phone, she said her name was Julia Pemberton, but when I asked her reason for seeking an appointment with Oxford's only redheaded private investigator with an Upper Second in English Literature (I didn't *really* say all that, of course) she was distinctly cagey. I suppose I could have insisted on knowing exactly why she wanted to see me before agreeing to the meeting, thus ensuring that she was not wasting my time. I'm sure there are many private investigators who would have done just that. But time is something I seem to have an abundance of (money is what I lack!) and I didn't want to put her off when she might just be bringing me a lucrative piece of work.

I hear the street doorbell ring, but I don't move. I have an arrangement with Gloria, the secretary at the exotic rubber goods company downstairs. She answers the door, and directs the visitor upstairs when appropriate, and I slip her a couple of pounds when I've got them.

I hear the staccato click-click-click of Gloria's stiletto-heeled shoes as she crosses the corridor, then her screeching voice announcing, 'She's at the top of the stairs. You can't miss her.'

People dream of winning big on the football pools so they can buy sports cars and villas in Spain, where they can sit drinking champagne from glass slippers as the sun gently sinks behind the hills. If I won the pools, I'd hire a personal secretary with a soft voice and sensible shoes.

I make it a habit of listening to the prospective clients' footsteps as they climb the stairs, because often the way they handle the stairs can give me some idea of what to expect.

Julia does not take the stairs at a rush (as if wanting to reach the top before losing her nerve) nor at a slow pull (thus temporarily postponing the inevitable). Instead, her steps suggest both competence and confidence.

She stops as she reaches the door. It is, in my opinion, a door worth studying. The upper half is frosted glass and engraved in that glass (at great expense) are the words:

Jennifer Redhead
Private Investigator

It is undoubtedly the most impressive thing about the whole office.

She knocks.

'Enter!' I say (because I think it sounds a little more impressive than plain, 'Come in.')

She is a good-looking brunette woman in her early to mid-thirties. She is wearing a conservative – but stylish – blue skirt and jacket, which don't have even the merest whiff of a chain store about them. In her left hand she holds an expensive handbag, in her right an untipped cigarette.

She enters the office, we identify ourselves (it turns out we are both who we are supposed to be), and she accepts my invitation to sit down opposite me.

She looks down at the desk. 'Do you have an ashtray?' she asks.

I open my drawer, take out my ancient Souvenir of Blackpool ashtray – pictures of the Tower, the South Pier, the Pleasure Beach, all the usual sights – and slide it across to her. Most people, I've observed, will examine the ashtray you've supplied, as if it will give them some insight into your character, but apart from registering its location, she hardly gives it a glance. Instead, she takes a packet of American Pall Mall out of her handbag and extracts a single cigarette, which she lights from the butt of the one she's already smoking, then she stubs the original one out on Blackpool beach.

'I would have offered you a coffin nail, but since you had to reach in your drawer for an ashtray, I assume you don't smoke,' she says.

She, on the other hand, seems to have a real habit, although I see no evidence of yellow nicotine stains on her fingers. What I do see, however, is that her nails, while short, are beautifully manicured.

The picture I have built up so far is that she is someone who takes a real pride in her appearance, and that whatever job she has is well paid, and probably involves working with Americans or in America itself. It is also probable that her work involves using her hands, but not in a hard-labour, pan-scrubber way, so maybe she is a doctor or a successful dentist.

She leans back as far as her chair will allow her to – which is novel enough to be almost shocking. What my potential clients usually do is hunch forward, as if they're either about to make a confession (and sometimes they are) or else reveal a deep hidden secret (and they do that, too).

'How can I help you?' I ask, and I'm thinking that since she doesn't look the type to go to a private investigator to find her missing cat, she probably wants me to dig up dirt on a troublesome neighbour or some rival at work.

'I would like you to find out who killed my mother,' she says, calmly and evenly.

I don't immediately respond, but that's not because I'm struck dumb – we hard-bitten, mean-street-pounding gumshoes are almost *never* struck dumb. Rather, I pause because I need to fully assess what is – you must admit – a rather melodramatic statement.

Is she winding me up, or being serious?

If she's winding me up, she can bugger off right now, because my work – as trivial as it might seem to some people – matters to me, and is the one thing I never joke about.

But what if she's being serious? That could be a problem, because people who are being serious tend not to take it well when they're turned down. Mostly they do no more than shout and scream – which I'd rather avoid – but sometimes they actually throw things, and my office is far too small for that kind of grand gesture. Besides, I've grown quite fond of my souvenir ashtray.

She is still waiting for a response, so whether I like it or not, I have to say something.

'I don't investigate murders,' I tell her, still watching for her reaction. 'That's a job for the police.'

She doesn't take it badly at all. In fact, she gives me a knowing smile, as if that was just what she'd been expecting me to say.

'The police!' she repeats, with just a hint of scorn. 'The police have pretty much given up on ever finding the killer.'

I sigh – partly because I feel genuine exasperation, and partly to signal to her that if she didn't like what I've just said, she's going to like what I'm *about to say* even less.

'If you'll forgive me, dismissing the police like that is a typical layman's reaction—' I begin.

'Lay*woman's*,' she interrupts.

'Laywoman's,' I agree. 'Yours is a typical laywoman's reaction. It may seem to you, looking in at the police from the outside, that they've given up but, though you're probably not aware of it, I've been on the inside myself and—'

'I'm *well* aware of it,' she interrupts again. 'You were a police officer for six years. You were forced to resign because you were on the verge of proving that a certain chief superintendent – whose name, I believe, was Dunn – was as dirty as a toilet brush in a dysentery outbreak.'

The way it's supposed to work in the gumshoe–client scenario is that the *gumshoe* studies the *client's* reaction for clues. But guess what: here, it's working the other way around as well. That's why she's leaning back in her chair – so she can study my face in cinemascope!

'I'm supposed to be shocked, aren't I?' I say.

'Yes,' she agrees. 'And are you?'

'Yes, I am,' I reply, because it would be pointless to pretend I'm not. 'But the question isn't really how you found out about me – it's why you would want to use it to shock me?'

She frowns, but says nothing.

'It's not the response you were expecting, is it?' I continue, scoring my first point on the comeback trail.

'No, it isn't,' she admits.

'What you thought I would be bound to ask you was how you knew so much about my chequered career?'

'Well, yes,' she says, lamely.

'But it's so obvious where your information came from – you got it from DCI Macintosh.'

This is a shot in the dark – but since Macintosh is one of the few people who know my whole story, it's a *calculated* shot – and from the expression on her face, it seems that I'm right on target.

'Why did you want to shock me?' I repeat.

'Because I needed to do something to knock you off balance before you started patronizing me.'

'And what exactly do you mean by that?' I ask.

'"The police are very busy people",' she replies in a voice which is intended to be a parody of mine and – in all honesty – comes a little too close for comfort. '"I'm sure they've done all they can to find your mummy's killer".'

'I never said that,' I protest, but my heart isn't really in it, because I know the words lack conviction.

'No, you didn't exactly say it,' she agrees, 'but if I'd let you run on, you'd have ended up saying something *just* like that.'

It's a fair cop – I wouldn't have used the tone, but the content would have run along those lines.

'I am a senior lecturer in the University of Cambridge Physics Department, and a visiting professor at the Massachusetts Institute of Technology,' she says. 'I advise both the British government and the North Atlantic Treaty Organization. I am an expert in my field to such an extent that much of my work is highly classified . . .' She pauses. 'And you – I have established through careful inquiry – are an expert in your field. I need your help . . .'

And here there is a slight tremble in her voice – the first indication that she is not completely in control.

'. . . but I don't need it at *any* price. If you can't respect me as a junior partner, then we'd probably better call it a day.'

The words have been carefully thought out, and are carefully delivered. She knows that I would never agree to her being an equal partner, but if we settle on the term *junior* partner, we can both interpret it in the way we each feel most comfortable with.

And then I realize what she's really done – that in getting me to think about how we might work together, she's made me half-acknowledge that I might take the case.

'If they found out I was investigating an unsolved murder, the police would have my guts for garters,' I say.

'No, they wouldn't,' she replies, with a confidence that I'm starting to find irritating.

'That's what they've told you, is it?' I say. 'They've said it would be all right for me to go blundering about in their case?'

'Is that sarcasm?' she asks me – when she bloody well already knows that it is.

'Yes,' I reply. 'It *is* sarcasm. It comes from the Greek, you know – and it means to tear the flesh.'

Actually, I'm suddenly feeling rather badly about it, because we both know that sarcasm is the lowest form of wit, and therefore a poor response from someone with a 2:1 in literature from Oxford University. Yet at the same time, there's a part of me that thinks I have every right to go in low and dirty, because – when all's said and done – the bloody woman has provoked me.

'I haven't police permission,' she admits. 'Not *per se*. But DCI Macintosh is willing to give it his unofficial blessing – and far from thinking you'll go blundering about, he seems to believe that there's just a slim chance that you'll find out something they missed . . .' She pauses. 'He appears to have a very high opinion of your detecting skills.'

That would come from us having worked together on what my own personal Dr Watson (if such a character existed) would probably have called the Strange Case of the Shivering Turn.

'How do you know Ken Macintosh?' I ask.

'He's a family friend.'

Macintosh is from Scotland, but has been based in Oxford for over twenty years. He used to have thick black hair, and a bushy beard which was reputed to be the home of a family of crows. These days, he keeps the beard trimmed and the hair is prematurely white, which, he claims, is proof positive that he's been doing his job properly.

'If Ken Macintosh is an old family friend, then you must have lived in Oxford once,' I say.

'We did. My father still does.'

I run through the names of people murdered in Oxford in recent years. It doesn't take long, because in this city of 150,000 people, two murders in a year are regarded as something of a bumper crop.

No one called Pemberton comes to mind, so though she's almost convinced me of her sincerity by invoking the name of DCI Macintosh, it's starting to look as if she was taking the piss after all.

'Listen, Miss Pemberton . . .' I begin.

'Mrs Pemberton,' she corrects me. She laughs – awkwardly, and with clear signs of embarrassment. 'You'd think a feminist like me would have insisted on keeping her maiden name after she got married, wouldn't you? But James was most insistent, and he looked so little-boy-hurt when I said I wouldn't be taking his name that eventually I gave way. I should have known then that the marriage wasn't going to last.'

'What *was* your maiden name, Mrs Pemberton?' I ask, trying not to show my impatience.

'What? Oh, sorry, it's Stockton.'

Stockton? Stockton . . .

Oh my God!

'Your mother was Dr Grace Stockton?'

'Yes, that's right.'

I remember, as an undergraduate studying western mythology, that I read a couple of her papers on the myths of Papua New Guinea to widen my perspective. And I remember becoming angry – some might even say almost bitter – when I realized that however much I worked, and tried and strained, I would never be as clever as the woman who had written those papers.

Happy days!

So how long is it since her body (or most of it, anyway) was discovered in the woods?

Two years?

Three?

Certainly no more than that.

It created a sensation at the time, because distinguished academics rarely get murdered, and even more rarely are decapitated.

For a moment, I forget who I'm speaking to, and am about to ask her if the head ever turned up, then I do a verbal swerve and ask her if her father is Dr Derek Stockton, Professor of Comparative Religion at St Luke's College.

'Yes, he is,' she says.

'St Luke's is where I read my degree,' I tell her.

'I know,' she replies.

And suddenly this is all starting to feel rather too close for comfort.

'No, they didn't,' she says, completely out of the blue.

No, they didn't?

'I'm not sure I understand,' I confess.

'When you asked me if my father was Derek Stockton, what you *really* wanted to ask was another question entirely.'

I say nothing.

'And what was that question?' she persists.

We sit there in silence for maybe thirty seconds, and then – because this is getting ridiculous – I say, 'I was wondering if they ever found your mother's head?'

'No,' she says, 'they didn't.'

There are three good reasons why I shouldn't take on this case.

The first is that even if the police are willing to co-operate with me (and I only have her word for that) it's still their business, rather than mine.

The second is that if the police have not come close to solving the murder in three years, then working on my own, I have absolutely no chance.

And the third – which shouldn't matter to me but does – is that I don't like the woman who would be my client, because I don't like anyone who tries to mess around with my brain.

Thus, there are three good reasons for backing away, and no good reasons for embracing the case.

Except that . . .

Except that she's expecting me to turn her down, and while she's not exactly pleased at the thought, she is sort of congratulating herself on having assessed me correctly.

Well, I'm not going to give the bitch the satisfaction!

'I charge seventy-five pounds a day plus expenses, and as far as results go, I can guarantee you absolutely nothing,' I say in a harsh voice which only vaguely resembles my own.

'That seems rather expensive,' she says. 'I've been checking around, and most detectives charge a lot less.'

'Those are my rates,' I counter, stubbornly. And so they are – for *her*. 'I'm sorry if you can't afford it.'

She laughs. 'Oh, I can afford it easily enough. I occasionally work on the American lecture circuit, which is obscenely well paid. I reckon I earn seventy-five pounds in the amount of time it takes me to stop and fart mid-lecture. Imagine that – seventy-five pounds for farting,'

She reaches across my desk and holds out her hand, and – against my better judgement – I take it and shake it.

# TWO

My new client drives away from my office, looking cool and sophisticated behind the wheel of a brand-new Lotus Esprit sports car. (I know this because I am lurking behind my bargain basement curtains, watching her.) Shortly thereafter, I set out myself, looking equally cool and sophisticated behind the handlebars of my three-year-old Raleigh pushbike (and if you believe that . . .).

I am on my way to see my usual contact in the Thames Valley Police, DS George Hobson.

The conversation that the two of us have just had over the telephone went as follows:

Me: How are you, George?

Him: I'm fine. What can I do for you, Jennie?

Me (slightly wheedling): Listen, George, I need to see you, when you can spare the time.

Him: Fine. How about meeting in the Bulldog in an hour?

Me (caught somewhere between suspicion, relief and incredulity): Did you say an *hour*?

Him: That's right.

Me: Just like that?

Him: Yes, just like that.

But it has never been *just like that* before. I wonder what George's angle is, because our relationship is a delicate balance of advantage, and I'd hate to fall off the seesaw just because I don't know the new rules.

I set off up the Iffley Road. It is already late October, and the air has a bite to it that holds out the promise of future runny noses and chilblains. On an empty plot of land to my left, children have already begun to build a bonfire on which they will burn an effigy of the traitor (or martyr, depending on your perspective) Guy Fawkes in a few days' time, and I notice that a couple of the shops I whizz past have large advertisements in their windows for Standard Fireworks and their biggest rivals, Brocks.

The buildings on the Iffley Road offer no evidence that the road constitutes a small part of something extraordinary. Indeed, as I cycle past the houses (some of them three-storied terraces, some semi-detached and a few standing completely independent), it is the very ordinariness which is most striking. This is a street which could be slipped into a free slot in Bedford or Gloucester (or a score of other towns), without being noticed, and to even suggest that it belongs to the city of dreaming spires seems almost laughable.

Then I cross the river, and things change, because I am suddenly surrounded on all sides by seven hundred years of monumental busyness and expansion.

To my right is Magdalen College, (pronounced *maudlin* after the emotion, rather than *Magdalen* after Jesus Christ's close companion). It is dominated by its square tower, built between 1492 (when Columbus sailed the ocean blue) and 1509. And what a tower it is! Its stonework glows golden, even in the weak autumn sun, and at 144 feet, it is still the tallest building in Oxford. It has four octagonal turrets, which look like nothing from the ground, but the northwest one (which is only slightly larger than the others) is big enough to have a spiral staircase running up it.

To my left are the University Botanical Gardens, entered by the baroque Danby Arch, with its framed niches from which statues of Charles I (who lost his head during the English Revolution) and Charles II (who didn't) gaze down haughtily. Beyond the gate I catch a quick glimpse of the islands of colour created by some of the 6000 species of plants grown in what is one of the oldest botanical gardens in the world.

A little further up the road is St Edmund's Hall, the only surviving medieval hall in the university, and across the road is the imposing Examinations Schools, where, at the end of Finals, it is common to see undergraduates throwing their mortar boards in the air with one hand, and quaffing champagne with the other.

How's all that for instant history!

On a more mundane (modern) level, an advertising poster – composed of two photographs and a message – is pasted on the side of the bus shelter outside Oriel College. The upper photo is of a man in late middle age, and is in colour. He is dressed for the races – top hat, binoculars, etc – and he has a glass of champagne in his hand. The photograph below it is in black and white, and features three miserable-looking children who are not *quite* dressed in rags, but are clearly concerned about where their next meal will be coming from.

The message – in accusing red letters against a black background – reads: 'What will *you* pass on to your children? Call in at Bradshaw's County Bank for free advice.'

The message is, in other words, that if you die leaving your kids absolutely nothing, you are a failure both as a parent and as a human being, whereas if you scrape and save and never have any fun out of life, then, when you breathe your final breath, your relatives will have your substantial estate to cushion the emotional blow of your departure.

I snort in disgust at the whole slick, manipulative con trick. There are times, you know, when I almost suspect myself of being cynical.

And what is *my* legacy from my cold and distant father? I find myself wondering.

A crop of red hair and the name Redhead!

Given the laws of genetics, the hair was inevitable.

But the name most certainly wasn't!

If my ancestor – the founder of the dynasty (ha! Some founder, some dynasty) – had been red-haired but *also* had lived near the edge of the forest, I could have been called Woodend (which coincidentally, was the name of one of my heroes – a detective chief inspector – when I was growing up in Whitebridge).

In fact, the possibilities of what I *could have* been called are endless. If that ancestor of mine had been a barrel maker, that would probably have mattered more than the hair, and I could have been Jennie Cooper. If he'd produced arrows for a living ('My forefather was a merchant of death,' confesses local PI in shockingly candid interview), I'd have been a Fletcher.

But instead, my forefather had handed his hair colour down through the generations. Some of the inheritors made no use of it themselves. My late father, for example, could have accurately been called Harold Mousybrownhead. But he conserved it in his genes, and when he engaged in successfully pro-creational sexual intercourse with my mother (the very thought of which brings me out in cold sweats and hot flushes simultaneously) he passed it on to me.

And this 'gift' is a curse for someone who needs to be taken seriously – because the ability to be taken seriously is about the only asset that a private investigator has.

Oh yes, it's quite true.

People who would never think of making a personal remark about her name to Jennie Cooper or Jennie Fletcher – 'Why isn't your head shaped like a beer keg?' 'Shouldn't your skull come to a sharp point in the middle?' – feel no compunction at all in pointing out to me (in case I've failed to notice) that the name goes with the hair – 'Or is it *vice versa* ha, ha, ha!'.

I have reached Carfax Tower, where the drunks from the Salvation Army hostel lie sprawled against the base, already overcome by the cheap cider they habitually drink.

I make a hand signal and turn down onto St Aldate's. My mental tsunami now all but over, I stop pumping the pedals quite so fast and take a few slow and steadying breaths in preparation for my meeting with my old friend (and ex-lover) Detective Sergeant George Hobson, who appeared, on the telephone, to be rather too willing to meet me.

# THREE

As I dismount my bike in front of the Bulldog, I'm still puzzling over the fact that George Hobson is making this rendezvous so easy for me.

Here's how it works under normal circumstances: I ring him up and ask for a meeting, and he invariably says he's busy (which, to be fair to him, he probably is). We arrange to meet later – usually the next day (if I'm lucky), or the day after – and we settle on a venue which, for reasons that will soon become very obvious, is always a pub.

The next day – or day after that – I arrive at the said pub (usually the Bulldog, since it is so convenient for St Aldate's police station), and my first action on entering is to buy George a pint of best bitter.

Then I sit and wait.

It is not until he is halfway down the pint that I diffidently make my request for information. He considers my petition much as a medieval monarch might, and while he is doing so, I buy him a second beer.

At this point, the conversation can go one of two directions. He may say that he doesn't have the information, or that he has it, but can't pass it on to me (and given the nature of things, can't even explain *why* he can't pass it on). In this case, as far as he is concerned, the free beer fountain dries up. Or, he may say that he can tell me what it is that I want to know, which is my cue to go to the bar, and order him another pint.

But what's happening today just isn't normal. Due to his ready acceptance, I feel like a wild animal following dangled bait which is leading it straight into a trap, though why the Thames Valley Police should want to trap one of the least important creatures of the jungle floor is anybody's guess.

I secure my bike, with a heavy chain, to the metal bracket outside the Bulldog which, in former times, was there for tethering horses. This chaining up is very necessary, because Oxford is the world capital of bicycle thefts (though no doubt our rival, Cambridge, would claim that particular honour for itself – as, like many younger sisters, it feels the need to try and claim *every* honour and distinction going!).

Detective Sergeant George Hobson is sitting in the public bar, with a pint in his hand. He hasn't seen me, and I pause for a moment to study him. He is not a heart-stoppingly handsome man, but he is easily good looking enough to pass most people's standards for acceptable partners, and, in addition, he is kind, he is generous and he is interesting, and, for a fleeting moment, I wonder why we broke up.

Except that *we* didn't break up at all, did we? I remind myself.

I think he loved me, and I'm almost certain he was about to ask me to marry him, which is why, despite the remarkably good sex we generated as a couple, I had to bring it all to an end.

Because *I* didn't love *him*, you see – at least, not in that way. I love him as a friend – I would die for him, if I had to – but I couldn't force myself to feel an emotion which simply wasn't there. The truth is, I've never been *in* love with anybody, and I don't think I ever will be. Maybe if I'd been a Woodend or a Cooper it would have been different, but romantic love is just not in the Redhead genes.

I take a few steps forward, and George becomes aware of my presence. He looks up, smiles, and gestures with a graceful sweep of his right hand that I should sit down opposite him.

'What's wrong?' I say, once we're at each other's eye level.

'Wrong?' he repeats, in a tone larded with innocence – which I don't believe for a minute.

'Whenever I ring you up and ask for a business meeting, you hum and hah and tell me how difficult it's going to be for you to find the time.'

'And it always is – because, as you know, I have a heavy work-load,' he protests.

'On this occasion, however, you said, without even thinking about it, that you could see me right away.'

'So you happened to catch me at a good time, Jennie. Don't be suspicious – be grateful!'

'Also, even when you get here first, you always wait for me to buy the drinks but . . .'

'That's not fair,' he says. 'I'm not the kind of man who sponges drinks off a friend.'

'Maybe not,' I agree, 'but you certainly seem to do a very good impression of one.'

'The reason I allow you to buy me drinks is that I know it will be your clients – the ones who pay your expenses – who have to cough up,' he says firmly

'And yet, this time, even though you will have assumed I'm meeting you on a client's behalf, you've still bought your own drink,' I reply.

He shrugs, unconvincingly. 'That was absent-minded of me. I won't make the same mistake again. I promise you that.'

I am still waiting for the trap to spring. I can almost feel the rope tightening around my ankle, ready to whip me up high into the air.

And then I notice what he's got under the table.

'What's in the bag?' I ask.

He shuffles his feet, slightly. 'What bag?'

'The bag you're now attempting to hide between your own leg and the table leg?'

He looks down. 'Oh, *that* bag.'

'There's something in it that you think might help me, isn't there?'

'Could be,' he admits.

'Which is very strange,' I muse, 'because I haven't told you yet what kind of help it is that I want.'

'You said on the phone you were investigating Grace Stockton's murder,' he says.

I shake my head firmly. 'No, I didn't.' I pause. 'I went out of my way *not* to say that.'

'So I made a lucky guess,' he suggests, unconvincingly.

'Do you want to know what I think?' I ask.

He pulls a face – as if that's going to put me off.

'No, I don't really want to know,' he says, 'but I imagine you're going to tell me anyway.'

Too bloody right, I am!

'I think the Thames Valley Police are much keener on me investigating this murder than I am myself,' I tell him, 'but whoever it is who pulls your strings has told you to make sure it's not that obvious.'

'You surely don't think . . .' he begins.

'You see, they can't bring themselves to admit they need me. Of course, it's all right, as far as they're concerned, for them to help me out – it's only charitable to help somebody who was once one of their own. But for them to accept openly that they need the help of a one-woman band with a scruffy office on the Iffley Road – well, that's swallowing enough pride to pack a double-decker bus with.'

'Maybe you're right,' he admits glumly.

'Julia Pemberton must have Ken Macintosh wrapped around her little finger,' I say.

'He's an old friend of her parents, but DCI Macintosh is only a small part of this,' George says.

'Then where's the real pressure coming from?' I ask.

'I don't know.'

'Where's the real pressure coming from, George?' I repeat, sternly this time, like a school matron who suspects one of her schoolboy patients of ejecting his semen onto the nice clean sanatorium sheets.

'The Home Office,' he mumbles.

'What was that you said?'

'Have you gone deaf? I said the bloody Home Office.'

'And why should the Home Office be interested in a purely domestic murder that happened over three years ago?'

'Dr Pemberton is a highly respected scientist, you know. She moves in all the top circles. I know for a fact that she's had dinner with the Prime Minister on at least two occasions.'

I'm not convinced – not even for a second. I drum my fingers impatiently on the table.

'Why?' I repeat.

George grins shamefacedly. 'The way I hear it, Dr Pemberton is bonking one of the junior ministers.'

Interesting! I wonder which came first – the chicken or the egg. Was she having an affair with the minister when she realized she could use him to put pressure on the police? Or did she decide that the best way to get the minister to pressurize the police was to have an affair with him? Based on our one meeting, I wouldn't dismiss either of those possibilities.

But whichever it is, it's delightful news, because it means I will be given a lot of leeway in my investigation, and should I choose to cut a few corners – which is not unknown, *entre nous* – it will probably be ignored by the people who could otherwise make my life very difficult.

'Well, who's getting the drinks, George?' I ask.

'What?' he says, in the sort of tone you might expect if I'd asked him to explain gravity – in Mongolian – while juggling with fiery torches.

'Whose round is it?' I elucidate. I put two fingers to my forehead, to indicate I am in deep thought. 'Now let me see, I've bought the last one thousand six hundred and forty-two, so I think it must be you.'

He rises reluctantly to his feet.

'What do you want then?' he says.

Like he doesn't know!

'A gin and tonic,' I say. 'Better make the gin Beefeater.'

'Isn't that the most expensive one?'

I'm loving this. I really am.

'Yes, it certainly is the most expensive one,' I agree, 'but I'm sure the Thames Valley Police can take the financial strain. In fact, given their vast resources, why don't you make it a double?'

Once we have our drinks sitting enticingly in front of us, George Hobson begins his narrative.

'The first we knew about it was when her husband – Derek Stockton – reported her missing. He'd been lecturing in the United States, and he'd been expecting her to meet him at Heathrow Airport. When she wasn't there, he rang home and got no reply. That's when he decided he'd hire a car.'

I take a sip of my G&T. Somehow the knowledge that the Thames Valley Police is paying for it makes it taste even better than usual.

'You've had all this stuff checked, have you?' I say.

'What makes you ask that?'

I shake my head disbelievingly. 'Come on, George, stop playing games,' I say. 'You know full well why I'm asking – it's because when a wife gets killed, it's more often than not the husband who's killed her.'

'I'm glad to see your time in the Force wasn't completely wasted,' George says, to cover his embarrassment at having been caught out. 'Yes, we did check it all. We checked that he hired the car at Heathrow and that he arrived there on the plane from Boston.'

'But did you also check to make sure that he didn't—'

'Fly across here and kill his wife, then fly back to the States, wait a day or so, then fly into Heathrow again?'

'Yes.'

'We most certainly did. And we discovered that on the three days before he flew back to England, he gave a lecture every day.'

Oh well, there's one easy option gone.

'Carry on,' I say.

'He rang us at four thirty in the afternoon. He said that he'd arrived home and—'

'Does that fit with the time he hired the car?'

'What a nasty suspicious mind you have,' George says. 'Yes, it does fit in – more or less.'

'More or less?'

George shrugs. 'It depends on the traffic. If he'd been lucky and had a clear run, he might have got home an hour earlier. If he'd hit any congestion, he could have been delayed for anything up to a couple of hours.'

'I see. Tell me about the telephone call.'

'I can do better than that,' George says, reaching into the bag he's brought with him. 'I've got a transcript.' He takes out a thick manila folder, and opens it at a place he's bookmarked. 'Shall I read it to you?'

'Why not? You've got such a beautiful reading voice.'

'Sarcastic bitch,' George says, *almost* under his breath. He clears his throat. 'Are you sitting comfortably?'

I say nothing.

'Are you sitting comfortably?' he repeats.

'Yes, I'm sitting comfortably. I've never been more comfortable in my entire bloody life!'

'Good! Then I'll begin.'

> Stockton: This is Dr Derek Stockton of Crocksworth Manor. I want to report my wife missing.
>
> Desk Sergeant: When did she go missing, sir?
>
> Stockton: I can't say exactly. I only got home ten minutes ago. I've been away on a lecture tour, but . . .
>
> Desk Sergeant: Have you considered the possibility that she might just have popped out to the shops, sir.
>
> Stockton: We live in the middle of the countryside, and the nearest shop is at least three miles away.
>
> Sergeant: Does your wife have a car, sir?
>
> Stockton: Yes, she does, and it's still in the garage. As a matter of fact, I was expecting her to use it to pick me up at the airport.
>
> Desk Sergeant: Ah!

George stops reading and lowers the transcript. 'And you can take that look off your face right now, Jennie,' he says.

'What look?'

'The look that says, "God, aren't uniformed desk sergeants just about the thickest of the thick?" He may sound thick in retrospect – but that's only because we now know for certain that Mrs Stockton is dead. What you have to do is put yourself in his place back then. As far as he was concerned, the odds were that the caller was unduly concerned or just wanted to waste police time. I could quote you a dozen calls made by absolute nutters which are almost carbon copies of this.'

'Fair enough,' I concede, because I know he's right.

'Now where was I?' he asks.

'Desk Sergeant: "Ah!"' I remind him.

'That's it.'

> Desk Sergeant: Ah!
>
> Stockton: What's that supposed to mean?
>
> Desk Sergeant: I was wondering if perhaps you and your wife might have had an argument before you left or while you were away.
>
> Stockton: We most certainly did not.
>
> Desk Sergeant: The problem is, sir, that even if she has gone missing, we can't do anything until forty-eight hours has elapsed.
>
> Stockton: But forty-eight hours *has* elapsed.
>
> Desk Sergeant: With all due respect, sir, you can't possibly say that, what with you having been away and all.
>
> Stockton: The plants in the garden are wilting for lack of water, and the cats met me on the doorstep, howling for food. My wife would never see the cats go hungry.
>
> Desk Sergeant: Maybe if you could get your neighbours to confirm that she hasn't been seen . . .
>
> Stockton: There are no neighbours, you bloody fool. As I've already explained to you, we live in the middle of the bloody countryside.
>
> Desk Sergeant: Listen, sir, you'll get nowhere with that attitude, so my advice to you . . .

George closes the file with a dramatic finality that points to only one conclusion.

'I take it Stockton hung up,' I say.

'Just so.'

'So what did he do then?'

'What do you *think* he did then?'

What would I have done in his position?

'I think he rang everybody he knew who might possibly have some influence with the police,' I say.

'That's exactly what he did, and when you're a senior professor at one of the greatest universities in the world, you're just bound to have some very influential friends, aren't you?'

'So you were there within the hour?' I hazard.

'Not quite that quickly,' George replied. He glances around him to make sure no one of any importance is listening, then continues, 'The chief constable is not exactly strong in the backbone department, but even he has *some* pride, and he held out until morning.'

'And were you involved at this point in the inquiry?'

'Oh yes. As a matter of fact, it was entirely my show. In the absence of any signs of foul play, you see, no one in authority saw any need to waste the time of any of the big hitters, so they put a humble detective sergeant in charge of the investigation.'

'They put a *humble* detective sergeant in charge?' I say. 'I thought you just told me that *you* were in charge.'

George grimaces. 'Ha, ha, ha!' he says. 'You're so funny you really should be on the stage.' He pauses. 'There's one leaving town at five o'clock. Make sure you've got a seat.'

The last time I heard that particular joke I was seven years old and in Walton Street Primary School playground, and I smile at it now just as I would smile at the sudden reappearance of any old friend.

# FOUR

*16th April, 1972*

Georgе Hobson arrived at Crocksworth Manor just as the birds were relaxing in the trees after their strenuous dawn chorus.

The first thing that struck him about the place was its isolation, for not only was it over half a mile from any other building, but it was at the end of a rough cart track which ran from the country lane to the front of the manor – and then stopped dead.

'So there's no chance of any passing traffic having seen anything, then,' he said to himself.

The second thing he noted was that even if the Stockton family had inherited the property, the amount of money that had been spent on what were obviously recent renovations would be enough to make a humble detective sergeant's eyes water.

Directly in front of the manor – and serving as a very upmarket turnaround – was a fountain. It was circular, and at its centre were three metallic dolphins – caught by the sculptor in the very act of leaping – from whose mouths a gentle stream of water cascaded into the pond below.

'Five years' overtime that would cost me – maybe even ten,' he muttered.

He realized that anyone sitting beside him would have taken it as a grumpy remark, but it was more ruminative than bitter. He liked the fountain, and though he could never have afforded it himself, he was glad that someone else was affluent enough to have called it into existence.

Hobson drove around the dolphin fountain, and pulled up at the front door. The door opened, and a man stepped out. He was late middle-aged, with hair that was beginning to make the graceful transition from black to silver. His jaw was square, his shoulders were broad, and his hands were massive.

Could this be Dr Stockton? he wondered.

If so, he did not fit Hobson's idea of him, because when he had been told that Stockton was a doctor of comparative religion, he had pictured someone mild and unassuming – a sort of gentle Jesus without the sandals.

'Are you the police?' the man demanded, not even giving him time to finish climbing out of his car.

'Yes, sir, DS Hobson,' George said.

'And have you found her?' the other man roared. 'Have you found my Grace?'

Yep, there was absolutely nothing of the New Testament pacifist about this man, Hobson thought. He looked as if he would be very much out of place delivering a sermon on the mount, but completely at home in a rumble, as a sidekick of one of the more violent of the Old Testament prophets.

'Well, *have* you found her?' Stockton asked again.

And deciding it wouldn't exactly be tactful to admit they hadn't even started looking yet, Hobson said, 'No, sir, we haven't. We were rather hoping you could give us some idea of where to look.'

'Yes, yes, of course, that would be a very positive step,' Stockton said. 'Please come inside, sergeant.'

He seemed suddenly much calmer, George Hobson thought. Perhaps that was because he'd given the doctor something to do – had, as it were, drawn him into the process.

The kitchen was such a massive room that the Aga cooker – which would have dominated most kitchens – fitted comfortably in one corner. The room had oak beams, from which hung curing hams and bunches of herbs. The air smelled pleasantly of generations of roasts and stews.

Hobson and Stockton sat facing each other across a large scrubbed wooden table.

'Have you any idea of when your wife might have left, Dr Stockton?' Hobson asked.

'She didn't *leave*,' Stockton replied, angrily. Then he took a deep breath, as if he was making a real effort to calm down. 'She didn't leave,' he repeated. 'She was *taken*.'

'What makes you say that?' Hobson asked.

'If she'd left, she would have written me a note to explain where she'd gone. Besides, she'd have packed a bag.'

'And how do you know she didn't?'

'None of her clothes were gone.'

'Again, how do you know?'

Stockton sighed. 'I know it because I checked her wardrobe and her drawers, and nothing was missing.'

'Do you know all your wife's clothes?'

'There may be some of her underwear I am unaware of, but other than that, yes, I do.'

Hobson thought about it. He'd never been married himself, but he had had a couple of long-term girlfriends, and he didn't think he'd ever come anywhere close to being able to describe their entire wardrobes.

'Are you absolutely sure about what you've just claimed, sir?' he said.

'Of course I'm absolutely sure,' Derek Stockton said, the irritation evident in his voice. 'It's no great trick – I just have that kind of mind.'

'What kind of mind?'

'A near-photographic mind.' Stockton studied Hobson's face for a second, then added, 'I can see you're still not convinced.'

Hobson shrugged. 'I've no wish to offend you, sir, but, as a rule, people always think they've seen more than they really have.'

'I am not one of those people,' Stockton said firmly.

If they'd been having this discussion in the pub, Hobson would have told him that he didn't know what he was talking about – that if it was once put to a real test, his cocky self-confidence would soon crumble away.

And perhaps he might yet have to do that with Stockton, but for the moment – taking into account the pressure the man was under – he resolved to move more gently.

'I've questioned any number of witnesses who were convinced they'd seen one thing, only to find, when all the facts were uncovered, that they'd seen something quite different.'

Stockton sighed again, and swivelled round so he had his back to the sergeant.

'Would you mind closing your eyes,' he said.

'Listen, sir . . .' Hobson began.

'Please,' Stockton said. 'This won't take a moment.'

Hobson did as he'd been told.

'You're a trained detective, Mr Hobson,' Stockton said. 'Would you mind telling me what I'm wearing, please?'

'You're wearing a red-and-brown check shirt with a yellow pullover which has an image of a polo player at the top right. You're also wearing brown corduroy trousers.'

'What about my shoes?'

'They're brown.'

'Lace-up or slip-ons?'

Hobson thought about it. 'Slip-ons,' he said, finally.

'You can open your eyes now,' Stockton said. 'That was quite good, but the shirt is brown-and-yellow check, you failed to mention the fact I'm wearing a green tie, and my shoes are actually moccasins.'

'Well, there you are,' Hobson said. 'I am, as you pointed out, a trained detective, and yet even I—'

'You are wearing a blue pin-striped suit and a white shirt,' Stockton interrupted him, still turned away. 'Your tie is blue, but has a red rugby club insignia on it. Your shoes are black lace-ups which are

reaching the end of their serviceable life, and your socks are blue
– though the left one is of a darker blue than the other one.'

Hobson glanced down, and saw that Stockton was right: he had
slipped on odd socks that morning without even noticing it.

'If you look at the cupboard behind your head, you will find a
number of tins of food that I stacked there just before I went to
America,' Stockton continued. 'There are tins of baked beans,
green beans, sweetcorn, artichokes and button mushrooms. I did
not deliberately memorize the number of tins, or the exact order
in which I stacked them, but I can describe the inside of the
cupboard perfectly. Would you care to open it and test me?'

'No, sir, you've made your point and that won't be necessary,'
George conceded.

'So when I say I am familiar with my wife's entire wardrobe
you are willing to accept that?'

'Yes, sir.'

'The only item missing is a sapphire blue casual dress which
she wears mainly around the house,' Stockton said. 'That's what
she was wearing when she was snatched.'

'I'm afraid we still can't overlook the possibility that she left
in a hurry and simply forgot to leave you a note,' Hobson said.

'However flustered or hurried she'd been, she would never have
forgotten to do that, because she knows how much I would worry
about her.'

'Is there any particular reason that you would worry about her?'
George wondered.

'What?'

'Is there any particular reason you worry about her?'

'She's my wife – my *raison d'être*,' Stockton said. 'Don't you
worry about your wife?'

'I'm not married,' Hobson said, adding mentally, but if Jennie
Redhead wasn't so terrified of commitment, I could have been.

'In that case, you couldn't possibly appreciate how I feel,'
Stockton said, somewhat dismissively.

'So it's your belief, is it, that if she's not here, it's because
someone is holding her?' Hobson asked, getting the interview back
on track.

'Yes, it is.'

'But you haven't found any signs of a struggle inside the house?'

'None. And before you ask, yes, I am sure of that, because Grace is as organized and orderly as I am, and if anything had been out of place, I would have noticed it.'

If that was true, there were three possibilities, George thought.

The first was that, despite what her husband seemed to think, she'd left home voluntarily.

The second was that she had been physically abducted, but her kidnappers had taken the time to clear up the mess.

If either of those scenarios was the correct one, then she could be almost anywhere, and launching a search without further, more specific information would be a complete waste of time.

But there was a third possibility, which was that she'd been attacked while she'd been outside the house.

'Did your wife – I'm sorry, *does* your wife – like going for walks in the countryside?'

'Yes, she does. She's very keen on fresh air. It helps her to think, and she goes for a wander most days.'

'And where do these wanders of hers usually take her?'

'Why do you want to know that?' Stockton asked, looking worried.

'Just answer the question, sir, if you don't mind,' Hobson said.

'Well, it depends. Sometimes she goes across the fields towards the river, sometimes down the lane that leads to the village. But the woods are her favourite place, by far.'

'Which woods are they? The nearest ones?'

'That's right. I don't know if they have an actual official name, but we call them the bluebell woods, because at this time of year, there's a thick carpet of bluebells.'

# FIVE

'First we searched the house and grounds,' George tells me. I nod. I wouldn't have expected anything else, because that's the approved procedure.

'You didn't find anything?' I say, and though it sounds like a question, it isn't really.

'Not a dickie bird,' George replies. 'It was a thorough search

– I supervised it myself – but there wasn't a hint of a struggle, and there was nothing that could have been bloodstains.' He pauses. 'So we widened the search to take in the area around the manor. I had a gut feeling that if we found anything at all, we'd find it in the bluebell woods – and my gut was right.'

'It often is,' I say.

'Yes,' he agrees, with perhaps a hint of complacency, 'it hasn't served me badly. Anyway, every available inch of the woods was covered with flowers, except for one small strip where there was just bare earth. We dug it up, and there she was.'

'Who identified her?' I ask.

'Dr Stockton himself.'

'That must have been hard.'

'It was – and not just on him.'

# SIX

*18th April, 1972*

George Hobson had never consciously counted up how many times he had taken a close relative of a murder victim to the mortuary, but as he and Stockton walked through the main entrance, he reckoned this was probably the tenth or eleventh gruesome visit on which he had acted as unwilling shepherd.

Reactions generally fell into two different camps. There had been one man and one woman who had immediately identified the corpse, and once that shocking admission had escaped their lips, they had gone slack, as if the bones in their legs had suddenly turned to rubber. The man had grasped the trolley on which the body lay for some support, but the woman had needed Hobson himself to grab her, or she would undoubtedly have collapsed.

That had been bad enough, but the other reaction – the majority reaction – was generally, if anything, much worse. Here, he would notice the relative's body stiffen, and would then know exactly what to expect next.

'It's not him,' they would say, in a tight, strained voice. And then, to reassure themselves, they would repeat it. 'It's not him.'

But that was only a part of their brains speaking – the part which refused to accept that the cold slab of meat they were seeing had once been someone they loved. And now that small part of the brain was doing its best to suppress the larger part, which recognized the truth.

'I want to go now,' they'd say, knowing that the longer they were there, the harder it would be to deny reality.

He was always gentle but firm with them.

'Please take another look. It's very important.'

And eventually they would break down – would admit that yes, it was Tom or Lucy.

Thus, for obvious reasons, Hobson had always regarded this particular duty as one of the worst jobs in policing. But this was going to be even worse than usual, because, unlike most identification procedures, where the body would be covered by a pristine white sheet and only the head visible, in this case the body would be on display, because there *was* no bloody head.

One of the mortuary assistants, white-coated and looking suitably grave, greeted them in the lobby and then said to Dr Stockton, 'Would you excuse us for a second?'

He led Hobson to the other side of the lobby, then whispered, 'Don't let the poor devil get too near to the stiff.'

Hobson bristled at the word 'stiff', but recognizing that now was not the time to get into a debate about showing the proper respect, he simply whispered back, 'Is there any particular reason for that?'

'We've done our best to make it look like she still has a head, but it won't bear close inspection,' the assistant told him.

Hobson understood exactly what he'd meant the moment they entered the viewing room. A sheet had been placed over the space where Grace's head should have been, and the bulge in it indicated that there was *something* there.

'You said the woman you dug up in the woods had been decapitated, but this body seems to have—' Stockton began.

'Don't worry about that, sir,' Hobson interrupted him. 'You just concentrate on the rest of her.'

The 'rest of her' was wearing a blue housedress with short sleeves and a hem which reached just below the knees. Hobson noticed that a swatch of material had been cut out of the hem. He wondered whether that had been done by Grace Stockton herself, or by her killer – and then he wondered why *either* of them would have done it.

Beside him, he felt Dr Stockton stiffen.

Oh God, he thought, this is going to be bad.

'It's not her,' Stockton said, looking away. 'It's clearly not her.'

'She's wearing a dress just like the one you said Grace was wearing,' Hobson pointed out.

'Maybe I was wrong about that,' Stockton said, with an edge of hysteria to his voice.

But he was never wrong about things like that, as he had convincingly demonstrated to Hobson only hours earlier.

'She's wearing a bracelet on her wrist,' Hobson said gently. 'It could be made of hair. Did Grace have a bracelet like that?'

'It's her!' Stockton moaned.

'Are you sure?' Hobson asked.

'Of course I'm sure!' Stockton said angrily. 'Do you think I can't recognize the legs of the woman who I've been married to for over thirty years?' Stockton demanded angrily. 'Do you think I don't know those arms, which have hugged me to her every single day we've been together?'

Hobson put his hand on the other man's shoulder.

'It's time for us to leave, sir,' he said.

But Stockton was having none of it. He lurched forward, took hold of the dead woman by the shoulders, and lifted her trunk clear of the trolley, with the obvious intention of hugging her to him.

The movement was enough to dislodge the semi-inflated football which had been serving as a head. It fell to the floor with a squelch, and rolled wobblingly away, in the direction of the door.

Stockton, seeing this, relinquished his hold on the corpse, bent over almost double – and vomited.

And who could blame him, Hobson thought.

# SEVEN

'How long had she been dead?' I ask.

'The police surgeon reckoned it was between two and four days,' George replies. 'He said the decapitation created circumstances that made it more difficult to calculate accurately the time of death – which is another way of saying that he was covering his own back. But his vagueness didn't really bother us, because we were certain she'd been dead for three days.'

'What made you fix on that?'

'It was three days earlier that our prime suspect suddenly appeared in Oxford – and then she quickly left again.'

I remember reading something about her, but after three years it was all a bit vague.

'Tell me about her,' I say.

George reaches into his bag, and takes out an A4-size photocopy. 'This is her.'

The woman is standing in Oxford railway station. Just beyond her, I can see other passengers. A couple of them are carrying coats, indicating they probably consider it too warm for heavy clothing, but the suspect has her duffle coat fastened up to the neck.

It is hard to say how old she is. She could be a well-preserved eighty-five or a totally wrecked thirty-five, but whichever she is, her hair is as unruly as Medusa's and her eyes are as wild as a mad woman's.

'We lifted that from the station CCTV camera,' George says. 'We also made several copies of the tape. There's one in the bag for you. You've got a VCR player, haven't you?'

'Of course,' I agree.

I don't know why I lie to George about that. With other people, I might play free and easy with the truth because I want to maintain my professional image – which is to say, I don't want them to suspect that my only assets are a tatty one-roomed office and a flat that even the cockroaches complain about. But

George knows all that. So maybe it's simply pride – one of the many sins which I skilfully manage to be guilty of on a daily basis!

'Tell me more about the suspect,' I say.

'She arrived on an early-morning train from London. She had with her a photograph of Dr Grace Stockton, cut out from a newspaper, and she was showing it around the station, asking if anybody knew where Dr Stockton lived.'

'Murderers don't, as a rule, like to draw too much attention to themselves,' I point out.

'Maybe she wasn't planning to become a murderer at that point,' George counters. 'Anyway, as luck would have it – luck from her point of view, that is, because it certainly wasn't lucky for Grace Stockton – one of the people she asked was a lecturer from St Luke's, who was off to London for the day. He was a little suspicious at first, but then she said she was Grace's cousin, and had simply lost her address.'

'And he believed her?'

'Granted, she looked a little eccentric, but Grace Stockton was a little eccentric herself, by all accounts.'

'In my experience, most anthropologists are,' I say.

'We lose track of her at that point, and don't pick her up again until she catches the bus which drops her off on the lane a good three-quarters of a mile away from Crocksworth Manor. The next time we see her, she's back on Oxford railway station.'

'She didn't take the bus back from the manor?'

'No.'

'And when's the next time she's spotted after her appearance on Oxford Station?'

'There isn't a next time.'

'What do you mean, "there isn't a next time"?'

'What I say. Nobody remembers her travelling back on the train to London, and nobody remembers her arriving at Paddington Station. We splashed her picture all over the newspapers and the television news, and hundreds of people called in. Several claimed she was their neighbour, but we checked it out, and she wasn't. Some said she worked in the local pub or chip shop. She didn't. There were callers who'd spotted her in Edinburgh at the same time as we know she was in Oxford. One woman said she was the ghost of her grandmother, and got quite hysterical when we didn't seem to believe her. We checked them all – as you have to – and they all turned out to be dead ends.'

'People don't appear out of nowhere and vanish into thin air,' I say.

'This one did.'

'So what other leads have you got?'

'Do you want a rough figure, or would you rather I was precise?' George asked.

'I'd rather you were precise,' I tell him.

'In that case – none.'

'None!'

'No other strangers were spotted, and none of the people Grace Stockton knew seemed to have a motive for wanting her dead, so if the woman in the duffle coat didn't do it, then we have no idea who did. And if the woman in the duffle coat *did* do it, we don't know who she is, why she did it, or where she is now. In other words, we have Sweet Fanny Adams.'

'But despite all that, you think that I can find your killer for you, do you?' I ask.

George shakes his head. 'No, not really,' he admits. 'But if you're working on the case, then at least it will keep Julia Pemberton and her Home Office boyfriend off our backs.'

Wonderful! I'm positively beside myself with joy.

# EIGHT

As I may have mentioned previously in this narrative, I do not own a VCR player – but I have a mate who does. The mate in question is called Charlie, or, to dignify him with his full title, Charles Edward George Withington Danby Swift, Fifth Lord Lostock.

Charlie is not *just* my mate, he is my *best* mate. I met him at my first college reception, held in the Master's Garden, where – an unsure working-class lass from the north of England – I found myself surrounded by a sea of confident young women who had previously attended schools like Cheltenham Ladies' College. I was drowning, and I knew it, and if Charlie had not appeared on the scene at that moment, it's more than possible I would have caught the next train home and never have returned to Oxford.

I might have fled even given his approach, if he hadn't gone about it in exactly the right way. But Charlie, who knew instinctively how to play me, didn't put a foot wrong. He offered no patronizing words of comfort and assurance. Instead, he took the piss out of me for feeling inadequate because I didn't fit into this environment. I knew he was right, of course, but my hackles were raised, and I said something withering in return. And all Charlie did was laugh and suggest we go to the nearest pub for a pint – which was exactly what we did.

Though we seemingly have nothing in common – I'm thirty-one and he's in his fifties, I was raised on a housing estate and he owns a vast stately home with extensive grounds in Wiltshire – we've been close for over a decade.

Oh my God, is it really *that* long?

What we share is more than a friendship – it is love. If he wasn't a homosexual, I'd ask him to marry me – and if he wasn't a homosexual, I suspect he'd probably accept.

Charlie is the bursar of St Luke's College, which means he gets to control the college's substantial fortune, and, as befits his status, he lives in rooms which overlook one of the college's more impressive quadrangles.

When he meets me at the top of the staircase which leads to his rooms, he is wearing a shot silk dressing gown which is all swirls and dragons. If it was anyone else wearing it, I would think he was imitating Noel Coward, but Charlie is a true original, and has never imitated anyone else in his life.

We exchange a gentle, asexual kiss, then I say, 'Could I use your video, Charlie?'

'Of course,' he agrees. 'And I'll make some tea. Darjeeling?'

'That would be lovely.'

Charlie makes an excellent cup of tea, but it is the only domestic task at which he is in anyway proficient. Fortunately, he does not need any other skills, since he has his scout to do his cleaning, ironing and shoe polishing, and the excellent college refectory to provide his sustenance.

I go over to the machine, which is resting on an exquisite rosewood occasional table.

'How do you work this thing?' I ask.

Charlie shrugs helplessly. 'My scout, Baxter, knows how to load it, but unless I say that I'll be needing him, he's not here in the afternoon.' He reaches for the telephone. 'I could call the lodge and ask them to send one of the porters up, if you like.'

I had my own scout when I was in college, but I've never felt very comfortable about other people doing things for me that I could perfectly well do myself. Thus, the prospect of summoning a porter sends a brief shiver of embarrassment coursing through my northern, working-class body.

'We don't need any help,' I say hastily. 'With a little application, I should be able to work it out for myself.'

The instructions are simple enough, and it's not long before I'm feeding the cassette into the machine and switching on the television. A black-and-white, slightly fuzzy, image of the inside of Oxford railway station appears on the screen. There are not that many people around, and looking at the clock at the bottom of the screen, I understand why.

9.43 a.m. Too late for the worker ants who commute in their thousands to the city of London (they will already be chained to their desks by that time) and too early for the tourists (doing the grand cultural excursion which invariably includes the Tower of London and Stratford-upon-Avon) to start arriving.

I spot my woman somewhere in the distance. She is too far away to see her face, but she is the only one on the concourse wearing a duffle coat. Besides, she keeps stopping and showing the piece of paper in her hand to passers-by.

*'Do you know this woman? Do you know where she lives?'*

She comes closer, and I freeze the image. This is more or less the frame that the police photograph was lifted from.

Charlie places a teacup down next to me (a fine china cup of some antiquity, of course) and says, 'Isn't that the woman who the police were looking for in connection with Grace Stockton's murder?'

'Yes,' I agree. And then, because he is clearly expecting more, I add, 'I've been asked to investigate the case.'

'I see,' he says, in a voice which ever so clearly indicates that he doesn't see at all.

The woman moves away. The screen goes blank for a second, and when the image comes back, it is from a different angle.

'What happened there?' Charlie asks.

'A second camera,' I tell him. 'They've spliced the tapes together.'

'Ah!' he says, as if I've just explained how to cast a magic spell or split the atom.

The woman is talking to another man.

'That's Philip Downes,' Charlie says. 'He's an expert in Assyrian relief sculpture during the reign of Ashurbanipal.'

Only in Oxford (and possibly Cambridge) would the second of those two sentences have been used as part of a personal description, I think. Still, it has established him as the St Luke's don who, on his way to London for the day, gave Duffle Coat Woman Grace Stockton's address, and thus, without realizing it, signed her death warrant

The screen goes blank again, and when the image returns, the clock at the bottom of the screen says it is 3.07 p.m.

The woman walks in through the main door, but she does it with a curious sideways motion, not unlike a crab, and since the hood of the duffle coat is now fully up, I cannot see her face.

We switch cameras, and once again, she is contorting her body into unnatural positions.

'Why is she doing that?' Charlie asks.

'She knows where the cameras are, and she's avoiding them filming her face,' I tell him.

'It didn't bother her in the morning,' Charlie points out. 'She made no effort to evade them then.'

'Maybe she didn't know she was going to kill somebody in the morning,' I suggest.

'Even so, it's nothing but a waste of her energy to evade the cameras in the afternoon, because she's already on film.'

He's making a good point. I give it my careful consideration.

'She's acting on instinct,' I say finally. 'If she'd thought it through like you have, she'd have seen it was pointless, but she's just cut another woman's head off, and most of her logical functions have probably shut down, to make room for blind bloody panic.'

The screen goes blank, and there is no more.

'We don't see her going onto the platform,' Charlie says.

'No,' I agree. 'That would have been on Camera Three, and Camera Three wasn't working that day.'

'You don't think she fixed it, do you?' Charlie asks.

'Are you being serious?'

'Well, you have to admit, it is rather a coincidence.'

God preserve me from amateurs!

'To disable the camera, she would have had to be part of a highly organized team, working to a delicate and intricate plan,' I say.

'Well, that's possible, isn't it?'

'And people working to a delicate and intricate plan don't usually need to ask passers-by where they should be going. Nor do they need get there by public transport.'

Charlie nods. 'I can be a real fool sometimes, can't I?'

'Not really,' I assure him. 'You've just strayed beyond the field of your expertise onto the highway of murder and mayhem.'

Charlie grins. 'Nicely put. So the camera just broke down?'

'That's the most likely explanation,' I say. 'Do you know what's bothering me?'

'What?'

'The timing.'

'How do you mean?'

'She couldn't have got to Crocksworth Manor much before eleven o'clock, and yet she was back here shortly after three.'

'So?'

'Assuming she had her argument with Grace Stockton soon after she arrived, it would still have taken close to two hours to carry her body to the bluebell wood and bury it.'

'You're probably right.'

'That would take it up to one o'clock. It's seventeen miles from Crocksworth Manor to the railway station. She didn't take the bus, and she didn't call a taxi. We know that because the police have checked both of those options out. And despite an extensive appeal on the television and in the newspapers, no driver has come forward to say that he picked her up hitchhiking. So how the hell did she make it back to the station by three?'

We have sauntered up Broad Street and are now in the Eagle and Child (also known locally as the Bird and Baby, and, occasionally, as the Fowl and Foetus).

The earliest record of it as a pub is 1684, and it was once the preferred meeting place of J.R.R. Tolkien (author of *The Lord of the Rings*), C.S. Lewis (author of *The Chronicles of Narnia*) and various other members of the literary society known as the Inklings.

That's the sort of literary trivia that impresses the hell out of you when you're a newly-arrived undergraduate, but by the end of the first year, the thrill is gone and it's no more to you than a pub you haven't yet disgraced yourself in by getting blind drunk.

But for me, it will always be a special place, because it was to the Eagle that Charlie brought me when he rescued me from that dreadful gathering in the Master's Garden.

It is only half an hour to lunchtime closing when we arrive, and a number of the regulars are fuelling themselves up in order to be able to survive the terrible drought that exists between three and six, when the pub door is barred, and they're the wrong side of it.

I nod to Father Jim O'Brien, a priest held in high esteem by his parishioners for his wisdom, kindness and understanding, and by drinkers in this pub for his ability to ingest more pints of draught Guinness than any other man they've ever met.

'How are you doing, Jennie?' he asks, with an Irish lilt to his voice and a beam on his face.

'I'm doing fine, Father Jim,' I tell him.

'And have you seen the error of your ways and decided to join the True Church – or are you still one of Satan's handmaidens?'

I grin. 'I'm still one of Satan's handmaidens. The hours aren't great, and the pay is appalling, but at least I can look forward to a warm retirement.'

He grins back. 'That you can,' he agrees. 'Think of me sometimes, when the devil is jabbing his fiery pitchfork into your cute little arse.'

'Cute little arse,' I repeat. 'Why, Father Jim, you really know how to flatter a girl.'

Charlie and I walk over to a table and sit down.

'I know the reason we're here,' Charlie says.

'The reason?' I repeat, to give myself time to think. 'Are you suggesting I have an ulterior motive?'

'Yes, that's exactly what I'm suggesting.'

'Does there really have to be a reason for me to suggest to my best friend that it's such a nice day that it would be a pity not to take a stroll?'

'And that reason,' Charlie continues, treating my remark with the contempt I suppose it so rightly deserves, 'is that you thought I'd be less inhibited talking about my colleague, Derek Stockton, if I was a mile or so away from the place in which we both work.'

Damn the man – he's too clever by half.

'My motives are pure,' I say in my own defence. 'I just want to bring an innocent woman's killer to justice.'

Charlie hums something which I recognize as the theme tune to an American television series. I think it's the one about the handsome doctor who is on the run for killing his wife, and is searching for the real murderer, who apparently only has one arm.

I sit there patiently waiting for him to finish, but he doesn't finish at all. Instead, he morphs straight into another theme tune.

There is more to this, I think, than meets the ear.

'What's this all about?' I ask.

'It's about teaching you a lesson,' Charlie says. 'If you want to find out something from me, just ask, and I'll soon let you know whether or not I can tell you. But don't try to soften me up first, because I have a whole repertoire of theme tunes I could assail your sensibilities with.'

I bow my head. 'You're right, Charlie, and I'm very sorry.'

'You're forgiven,' Charlie says. 'Now ask me what you could have asked me back in my rooms.'

'Will you tell me about the Stocktons?' I ask, in a meek voice which is half mock contrition and half the genuine article.

'Of course I'll tell you,' Charlie says. 'But I don't think you'll like it.'

'Why won't I like it?'

'Because your job involves searching out weaknesses and flaws, and everything I have to say about the Stocktons is positive.'

I'm impressed, because Charlie is highly observant and rarely guided by prejudice, and I've always found everything that he's said about other people to be spot on.

'Go ahead anyway,' I say.

'They were the perfect long-married couple,' Charlie says. 'They no longer looked as if they couldn't wait to tear each other's clothes off, but they were clearly still very much in love. I don't mean they didn't have the occasional argument – all married couples do – but it was never serious, and it never lasted long. They did all kinds of things for each other – some little things, some much bigger things. Let me give you just one example. Shortly before she was murdered, Grace and Roger Quinn, Derek's best friend, spent days and days organizing a surprise fifty-fifth birthday for Derek – a party which, sadly, never happened.'

'Are you sure that's what they were doing?' I asked sceptically.

'Oh yes. It was going to be a very elaborate affair. But, of course, after Grace's murder . . .'

'What I meant was, are you sure they weren't having an entirely different kind of affair?' I ask.

'I knew what you meant,' Charlie says, 'but Grace Stockton was a strictly one-man woman.'

'And what about him?' I ask, because I know he has a watertight alibi in America, but I can't quite bring myself to forget that in so many cases it is the husband who's responsible.

'He's a one-woman man,' Charlie says. 'He wouldn't look at another woman.'

'How can you be so sure?'

'Call it a shirtlifter's instinct,' he says.

And suddenly – totally unexpectedly – I am thrown into a rage.

'Don't you dare call yourself that!' I say, before I've even had time to analyse my feelings.

'What?' he asks.

'A shirtlifter!' I reach across the table, and grab him by the lapels of his stylish jacket. 'That's as bad as "queer" or "queen" or "bum bandit". It degrades you and it degrades your sexual life, and I won't stand for it! Do you understand what I'm saying?'

He laughs, uncomfortably. 'Steady on,' he says, 'I was only using the term satirically.'

'It's not satirical – not in any true sense of the word.'

'All right, then, if you want to quibble over terms, I was using it in a humorous manner.'

'But it's not funny,' I say. 'You'll never get other people to respect you for what you are unless you can show them that you respect yourself.'

Am I talking from personal experience here?

What do you think?

My anger has subsided, and I'm beginning to feel a little foolish. I release my hold on his jacket, and my arms flop onto the table, as if ashamed of themselves and their actions.

'I'm only saying this because I love you,' I tell him in the voice of a five-year-old.

He takes my right hand. 'I know that. Shall we start again?'

'Yes, please,' I say.

'We homosexuals . . . or may I call us gays, as it's becoming quite a common term, and it's not considered pejorative at all?'

'Yes, you can call yourself gay,' I concede.

'We develop this instinct. When I see a man, I can tell whether or not he's gay almost immediately. And it goes beyond that. I can tell if he's in a relationship he's happy with, or if he's likely to fall victim to my manifest charms.'

'What's this got to do with Derek Stockton? Are you saying he's a secret gay?'

'No, no, not at all. But this instinct I have for gays can be applied to heterosexuals, too. I can tell if a man is looking out for an opportunity to play away from home, and Derek never was. Nor is he now. I see him nearly every day, and not once has he shown any interest in a woman since Grace was murdered. If you want my opinion, it's only by a supreme effort of will that he shows an interest in *anything*. He's a shell of the man he used to be. It breaks my heart to see it, but I know there's nothing that I – or anybody else – can do about it.'

'Thank you for that,' I say.

'Are we all right with each other?' he asks, with a trace of anxiety in his voice.

'Of course we are,' I assure him. 'As you pointed out yourself, all old married couples have arguments now and again, but it doesn't mean a thing.'

Still, we are both relieved it's over.

A look comes to Charlie's eyes which tells me that he's about to be mischievous.

'If you really want to find out about Derek, the person that you should be talking to is Father Jim,' he says, indicating the priest who is just draining a pint of Guinness.

'Why, is he a close friend of Derek's?' I ask, falling straight into the trap he's set me.

'No,' Charlie says, 'he's not his close personal friend at all – he's his confessor.'

It has never occurred to me that Stockton could be a Roman Catholic, but there's no reason why he shouldn't be.

'What about Grace?' I ask. 'Was she a Catholic, too?'

Charlie shakes his head. 'No, Grace hadn't got much time for western religions.'

We've still not ordered any drinks, and now there's no time to.

'I'm sorry, but I have to go,' I say.

'Have you got an appointment?'

'Yes.'

'Who with?'

'The man we've just been talking about.'

'I don't think Derek is in college today,' Charlie says.

'He isn't,' I confirm. 'I'm meeting him at Crocksworth Manor. I need to see the scene of the crime.'

# NINE

*Camden Town, London*
*26th April, 1944*

Although it was early summer, there was a chill wind blowing in off the river, and since many of the buildings in Camden Town had been flattened by bombing in the early years of the war, there was nothing to stop that wind as it wrapped its icy fingers around Jane as she stood on the opposite side of the road to the King's Head public house.

The girl pulled up the collar of her coat, but the coat was cheap and thin, and provided her with very little protection. She wished she could abandon her post and go back to her hovel, but she knew that if she did that, she would have no money for booze, and spending a night without drink was unthinkable.

So there was no choice but to remain there long enough for one of the customers in the public bar to leave drunk. And he did have to *be* drunk, there was no doubt about that, because she had never been attractive enough to find it easy to persuade men to part with their money, and now she was visibly pregnant, it was getting more and more difficult.

There was no doubt she'd had a hard life, but she never thought of it in those terms. Life was life, and you endured it because there always came a point at which you could drown yourself in alcoholic oblivion.

Her father had abandoned the family when she was six, and her 'step-father' had moved in when she was eight. He waited until she was eleven before he started visiting her at night, but when he did, he was as rough with her as if she'd been a hard-bitten, seasoned whore. She did not think of complaining to her mother, because the poor woman was already so cowed that she would not have dared to say anything. So Jane had endured it, two or three nights a week, until she was thirteen, and then she had run away.

Since then, she had lived with a variety of men, most of whom had treated her badly, and sometimes loaned her out to their friends. She had thought she'd finally got lucky with the last one – Archie. True, many women would not have considered him much of a catch – he was thin, with a lazy eye and bad teeth – but he'd occasionally said he loved her and he hadn't knocked her about half as much as some of the others had.

Then she had fallen pregnant, and he had walked out of the condemned house in which they lived one morning, and never come back. To be fair, he had left her with enough forged ration books to feed her for a couple of years, but she didn't eat much anyway, and what she really needed was money for booze.

A man came out of the pub, swaying slightly, and crossed the road.

She stepped into his path.

'Would you like a good time?' she asked.

He looked at her through bleary eyes. He was a big man, but he had let himself go to seed, and now he had three double chins and a stomach which arrived at his destination a good few seconds before the rest of him did.

'How much?' he asked.

She did a quick calculation. Ask too much, and she'd lose him. Ask too little and she'd have to go through this whole disgusting procedure again before she had enough money for her needs.

'Five shillings,' she said.

He thought about it, while, with his free hand, he jangled the coins in his pocket. And then he took a closer look at her.

'You're in the club!' he said, accusingly. 'I'm not screwing a woman who's in the club.'

'I'm only four months' gone. It'll be quite safe for a couple more months yet,' she said reassuringly – even though she knew it was not the baby's health which was concerning him.

'I'm not wasting five bob of my own good money on somebody the size of an elephant,' he told her.

'Look,' she said, desperately, 'maybe we can find some other way to do it. Maybe that will be even better.'

'What do you mean?' he asked.

'Well, I could bring you off by hand.'

He laughed, scornfully. 'I've got a hand of my own. Why should I pay you five bob to do what I could do for free?'

She gulped. She had been hoping to avoid this, but she saw that she had no choice.

'I . . . I could use my mouth,' she said.

'You'd do that, would you?' he asked. 'You'd actually do that?'

She hoped the ground would swallow her up, but it didn't, and she said, 'Yes.'

And even then – even after she'd offered him something he probably only read about in dirty books – he still needed to think about it.

'I'll tell you what,' he said finally. 'I've got a pal back in the pub. I'll go and fetch him, and you can do us both.'

'All right,' she said dumbly.

'Just to make sure we're clear on this, you'll do both of us for the five bob we've already settled on. Are we agreed?'

'Yes,' she said, hating him – but hating herself more.

# TEN

For reasons of an impecuniary nature, I don't possess a car of my own, but wheels are sometimes provided for me by one of my drinking companions, a mechanic called Sylvester, who runs his own repair garage and occasionally lends me one of the vehicles he's just finished working on.

'Are you sure the owners won't mind me using it?' I asked the first time he made the offer.

'If I don't tell them, the owners won't know about it,' he replied blithely. 'Besides,' he added, when he saw the dubious expression on my face, 'look at it this way, Jennie – I'd have to test drive the vehicles once I'd repaired them, now, wouldn't I?'

'Well, yes, I suppose so.'

'So by driving the cars around, you're not only doing me a favour, you're doing the owners a favour. You're a veritable registered charity – except that you're not registered.'

'And I'm not a charity,' I pointed out.

'Well, there you are then,' Sylvester said, as if I'd proved his point for him.

And the matter was settled.

The vehicle Sylvester has lent me this fine autumn afternoon is a Mini Cooper, just like the ones used in *The Italian Job*, but I resist the urge to imitate the film and pull off a spectacular stunt in the middle of Oxford traffic, and instead drive sedately out of town in the direction of Crocksworth Manor.

The country road I follow is a pleasant lane, lined by hedges which were probably first planted out a couple of centuries ago. The hedges are positively weighed down by red berries, which, according to popular folklore, is a sign that a harsh winter is coming. I shiver at even the thought of it, and wonder if I could make a living as a private eye somewhere warm, like the Canary Islands or the Bahamas. But I know deep down this is no more than pointless speculation, because Oxford is like a powerful drug, and once it has got a hold on you – as it has on me – you can never bring yourself to break away.

About three miles down the lane, there is a five-barred gate at the side of the road, and a rough track beyond it. There is no sign to indicate that Crocksworth Manor lies at the end of the track, but there is no lock on the gate, either. I unlatch the gate, drive in, and then dutifully obey the country code by closing the five-barred gate again behind me.

The track looks rough from the other side of the gate, but that is nothing to what it feels like when you're driving along it. There are sudden unexpected dips which test the suspension of the Mini Cooper, and deceptively steep rises which have the gears – caught unawares – howling in complaint.

Surely the Drs Stockton could have afforded to get this fixed years ago, I say to myself, as my spine alternates between trying to leap free of my body and to stab me in the brain.

Yes, they clearly could, because just in front of the manor I can see a large ornamental fountain with three dolphins leaping joyously in the air, which I'm certain must have cost as much as a reasonably sized terraced house would have done back in Whitebridge.

So, leaving the track in this deplorable state was clearly a matter of choice. And the reason for that choice, I speculate, is that it serves as a kind of barrier between the manor and the outside world, (a bit like a medieval moat, in a way, but less likely to start stinking in the summer heat).

Body and vehicle still both intact (just!) I pull up beside the fountain, and get my first judder-free look at the building. It is a manor in the truest historical sense – i.e. a large farmhouse from which the local aristocrat ran the surrounding villages very much in the style of a late medieval mafia boss. It's clearly Elizabethan, and I would date it at around 1560, though I could be out by twenty or thirty years. But whenever it was built, it is in fantastic nick.

The front door is a magnificent example of artisan craftsmanship – solid planks of seasoned oak, cunningly held together by hidden joints which even two teams of horses, pulling strenuously in opposite directions, would have difficulty in separating.

'I see you're admiring the workmanship,' says a deep voice from somewhere behind me.

I turn around, and see Dr Stockton standing there. He is a tall man, broad and in his late fifties. I remember observing him in college, when I was an undergraduate, and putting him at the very top of my fantasy list of dons I'd like to bounce up and down on the bedsprings with.

But though I may have fancied him back then, I don't think I've ever been this close to him before, so feeling the aura that emanates from him is a new experience for me. It is not easy to say which elements make up the aura. There is confidence, certainly. There is intelligence, too. But there is also – and I hate to say this, because as a hard-bitten gumshoe it sounds far too fanciful – an integrity based on decency and honesty.

'Miss Redhead?' he asks.

I see what Charlie means about him – he so clearly *isn't* the man he used to be.

'Yes, I'm Jennie Redhead,' I admit.

'I remember you as an undergraduate.'

Had he fancied me, too? Had he yearned for my body as he watched me cross the quad?

I suspect not. It's much more likely that the reason he remembers me is that not many students had hair that reminded him of a red traffic stop sign.

'I want to be honest right from the start,' he tells me. 'There is only one reason I've agreed to see you, and that is that my daughter asked me to. If it had been left up to me, I would have refused.'

Great! Tremendous! Truly wonderful!

But at least it's good to know where I stand.

'Would you care to tell me why you would have refused to talk to me?' I ask him.

'My reasoning is simple enough – all that your investigation can accomplish is to stir up unhappy memories for both of us,' he tells me.

'And possibly find your wife's murderer,' I respond.

He snorts with mild contempt, like a Spanish fighting bull watching a fat picnicker wander all unknowingly across his pasture.

It is an instinctive reaction, and I can see from his expression that he instantly regrets it.

'I'm sorry, I don't want to appear rude,' he says, 'but if half a dozen regional police forces – working together on the case, from the very beginning – have not been able to establish even where the mad woman came from, then what chance do you think that you, a single individual working alone, will have after a full three years have passed?'

He has a very important point. And he is not the first to make it – I said as much to his daughter, when she came to see me in my office. But despite my own doubts, I still made a promise to her that I'd look into it, and here I am, fulfilling that promise to the best of my ability.

'Well, how do you answer that?' he asks.

I have sat through enough seminars in my time to recognize the tone of his voice. At this particular moment, Dr Stockton is very much the college tutor, gently leading his student towards grasping the truth for herself.

'I don't think I have much of a chance at all of doing something the police failed to do,' I admit. 'But isn't it worth taking the gamble, just to see if we're both wrong?'

He sighs, heavily. 'But even if you succeed, it won't bring my wife back, will it?'

'No,' I agree, 'it won't do that.'

'But you're right, Miss Redhead,' he concedes. 'Punishment is meaningless in this case, because I do not believe that the poor woman was responsible for her actions, but I still have a duty to do all I can to see she is apprehended.' He gestures towards the front door. 'Please come inside.'

He could have taken me into one of the manor's reception rooms, but instead we go to the kitchen. It is a large room – almost vast! – with an Aga cooker, a stone fireplace and big scrubbed table. Looking around it, I get the definite sense that when the whole family was living here – when Grace was still alive, and Julia was growing up – this was the very heart and soul of the house.

Dr Stockton gestures me to sit down at the table.

'Would you like something to drink, Miss Redhead?' he asks. 'A cup of tea or coffee? Or perhaps a glass of whisky?'

For any number of reasons, I am finding this whole situation straining, and the urge to ask for a gin and tonic is almost irresistible. Then I remind myself that I'm working, and say, 'A cup of tea would be delightful, thank you very much.'

*A cup of tea would be delightful, thank you very much!*
Whose words are those?
Certainly not mine!
So what's suddenly making me talk as if I've just stepped out of the pages of a Jane Austen novel? Is it this room, soaked in family history? Or is it Derek Stockton himself?

He brews a pot of tea and places it on the table between us. Most men would ask if I'd like to be Mother, but he – thank God – just says, 'Would you like sugar? Milk?'

I'd really like lemon, but how many households can provide you with fresh lemon?

'Or would you prefer lemon?' he asks.

Is he a mind reader – or just a thoughtful host?

'A dash of milk would be fine,' I say, reminding myself that this is supposed to be an interrogation, not a tea ceremony.

He gives me my dash of milk – perfectly judged – then says, 'So what is it you want to know?'

'I'd like to know what motive you think the murderer had for killing your wife,' I tell him.

He shrugs. 'She was a crazy person.'

I shake my head. 'With all due respect, Dr Stockton, that's really not good enough,' I say.

'What do you mean, "it's not good enough"?' he shoots back at me, his tone taking on a hard edge that is meant to be a signal that he is on the verge of being offended.

'You're an intelligent man. You must have considered what happened from all possible angles, so I think it's unlikely that you don't know *exactly* what I mean,' I tell him.

He gives me a half-smile. 'Maybe I do know – but I'm not the one being tested here.'

'I wasn't aware that either of us was being tested,' I say.

His smile widens a little. 'Yes, you were.'

'Yes, I was,' I agree, and I smile too, because that's the best thing to do when you've been caught out.

'So why don't *you* tell *me* why my answer isn't good enough for you?' he suggests.

'If your wife had been murdered in some public place – say, for example, at a railway station – then the murder could be seen as a random attack by a deranged person. In that case, your wife would just have been unlucky to be in the wrong place at the wrong time. But it wasn't like that at all, was it?'

'No, it wasn't.'

'In this case, the killer took a train from London, then a bus, and then walked nearly a mile. So her motive for murder may not have been a logical one, but she *did* have a motive.'

'Go on,' he says.

'There are two possibilities. The first is that the woman had something against anthropologists in general, so your wife was killed not for who she was but for what she represented. If that's the case, then I'm no use to you at all, because I'll never be able to find her. But if it was just any old anthropologist she was after, then surely she would have chosen one in a more convenient location.'

'Agreed,' he says.

'The second possibility,' I plough on, 'is that the killer knew your wife at some point in the past, and your wife did something which offended her so much that her only possible response was to commit murder.'

Stockton nods again. 'Five minutes ago, I would have said you had no chance of catching the murderer,' he tells me.

'And what would you say now?' I ask – because that's what he wants me to do, and if being his dupe is the way to get his cooperation, then I'll put on a jester's cap with bells on if needs be.

'Now, I would say you have *almost* no chance.' He takes a sip of his tea, though it must be lukewarm by now. 'What is it you would like to ask me, Miss Redhead?'

'I'd like to know about the times in her life when your wife wasn't living in Oxford.'

'Since when?'

'Forever.'

'Grace was born in the Far East,' he says. 'Her father was a missionary out there. He went out on a two-year posting and never left. He and his wife are both buried in Papua New Guinea.'

'Did they send Grace back to boarding school in England?'

Stockton laughs. 'The missionary society couldn't afford fancy things like boarding schools.'

'So where was she educated?'

'In the local school, where there was one, and by her mother when there wasn't. When she was seventeen, the head of the

London office of the missionary society – who'd met her briefly
on a fact-finding visit to PNG, and been very impressed by her
– suggested that she should be tested by London University. The
university agreed, and she took the examination at the British High
Commission in Port Moresby.'

'And passed with flying colours?' I ask.

Stockton looks at me almost pityingly.

'Of course she didn't pass with flying colours,' he says. 'The
exam was aimed at students educated in the Home Counties, and
she'd been brought up in the Papuan rain forest. She simply didn't
have the cultural background or values that were implicit in the
examination, and she failed it in quite a spectacular manner.
Fortunately, however, the tutor who marked the paper was percep-
tive enough to see that the brain behind all those wrong answers
was a quite exceptional one. And then, of course, she had her
languages in her favour.'

'Languages?'

'Do you know how many languages are spoken in PNG?'

'No,' I admit, 'I don't.'

'It has been calculated there are 820 languages, which is twelve
per cent of the world's total number of languages. And this, mind
you, in a population of only five million. The majority of languages,
in fact, are spoken by less than a thousand people.'

'And Grace spoke one of these languages?'

'Better than that. Because her parents had moved around so
much, she was fluent in two of the languages, and had a good
working knowledge of three more. That more than made up for
any deficiencies, and she was immediately offered a scholarship.'

'So she came back to England?'

'No.'

'No?'

'In order for her to come back, she'd have to have been here
before. And she hadn't. She'd visited Singapore once, but that had
been the full extent of her travel. The rest of her life had been
spent solely in Papua.'

'It must have been a great shock to her.'

'It was – and to make matters worse, she arrived in Britain just
as the war was starting to hot up. In fact, she'd hardly settled into
her college accommodation when the Germans began bombing

London almost on a nightly basis, and the college was evacuated to Cambridge. But she didn't go with them.'

'Why not?'

Stockton laughs. 'She told me that the reason she stayed was because a Trinka woman does not run – she stands with her people,' he says.

'What's a Trinka woman?'

'They're one of the tribes her parents tried to convert, and they're also the subject of her Ph.D.' He laughs again. 'She was half-joking, of course. What she really felt was that pursuing her own education was a self-indulgent luxury while there was a war going on, and she'd be far better employed making herself useful.'

'What did she do?'

'She worked part-time for the Ministry of Food, and part-time for a girls' school in Southwark. That was in the daytime. At night-time, she was a fire warden. She wanted to operate an anti-aircraft gun, but everyone agreed that you could never have a woman doing that. They were wrong, of course – she'd have made an excellent gunner.'

'When did you meet her?' I ask.

'I was just coming to that. We met in 1943. I'd been serving as a commando in North Africa, but I got unlucky and had to be invalided out. Anyway, they'd patched me up nicely in hospital and I'd managed to convince the powers-that-be I was fit enough to take part in the invasion of France.'

'What rank were you?' I ask.

'Does it matter?'

It didn't a minute ago. But it does now – because you can sometimes learn as much from the questions that people *don't* want to answer as from the questions that they *do*.

'No, it doesn't matter,' I say, then add the cunning kicker, 'not if it really bothers you to tell me.'

'It doesn't bother me at all. I just can't see the point.'

'Humour me, then.'

'I was a major.'

'You must have been rather young to be a major.'

'There was a war going on, and with all the bullets and bombs whizzing around, there was quite a lot of what we euphemistically called "staff turnover", so there was plenty of scope for stepping into dead men's shoes – I mean that literally. And since you seem so interested in my military progress – though I can see no reason why you should be – you'd perhaps like to know that I was a lieutenant colonel by the time the war ended.'

'Did you win any medals?'

'No,' he says – and I'm sure that while it's not actually a lie, it's not entirely the truth, either.

'What are you hiding?' I probe.

'I'm not hiding anything,' he says, evasively.

'Come on, now, Dr Stockton,' I coax.

'All right, I was offered the VC,' he says.

'What do you mean, you were *offered* it?'

'I turned it down.'

The Victoria Cross!

The highest of all the military awards.

For anyone who doesn't know, it was created in 1857 by Queen Victoria (surprise, surprise!) and despite the fact that millions of British soldiers have been involved in all manner of warfare since then, it has been awarded less than fourteen hundred times.

And he says he turned it down!

'Why did you do that?' I ask.

And now I'm fired with a genuine curiosity that has little or nothing to do with the case.

'I killed some men – more than I care to remember – because that was the only way I could think of to fight the evil which was afoot in Europe,' he says. 'But I'm not proud of it – and I certainly didn't want to be rewarded for robbing other human beings of their lives.'

'You weren't awarded it for killing people,' I point out. 'You were awarded it for your courage.'

'Courage!' he repeats, bitterly. 'When Jesus and his disciples were in the Garden of Gethsemane, the High Priests' men came and seized Our Lord. But when one of His own people fought back, and cut off the ear of one of the High Priest's men, Jesus told him to desist. That is courage.' He stops, and suddenly looks rather embarrassed. 'I'm sorry,' he says, 'I was preaching to you.'

'That's quite all right. Tell me more about meeting your wife.'

'We met in '43. We fell in love almost immediately, and were married within weeks. We both desperately wanted children. It would have made sense to wait until after the war before we started trying, but given the kind of soldier I was, we both accepted there was a good chance I would be killed, and a child would be my way of leaving a little of me behind.' Stockton pauses, and – for once – looks uncomfortable. 'Grace was a virgin.' He pauses again, to take a breath. 'We were both virgins, as a matter of fact. But we were lucky, and just before I re-joined my unit, we found that Grace was pregnant.'

'She didn't come with you?'

'Absolutely not! She *couldn't* have come where I was going. I wasn't even allowed to tell her where that was.'

'So what did she do?'

'She stayed in London – she insisted on it. She still had her two jobs, and once the Blitz had ended, she devoted the time it freed up to what I suppose we would call social work these days, but back then we simply thought of as lending a helping hand where a helping hand was needed.'

# ELEVEN

*7th May, 1944*

The reason why Grace chose to cross the road outside the King's Head to talk to Jane, who was standing on the opposite corner, could have been that Jane looked so forlorn and miserable that only someone with a heart of stone could have ignored her and just walked by on the other side.

It could have been that – but it wasn't.

It could also have been that she felt an affinity with the other woman, because they were both so visibly pregnant.

But it wasn't that either.

What compelled – almost commanded – Grace to cross the road, was that, even at a distance, she could tell that this woman, who was so totally different to her in every possible way on a superficial level, was her *kimpum*.

She would have found it hard to explain to anyone else on this cold damp island what *kimpum* (which was a Trinka word) actually meant. She supposed the closest translation would be 'secret sister' or perhaps 'hidden sister', but neither of these words came anywhere near to really pinning down the concept.

Family duties and responsibilities were at the core of Trinka beliefs, and the *kimpum* was merely an extension of that system. There was no rule by which you could recognize a *kimpum* – no criteria you could use to judge whether or not this person was the real thing. Indeed, not every woman even had a *kimpum* – but if you were one who did, you were expected to recognize her immediately when you caught sight of her, and to make yourself at one with her as soon as you could.

So Grace crossed the road.

'Hello,' she said, 'I'm Grace.'

Jane looked her up and down – without *really* looking at all – then said, in a semi-wheedling voice, 'I'm Jane. You haven't got a cigarette, have you?'

'No, I'm afraid I haven't. I don't smoke.'

'Well, then, you're no bloody use to me, and you can just piss off,' Jane said harshly.

'I'd like to talk.'

'Well, I wouldn't. If you're on the game, you're competition that I don't want. And if you're not on the game, you'll only put customers off by standing there. So, like I said, you can just piss off.'

On the game! Grace would have had no idea what Jane was talking about when she first arrived in London, because prostitution simply did not exist in Trinka society. But she had been there for nearly five years now, and she was getting to know how things in the corrupt and rotting so-called 'civilized' world actually worked.

'I'm not "on the game",' she said, realizing, as she spoke them, how awkward the words sounded coming out of her mouth. 'I'm only in Canning Town because I'm conducting a survey for the Ministry of Food.'

The look in Jane's eyes said she had absolutely no idea what any of that meant – and really didn't care one way or the other – and Grace realized that she would have to adopt another approach.

'How much do your customers usually pay you?' she asked.

'What's that got to do with you, you nosy bloody cow?'

'If you take me back to your place for a little talk, I'll pay you a pound,' Grace said.

'I don't do women,' Jane told her, contemptuously. 'Everybody's got to draw the line somewhere, and that's mine. To tell you the truth, I think the whole lezzie thing is bloody disgusting.'

'I don't want to have sex with you,' Grace said – and she found herself wondering just how two women could possibly *have* sex. 'All I want is for us to have a talk.'

'So we just have a talk, and you give me a pound?'

'That's right.'

Jane held out her hand. 'Give it to me now then.'

To give her the money would be a mistake, but it would also be a mistake *not* to give her the money. Grace took a one pound note out of her purse, tore it neatly down the middle, and handed one half to the other woman.

'You're not stupid, are you?' Jane asked.

There was a certain grudging admiration behind the comment, and that, Grace supposed, was at least a start.

# TWELVE

'Grace stopped working at the ministry and the school about two weeks before Julia was born,' Derek Stockton says. 'She never returned to the ministry, but after a couple of months she did go back to the school for a few weeks.'

'And then?'

'And then she left.'

'Do you mean she left the school or that she left London?'

'Both. She came to Oxford.'

'Which raises two questions,' I say. 'Why did she leave London, and why did she choose Oxford?'

'She left London because she was almost hit by a doodlebug . . .' Dr Stockton pauses, and looks at me inquiringly. 'You do know what a doodlebug is, don't you?'

'Yes, it's a V-1 missile – a flying bomb.'

'And that made her realize it was not just her life she was risking by staying there – it was our baby's as well. Your second question is, why did she come to Oxford? And the answer is that she came here because she already had somewhere to live.'

'She had relatives here?'

'No, her only living relatives were her father and mother. But I'd started studying at the university before war broke out, and I owned a flat on St Giles.' He pauses again, as if he wants to assess how I'm taking this, and when my face gives nothing away, he continues, 'I've never been what you might call rich, Miss Redhead, but I've always been comfortably off.'

'And she stayed here until the war ended?'

'Yes, by the time I came back, she'd already transferred her studies from London University to St Luke's, and was well into her bachelor's degree.'

'I don't ever recall seeing her in college,' I admit.

'That's because we didn't think it was healthy for us both to work in the same college, and so she accepted a fellowship at Balliol.' Stockton takes another sip of his cold tea. 'We were married for nearly thirty years,' he resumes. 'We weren't constantly together – we both did lecture tours, and she went to New Guinea several times to conduct fieldwork – but we were together more than we weren't, and it's sometimes difficult to accept that it's all over.'

I want to ask him if his religion makes it easier to bear – if he can accept it all as part of God's plan, and if he believes that when he dies they will be reunited. But this is just curiosity on the part of Jennie the atheist (who is searching for something – anything – to commit herself to), and it has nothing to do with Jennifer Redhead PI's work, so instead I say, 'Since you don't recognize the woman on the CCTV, it's most likely she will have known Grace either in London during the war, or on the lecture circuit, although we can't dismiss the possibility that they met when Grace was doing her fieldwork.'

'Agreed,' Stockton says.

'How likely is it that the killer knew her in London?'

'Not very likely, I would have thought. If she hated Grace that much, why did she wait nearly thirty years to do anything about it?'

That's true, but it's hard to see one of the people from the rarefied society in which she'd moved since then doing it either.

'Whatever part of the past the woman came from, I don't think she was intending to kill Grace when she arrived here,' Stockton says.

'What makes you say that?'

'The weapon she used.'

I frown. 'There's nothing at all in the evidence folder about a murder weapon.'

'That's true, but the officers conducting the case privately agreed with me that it was probably a Trinka battle knife.'

'Explain,' I suggest.

'I'll do better than that,' he says. 'I'll show you. Follow me.'

# THIRTEEN

*7th May, 1944*

It was not a long journey from the King's Head to Bombay Street, where Jane said she lived, but they had to take a zigzag path, in order to avoid the mountains of rubble which had once been houses in which decent, hardworking people had led their uneventful lives.

The whole of London had suffered from the Blitz – the German bombing of the city between September 1940 and March 1941 – but Canning Town, being close to the docks, had been particularly badly hit, and because any money or time that might have been available for reconstruction was instead being poured into the war effort, the rubble was still there for all to see.

The government was keeping quiet about just how many bombs had been dropped, of course, but Derek Stockton, Grace's new husband, had seen many of the statistics, and when he had been trying to persuade her to leave London, he had told her (though officially he should not have done) that the estimated figure was close to twenty thousand tons. He had added – in an attempt to strengthen his argument – that the government had also underplayed the civilian casualties, and the true number was over forty thousand dead and well over one hundred thousand injured, which was why anyone with the wherewithal was getting out.

'All the more reason for me to stay,' she had countered, 'because if most of the able people are fleeing the city, then those able people who remain become even more necessary.'

'Grace . . .' he had said.

'I work for the Ministry of Food now. That may not seem very important to a soldier who will soon be risking his life in battle, but believe me, for the people who live here, the work I do is vital.'

Thinking back to that conversation, she smiled as she carefully picked her way through the rubble. Derek had never met her mother, but if he had done, he would have recognized the look of stubbornness which filled Grace's face at that moment, as something she'd inherited.

There's definitely something of the missionary about me, too, she thought.

# FOURTEEN

Derek Stockton leads me down a long, low corridor. It is well lit-up by electric lighting now, but there are brackets on the walls which once held flaming brands soaked in pitch, and behind those brackets, the dressed stonework is black from centuries of singeing.

We turn off the corridor into a light, airy room.

'This was Grace's study,' Stockton says.

I look around me. It is obvious it is not used now – it has the sort of feel to it that 'period' rooms in museums have – but someone has kept it scrupulously dusted. One wall is taken up by a large window which looks out onto the garden, another two walls are hidden by bulging bookcases, and the fourth is dominated by a huge stone fireplace.

But it is the bits of wall on each side of the fireplace that are especially interesting, because Grace Stockton had chosen this as a display area for her artefacts. There are masks and aprons, tools and fetishes. But there is one space where something once hung but hangs there no longer.

'That's where the Trinka battle knife was,' Stockton explains. 'The Trinka are one of the tribes that Grace was studying. Until recently, they were headhunters and cannibals. The battle knife was there when I left for the States, and missing when I came back – and it hasn't been seen since.'

'In other words, you're saying that Duffle Coat Woman – that's what I'm calling the killer for convenience – came to the manor with no intention of doing harm, but when she did lose her temper, she searched for a weapon, found the knife and used it.'

'Correct.'

I take a deep breath, because what I'm about to say has to be said, but I don't want to say it to this particular man.

'So let's get this clear, Dr Stockton – Duffle Coat Woman used this missing Trinka knife to cut your wife's head off.'

He barely flinches, but when he speaks again there is a notable tremor in his voice.

'Yes, that is what I believe happened. The knife was crafted for just that purpose.'

More unpleasant questions: 'Why did she bury your wife's head separately?' I ask.

'We don't know she did bury it,' Stockton replies. 'Perhaps she took it with her.'

'And why – in God's name – would she do that?'

'She *didn't* do it in God's name,' he says heavily.

It is a serious rebuke – no doubt about it.

I would have thought that given the scope of our general conversation, taking the name of his god in vain was something that could be overlooked, but I was clearly wrong.

'I didn't mean to offend you,' I say.

'It's all right,' he says, milder now.

But a feeling of awkwardness has suddenly grown up between us, and it is perhaps because of this that he says, 'Let me show you something.'

He walks over to the fireplace, and indicates that I should follow him.

'Do you know what a priest hole is?' he asks.

I'm not sure how he wants me to react to the question – whether he wants me to profess ignorance, or whether it will simply annoy him to have to explain it all to me. I think about it for a moment, then I decide – what the hell! – I might as well be honest.

'It's a kind of hiding place that was secretly built into some covertly Catholic houses during the reign of Queen Elizabeth I,' I say. 'Catholic priests needed to hide from the queen's secret police, because if they were caught, they stood a very good chance of being hanged.'

He nods, and it seems I've chosen the right course.

'There's a priest hole here in the fireplace, Miss Redhead,' he says. 'See if you can find it.'

I give a couple of the dressed stones above the hearth a gentle push, and nothing happens. I try a couple more, with the same result. I'm getting annoyed now, because I don't like being defeated by something that was constructed over three hundred years ago, and my gentle pressure soon gives way to maximum force – which gets me no further at all.

'You'll never find it, however hard you try,' Stockton says confidently, from somewhere behind me.

I bloody will, I think. Oh, yes, I most certainly bloody will.

But after five minutes more searching, I'm forced to admit that no, I bloody won't.

I step out of the fireplace, and Stockton steps in.

'They had to be made difficult to find, because the authorities were constantly raiding Catholic houses and looking for them,' he says.

And then he runs his hands over the wall next to the fireplace, before resting them on two stones about eighteen inches apart. He presses both stones at exactly the same time, and a section of the wall swings out on a creaking hinge to reveal a small room.

'It was probably built by a carpenter and stonemason called Nicholas Owen,' he says, 'because Owen was responsible for most of the priest holes in England. He travelled secretly from manor to manor, taking no more in payment for his labours than what he needed to survive.'

'Did they catch him in the end?'

'Oh yes, his luck ran out eventually, as he'd always known it would. The authorities incarcerated him in the Tower of London, and tortured him to make him tell them where all the priest holes were. They had some particularly nasty methods of torture in those days, but he never said a word, and eventually the torture killed him. Now *that* is what you call faith.'

Ah, so that is what this was all about – another object lesson on the nature of faith for the redheaded atheist!

Stockton swings the wall back on its hinge, and it looks so permanent that it is hard to believe – though I've just seen it for myself – that there is a room hidden behind it.

The diversion is over, and the banished feeling of awkwardness rushes back in to fill the gap.

'Your wife's private papers are being held in the police evidence room, and I need your permission to look at them,' I tell Stockton, partly because it's true and partly because I just feel the need to say *something*.

'All right,' he agrees gravely. 'You have it.'

'I don't want to be difficult, but I need it in writing.'

'Of course,' he says. 'Come through to my study.'

# FIFTEEN

*7th May, 1944*

T hey finally reached Bombay Street. Once, a row of terraced houses had run the whole length of it, but now it was reduced to the four end houses, which creaked and tottered in the wind, as if they might fall down at any moment.

A poster had been pasted onto the crumbling brickwork of the end terrace. It read:

**Ministry of Housing**
**Warning! Unsafe!**
**This building is condemned**

Jane led Grace to the second of the two houses, and pushed the front door open.

'The place is a bit untidy at the moment,' she said apologetically. 'I must admit, I get very lazy when my husband's not here to bully – I mean, to encourage – me.'

It was worse than untidy, Grace thought as they walked down the hallway and entered the back room – much, much worse.

To be fair, it would have been difficult to make this crumbling house presentable whatever she did. The walls were so damp that it was shedding the wallpaper like a snake sheds its redundant skins, and crumbling plaster contributed its own particular musty smell.

But there were other smells, too – like cheap alcohol and vomit. And the room was not just dingy, it was filthy.

It was tempting to comment on this immediately – to point out that Jane owed a duty to her unborn child, and that living in this squalor was the worst thing she could possibly do for it.

She sensed Jane tense, as if she were expecting just such an attack, but Grace knew that this was not how you approached your *kimpum*, and so she sat down at the table as if she didn't even notice the dirt, and smiled.

'Well,' Jane said, clearly knocked off balance by the other woman's ready acceptance, 'what sort of talk are you paying for? Do you want to hear all about the men I've been with, and what I've done with them?'

'Why would I want to hear about that?'

'I thought that's why we were here. I thought it was how you got your kicks.'

'It isn't. But if your experiences with men are what you really want to tell me about, then I'm happy to listen,' Grace said.

'Well, what else would you like me to tell you about?' Jane asked – meaning, What else could somebody like me say that would be of any possible interest to somebody like you?

Grace shrugged. 'I don't know. I hadn't really thought about it. You could tell me about your childhood, I suppose.'

Jane returned the shrug. 'It's your money.'

She started cautiously, giving a heavily edited version of her early life, but as Grace listened – with a kindly, understanding half-smile on her face – Jane grew more confident and more candid. She talked for over half an hour, and when she reached the end, she was both more exhausted, and more at peace, than she could ever remember being before.

'What about you, then?' she was surprised to hear herself say. 'I expect you were brought up in a big house full of servants.'

Grace laughed. 'No, it wasn't like that at all.'

She described her childhood in the jungle – how there were no other children to play with, and how, even if there had been, she wouldn't have been allowed to, because her parents considered play to be at best frivolous, and worse sinful. She talked about the time when she was feverish for two weeks, and none of the medicines in her parents' modest cabinet seemed to have any effect.

'The nearest doctor was a hundred miles away,' she explained, 'and a hundred miles by canoe is much, much further than a hundred miles by road.'

'How bad were you?' Jane asked.

'It was touch and go. My father even had one of the natives dig a grave for me.'

'How do you know that?'

'He told me.'

'When you'd got better?'

'No, when I was still very ill.'

'How could he do that?' Jane gasped. 'How could he be such a monster?'

Grace laughed, a little unconvincingly. 'He wasn't being a monster – at least, not in his terms. To him, my physical life was of no importance, because I'd already been saved. And as for me – I should be glad I was being given a short cut to heaven.' She shivered. 'I think that was the moment I stopped being a Christian.'

And I thought I'd had it rough, Jane reflected.

'But your dad was very happy when you recovered, wasn't he?' she asked hopefully.

'Yes, I suppose so,' Grace agreed, 'but I think he also looked on digging that grave as a waste of effort that could otherwise have been devoted to doing the Lord's work.'

'It must have been terrible for you,' Jane said.

'Oh, it wasn't all bad,' Grace said lightly. 'Sometimes the missionary society would send us a can of corned beef, and then I felt like just about the luckiest girl in the world.'

'Corned beef made you feel like that?' Jane asked incredulously. 'Ordinary corned beef?'

Grace smiled. 'I can assure you, it wasn't ordinary to me.'

'But even we had that – and we had nothing. To tell you the truth, we had so much of it that I got sick of it.'

'I never did. It was magic.'

It was time to risk taking the next step, Grace decided.

'I like you,' she said. 'Do you like me?'

'Yes,' Jane said – and then looked around the room as if to find out who had spoken.

She wondered why she felt like that. Maybe it was because Grace was not as posh as she'd seemed at first. Maybe it was because the other girl seemed willing to accept her for what she was. And maybe – maybe – it was because she felt so sorry for the younger Grace, who *this* Grace had just so vividly described to her.

'I don't have a sister,' Grace said. 'Do you?'

'No.'

'Back home – in Papua New Guinea – we have what we call an adopted sister,' Grace said. 'Will you be mine?'

'Yes,' Jane said, and this time she had no doubt that the voice which agreed was her own.

'In that case, we have to go through a ritual,' Grace said.

Alarm suddenly filled Jane's face.

'Will it hurt?' she asked.

Grace laughed. 'No, it won't hurt. But I have to take a lock of your hair. Would that be all right?'

'Yes.'

Grace took a small pair of scissors from her handbag and snipped at Jane's hair. Then she took a lock of her own. She laid one lock on top of the other, and mingled the two samples. Then she divided the pile into two equal heaps.

With skilled hands, she wove each new pile into a hair bracelet.

'One is for you, and one is for me,' she said. 'You must wear it at all times.'

'I will,' Jane promised.

'I know people in the Ministry of Housing,' Grace said. 'I'll see if I can get you better accommodation than this.'

'No!' Jane said, with sudden violence.

'But this place is so unhealthy and—'

'I'm safe here – because nobody knows I live here.'

'Safe from what?'

'Safe from the people who will try to take my baby away from me.'

For a second, Grace was about to ask her why she thought they would try to take her baby away. But the answer was obvious – they would try to take it away because she was not fit to be a mother.

'Do you really care about your baby?' she asked.

'I love him,' Jane said, and her face glowed with that love. 'I'd die if I didn't have him.'

Well aware that she was about to take a huge gamble from which there was no retreat if it failed, Grace said, 'If you really love him, then you'd better start taking care of him, even before he's born.'

This was the moment at which Jane could explode and demand she leave the house.

Instead, the other woman lowered her head and said very quietly, 'Yes, I know.'

'That means you're going to have to stop drinking . . .'

'Yes.'

'. . . and going with men . . .'

'Yes.'

'. . . and if you refuse to leave this place, then the least you have to do is give it a thorough cleaning.'

'Yes.'

'I'll help you with the cleaning, but you'll have to manage the other things on your own,' Grace said.

'It will be so hard – I've been drinking since I was twelve – but I'll try. I promise I'll try.'

Grace reached across the table, took Jane's hand, and gave it an encouraging squeeze.

'I'll be back tomorrow with the cleaning materials,' she said, 'and I'll bring a locksmith with me, so we can get some decent locks put on the front and back doors. Whenever you need anything, I'll do my best to provide it – as long as it isn't booze. And I'll visit you as often as I can.'

She stood up, and so did Jane. The two women hugged each other.

'Goodnight, sister,' Grace said.

'Goodnight, sister,' Jane replied.

# SIXTEEN

Derek Stockton's study is at the other end of the corridor, and though it is of similar size and shape to Grace's, the choice of furnishings gives it an altogether much more masculine feel.

Stockton walks over to a large roll-top desk that dominates

the centre of the room. Beside it is a table on which books and papers are laid out with such apparent precision that they almost form a rather attractive geometrical pattern.

Stockton sits down at the desk, opens one of the drawers, and extracts a large sheet of headed notepaper.

'Grace and I chose this place because of its relative isolation,' he says, uncapping his fountain pen. 'There are times when you need a few days completely to yourself, so you can think and work, and in town you're always getting interrupted, however clear you make it to your friends that you don't want to be. I used to congratulate us on our cleverness in choosing it, but now I feel that if only we'd settled somewhere closer to other people . . .' His voice falters.

'Then your wife would have been found earlier than she was, but she would still have been dead,' I interject.

He nods. I'm sure it is not the first time he has heard that particular argument, but he seems to draw some small comfort from it anyway.

He quickly fills the page with clear, decisive handwriting, folds the paper neatly, and inserts it in an envelope that he produces from one of the other drawers in the desk.

He holds out the envelope for me, but as I reach out for it, he suddenly jerks it away.

'I want something in return for this,' he says.

'What?' I ask.

'I love my daughter with all my heart and soul,' he tells me with an intensity which electrifies the air. 'I would do anything for her.'

'I can see that,' I reply.

'I want you to promise that if you uncover anything that will hurt her, you will keep it from her,' he says.

'What kind of thing?'

Stockton waves his hands helplessly in the air. 'I don't know,' he says. He pauses. 'Have you ever had a dream where there is no image – just a deep, all-pervading darkness?'

I shudder slightly, because I know exactly what he means.

'Yes,' I say.

'And there is something in that darkness that you fear, though you have no idea what it is?'

I nod.

'It's like that. Perhaps, in that darkness, my wife committed some terrible act – and it was that which got her killed. Like most of our fears, it's probably baseless, but if it turns out that she did do something terrible, finding out about it would have a devastating effect on my daughter.'

'And what effect would the discovery have on you?'

'It would devastate me, too, of course – but I don't matter.'

'So you want me to hide anything hurtful from her, even if it means that her mother's killer goes unpunished?'

'Even then.'

I shake my head. 'I can't make that promise.'

'Why not?' he sneers, his face suddenly filled with contempt. 'Is it because when you chose your so-called profession you signed some seedy investigators' version of the Hippocratic Oath?'

'No,' I reply, coldly. 'It's because it was her mother who was killed, and she's entitled to know the truth.'

The mask of contempt collapses, to reveal that what it was hiding was the face of an injured puppy.

'You're quite right,' he says. 'She is entitled to know. And I'm so sorry for suggesting that you were a seedy investigator.' He hands me the envelope. 'Good luck, Miss Redhead. I hope we never need to meet again, but if we do, you know where I am.'

# SEVENTEEN

*7th May, 1944*

Grace went straight back to the King's Head. She had been there filling in her survey just before she met Jane, but then she had been in the saloon, and now she entered the public bar.

It was a much rougher looking place than the saloon (the latter had pictures on the wall and was carpeted, the former had brass spittoons and sawdust on the floor) – and the customers perfectly reflected the decor.

The landlord looked slightly alarmed to see her there.

'Back again so soon, miss? Well, I suppose it must be very thirsty work talking to all those people, and if you'd care to go round to the saloon bar, I'll pour you a nice glass of shandy on the house.'

'I'd like to address your customers,' Grace said.

'What? In here?' the landlord replied – and now he was definitely looking worried.

'In here,' Grace agreed. 'And to be perfectly honest with you, I'm going to do it with or without your cooperation.'

The landlord's concern grew visibly, but he banged on the counter with a pint pot and said, 'Pay attention, lads. This lady from the ministry wants to talk to you, and you'll listen politely or have me to answer to.'

Grace stood with her back against the bar, facing the drinkers. They were a rough lot, with missing teeth and prominent tattoos. Most of them would be dockers and labourers, she thought, but there was probably a fair smattering of minor criminals as well.

'There's a woman who sometimes stands across the road from this pub and sells her sex for money,' she said.

'I've seen her, and I wouldn't touch her with a barge pole,' one of the men called out.

'No, you wouldn't,' another man shouted. 'I've seen you with her, and it definitely wasn't a barge pole you were using.'

The other men burst into ribald laughter, and the landlord said, 'Now then, now then, remember you're in the presence of a lady, lads.'

'She is pregnant, and she uses the money she gets from you to buy drink, which is very harmful to her unborn baby,' Grace said. 'That's why I don't want any of you to have anything to do with her anymore.'

'Why don't you mind your own business, you posh bitch,' one of the men called out from behind his hand.

'Yeah, keep your nose out of it,' another added.

Grace spoke a few sentences in slow, heavily ceremonial Trinka, and the bar fell uneasily quiet.

'I was brought up in Papua New Guinea, and that is a Trinka curse,' she said, reverting to English. 'I have been trained in the mysteries of Trinka magic, and I have the power to do many terrible things, but the one that's probably of the most interest to you is that I can make a man's testicles rot and fall off – and that is the power I will use on any man who goes near that woman again.'

Most of the men twitched uncomfortably – some even felt their crotches for reassurance – but one brave soul said, 'What a load of bloody rubbish. I don't believe a word of it.'

'Put your tackle on the table, and I'll prove it,' Grace said. 'With everyone watching, I'll make your balls turn green.'

'Go on, do it,' someone said.

The 'brave' man shrugged his shoulders, awkwardly. 'No, I don't want to,' he said. 'I'm not the sort of bloke to expose his crown jewels to a woman he doesn't know.'

'Or, at least, to a woman who you haven't paid for,' one of his pals ribbed him.

'I don't need to look,' Grace told him. 'It will work even if I've got my back turned. So go on – get it out, and give your mates a laugh.'

'This is bloody ridiculous,' the man said. Then he stood up and rushed towards the exit.

'This is your only warning,' Grace said to the rest of the men, in her most impressive voice. 'If you disobey me, I will know – and I will punish you.'

To stay longer would be to diminish her effect. She left through the same door the frightened man had, but whereas he had done it in a mad, embarrassed dash, she made an awesome, stately progress.

Once outside, she took a deep breath. Her hands were trembling and her heart was thumping, but she thought she had pulled it off.

The men would not go near Jane again – the rest was up to Jane herself.

# PART TWO
## Tuesday 28th October, 1975

# EIGHTEEN

When I woke up this morning there was a light layer of frost covering my window panes, and opening the window to clean it off, I caught sight of my first robin redbreast of the year.

Ah, the cute little robin. There may be Christmas cards of winter scenes which do not contain images of this best known – and best loved – of winter birds, but they are few and far between, because robins are small and delicate and beautiful, and just the sight of one of them conjures up ideas of sleigh rides and Christmas trees, log fires and chestnuts roasting. They are, in so many ways, the harbinger of the festive season.

They are also extremely vicious creatures that have been known to attack other species without the slightest provocation.

Any other robin which invades their territory is, equally, shown no mercy. Up to ten per cent of robins are killed by other robins. They have tiny beaks, but driven by determination and bloodlust, a robin will peck the interloper to death – the equivalent, I suppose, of me killing someone with a penknife.

But even though a robin may well have had the stomach for it, it was not one of our little feathered friends that decapitated Grace Stockton, which is why I am now in one of the interview rooms in St Aldate's police station, with the file on the investigation into Grace's murder laid out on the table before me.

I am not alone in this confession extraction chamber. Beside me at the table, and acting like someone completely at home – which, in fact, he is – sits my old friend DS George Hobson.

'Take your time with it, Jennie,' George says expansively. 'There's absolutely no rush.'

'There isn't any need for you to stay,' I tell him.

'You might get lonely by yourself,' he says, with an awkward, lop-sided grin.

'I won't,' I promise him. 'I'll be perfectly happy with my own company, George.'

'Or you might need something explaining to you.'

'If I do, I'll make a note of it, and ask you later.'

He doesn't move.

'I'm sure you have some very important detecting work that you need to be doing, and since we don't want the wheels of justice to grind to a halt, why don't you just run along,' I say helpfully.

'I've been assigned to stay with you for the whole of the morning,' George replies.

'In other words, the Thames Valley Police may have asked for my help – I might say, almost *pleaded* for it . . .'

'I wouldn't go that far.'

'. . . but they don't entirely trust me.'

George shrugs. 'You're a civilian,' he says, as if that explains it all – and in a way, I suppose it does. 'Besides, you can never *quite* trust somebody who is offered her old job back – with a virtual guarantee of promotion built into that offer – and yet turns it down.'

It's quite true what he's saying. I *was* offered it by DCI Macintosh, and I *did* turn it down – because although it had almost broken my heart when I was forced to resign, I soon grew to like the freedom that the precarious life of a private eye affords me.

George tips back his chair and folds his arms. Whatever I say, the gesture informs me, he has no intention of going anywhere.

I open the file. The narrative begins with the transcript of the phone call Dr Derek Stockton made to the police on the afternoon when he realized his wife was not at home, and then continues with details of the interview that George had conducted with him.

'How did Stockton seem to you?' I ask.

'Like a man who was used to being in control of himself, and who was trying his best to maintain his front despite the nightmare he seemed to be living through,' George says.

And still, three years on, that description would still pretty much fit him, I think.

The report continues with details of the meticulous police work which led to the tracking of Duffle Coat Woman's movements.

'Dr Stockton thinks Duffle Coat Woman never intended to murder Mrs Stockton,' I say.

'That's good to know,' George replies, 'because I always like to hear whatever assessment amateurs make of a murder – and it's particularly valuable when the amateur in question is personally emotionally involved.'

'Fair point,' I'm forced to agree. Then I think back to the conversation that we had in the Bulldog. 'Hang about,' I tell him. 'You said yourself the fact she was asking for Grace's address on Oxford station probably meant that she had no intention of killing her.'

'I didn't claim it wasn't a possibility,' he answers, blithely. 'I merely said that I rarely appreciate advice from amateurs. The fact that she didn't seem to mind the cameras when she arrived, but took care to avoid them when she was leaving, *would* seem to indicate she was aware of some change in her circumstances. On the other hand, if she was trying to look inconspicuous, why didn't she ditch that bright red duffle coat much earlier?'

'What!' I exclaim. 'Say that again.'

'She left the duffle coat in the women's toilets at the railway station, but if she'd wanted to go unnoticed, she should have got rid of it before she even arrived at the station.'

'It's not that bit I'm interested in,' I say, impatiently. 'It's the bit about the colour of the duffle coat.'

'It was bright red – almost scarlet.'

Almost scarlet! There was no way you could tell that from the surveillance tape, because that was in black and white.

'I didn't know they made duffle coats in red,' I admit. 'I thought they only came in dark blue and green.'

'You're wrong about that. They make them in brown and yellow, as well,' George tells me. 'But where you are right is that they don't make any duffle coats in red.'

'Well, then?'

'It had been dyed. And according to the boys in the lab, whoever dyed it knew what he was doing.'

Why would someone dye a duffle coat? I ask myself.

Maybe a young art student, trying to show originality, might do it.

But would a woman in late middle age feel such a need?

That seems highly unlikely.

The file goes on to reveal the use that had been made of the still photograph. It had been published in the national press – which

I vaguely remember from the time – but in addition, copies had been sent to any police station which was situated in close proximity to the London to Birmingham railway line. As always, police switchboards had been jammed with people claiming to know the woman, but they had all been mistaken, deluded or mischievous.

The report continues with a description of how the body was found in the bluebell woods, and how, once it had been disinterred, the team conducted a fruitless search for the head.

'So looked at all-in-all, the investigation really doesn't add up to much, does it?' I say to George Hobson.

'That's a bit harsh, Jennie,' he replies. 'I admit, it hasn't exactly achieved a lot, but . . .'

'Let's have a look at what it *hasn't* achieved,' I suggest. 'You've no idea who the woman was, where she came from, why she killed Grace Stockton or where she went after that. Is that fair enough?'

'I suppose so.'

'You don't even know that she did actually kill Grace. Maybe Grace was already dead and buried by the time she got to the manor.'

'Now that's not likely, is it?' George asks. 'It would be too much of a coincidence that some other person – the real killer – *and* our mystery woman both visited the place within a few hours of each other.'

'Coincidences do happen,' I point out.

'So say for the moment that Duffle Coat Woman is an innocent party,' George says. 'There was no sign of violence at the manor – I know that because I was there myself – so when she arrives, there's neither hide nor hair of the woman she's come to see. OK?'

'Yes.'

'But instead of waiting around to see if Grace Stockton turns up, she takes the next train back to London. And after coming all that way, she doesn't even bother to leave a note. Is that what you're saying?'

'Maybe.'

'All of which means that she's completely unaware that any crime has been committed? Am I right?'

'Perhaps,' I agree, but I'm well aware that the ground I'm standing on is turning out to be a bit of a swamp.

'So why, when she reads about the murder in the paper – when she sees her own picture in the paper – and realizes the police are looking for her, doesn't she report to the nearest police station?'

'Perhaps she's too frightened to.'

'OK, that's a possibility,' George concedes. 'But let's go back a little – if she doesn't know a crime has been committed, why does she hide herself from the cameras at the railway station?'

He has a point.

'Is it possible she was deliberately drawing attention to herself when she arrived?' I ask.

'What do you mean?'

'By stopping people and asking them where Grace Stockton lived, she was making herself memorable. And that would have been so easy to avoid.'

'Go on.'

'Finding out where Grace lived before she arrived wouldn't have been very difficult at all. She's in the phone book, and she's in the university listings. And even if she wasn't, there's probably some sort of institute of anthropologists with the information, and her publishers will certainly have had an address that they could have been conned into revealing. If I'd been looking for her, I'd have tracked her down in less than an hour.'

'And if I'd have been an American with lightning reactions, who wasn't afraid of flying, I could have a souvenir sample of moon rock on my mantelpiece right now.'

'What's that supposed to mean?' I ask.

'Maybe you would have tracked her down in less than an hour – but you're a college graduate, an ex-copper and a private detective,' George says. 'You know how to do research. But there are a lot of people who don't.'

Again, that's true enough. It's either the height of arrogance or the depth of humility to assume that if you can do something yourself, it must be easy – and maybe it's both (or neither) depending on the circumstances.

'Which newspaper was it that Duffle Coat Woman was showing around the station?' I ask.

George takes the witness statements out of the folder, and flicks through them.

'None of the witnesses could identify the newspaper,' he says, 'because she didn't show them a whole page, or even a complete article. All she had was the picture of Grace Stockton. Does it matter?'

'It could be vital,' I tell him. 'If it's a national newspaper, she could have seen it anywhere in the country, but if it was a local newspaper, then that narrows down the area in which we need to search.'

'In other words, if you find out it came from the *Manchester Evening News*, you'll only have a city of over a million people to search, which should make it an absolute doddle.'

'Well, you must admit it's a start,' I say, and I'm surprised to hear how defensive I'm being.

'And, of course, before you can even begin that nigh-on-impossible search, you need to find out which newspaper she took the photograph from. And how do you propose to do that?'

'I'm working on it,' I say, sounding much more optimistic than I feel.

# NINETEEN

My working assumption is that Duffle Coat Woman – now known to be *Red* Duffle Coat Woman – saw Grace Stockton's picture in the newspaper no more than two weeks before Grace herself was murdered.

Why have I settled on two weeks?

There are a couple of reasons.

Reason number one: the fact that Red Duffle Coat Woman came to Oxford, even though she didn't know precisely where Grace lived (and was therefore taking a gamble on finding out), would seem to imply she felt an urgent need to talk to the other woman.

Reason number two: the fact that she then killed Grace (as we are all assuming she did) is just a way of underlining that the mission really was urgent.

So given both those facts, is it likely RDCW would have put off the visit for *more than* two weeks?

Definitely not!

Well . . . probably not.

There are circumstances, I must admit, which might have forced her to put off making an appearance for longer than she might have wished. She could have been nursing a dying relative, for example, or have broken her leg. She could have been banged up in prison, or living abroad.

Now that I stop to think about it, I can come up with a dozen reasons for a delay, right off the top of my head.

But I have to start somewhere, and having settled on the two-week time limit, I go to Oxford's very excellent central public library on Westgate, and search the newspaper archives.

I've been using the library a great deal since I started my agency (I love that word – agency – it gives my shoebox office a little of the gravitas it is badly in need of), and I have several friends there, including assistant librarian Elaine Williams, who greets me with a positive whisper of joy.

Elaine was one of my first clients, and I'm as grateful to her for giving me the work as she is to me for solving her problem.

Elaine Williams' problem went by the name of Jack Stone. He was a six-foot-three, rugby-playing fireman. He also happened to be Elaine's ex-boyfriend, and he had been persecuting her ever since she decided to break up with him.

The persecution started with phone calls in the middle of the night – calls during which the caller himself said nothing.

Next came the anonymous letters accusing her of every kind of moral weakness and sexual deviance known to man.

That had been bad enough, but then the hate campaign began to escalate. What had been suggested in the poisonous letters now appeared as poisonous graffiti – large-lettered, poisonous graffiti – on the side wall of the greengrocer's shop near to Elaine's flat, and on the bench next to the bus stop she used.

The late-night calls resumed, too, but this time they were not silent – this time they came from a number of foul-mouthed men who wanted to know where she lived and how much she charged.

At first, she had no idea what the origin of this latest horror was – and then she saw the business card in one of the local phone boxes.

Down both edges of the card, there was a silhouette of an obviously naked woman, and in the centre was the message:

Sexy Elaine
I'll let you do anything you want to me.
Nothing is too dirty!

Her telephone number was listed below.

'It's turning me into a nervous wreck,' she'd told me, with tears forming in her eyes even as she spoke. 'I can't eat, I can't sleep. I was Oxfordshire Library Assistant of the Year, last year, but now I've started making so many mistakes that I've been given my final warning. I'm going to lose my job. And I love my job, Miss Redhead. I really, really do.'

'Why haven't you reported it to the police?' I'd asked her.

'I have reported it, but they say that unless I can produce something to show that it is Jack doing all these horrible things, there's nothing they can do. So find a way to prove it for me, Miss Redhead. Please find a way!'

I tried. I honestly did. I searched for a witness who had seen the graffiti being sprayed, but it seemed to have been done in the dead of night, when everyone was asleep. I tracked down the printer who had produced the cards, but he would say nothing, and I had no means of compelling him to.

It was soon obvious to me that Jack had been very careful, and that without the backing of a full police forensic lab, I was never going to be able to pin anything on him.

By rights, I should have reported this to my client, but I knew that it would break her heart.

It was then that I discovered I was losing all objectivity – that I was taking it personally.

It was the first time that it had ever happened – but it certainly wouldn't be the last.

Oh dear me, no!

Not by a long chalk!

I decided to beard the lion in his den, the den in this case being the local rugby club, where, after the Saturday match, I knew he would be drinking with his mates.

Wait, Jennie! I can hear you shouting silently. Wasn't it foolish to go onto his territory, especially when he was surrounded by his mates, and full of ale? Under those circumstances, there was probably little chance he would listen to a reasoned and reasonable argument, and it might actually turn quite nasty.

This is quite true. In fact, I was banking on him turning nasty, because that would create the ideal scenario for testing out the old adage that while calling names can never hurt you, sticks and stones might well break your bones.

The rugby club consisted largely of a big square room which served as a meeting room, boozer and dance hall. Women often graced it with their presence, but on Saturday afternoons, it was a strictly male preserve, thick with coarse language and testosterone. On the small stage, a trio was lethargically performing their repertoire, no doubt conscious of the fact that it little mattered to most people whether they were there or not. Waiters rushed back and forth, carrying trays weighted down with pints of bitter, and the gentlemen's toilet was doing thriving business.

Jack and his bunch of mates were sitting at a table near the stage, waiting for the stripper – 'All the way from Droitwich – Miss Lola Perez' – to make an appearance. They were all dressed in blue blazers and rugby club ties. They had already drunk quite a lot (as was evidenced by the number of empty glasses on the table) but their eyes had not yet acquired the dullness that only comes with true rat-arsed drunkenness.

I looked from one to another. I'm not prejudiced, I've known any number of intelligent, sensitive rugby players – and even slept with a couple of them – but what I was viewing now was a prime selection of absolute meatheads.

'Take a seat, Ginger,' Jack Stone said, patting the chair next to him. 'Or if you like, you can sit on my knee.'

I was quite grateful to him for his chauvinism, since it was making it all that much easier for me to do what I had to do.

'Yeah, sit on his knee,' called one of Jack's mates. 'Or sit on his thing, if you'd like it better.'

I shook my head. 'I'm here on business,' I told Jack.

He smiled. Here was an unexpected opportunity to have some sport, he was thinking.

'What kind of business?' he asked.

'I want you to stop playing all your nasty little tricks on Elaine right now,' I told him.

'Are you talking to me?' he asked, looking round expectantly, to make sure that all his mates were listening.

'Talking to you?' I answered. 'No, certainly not.'

'Good, because—'

'Unless, of course, you happen to be a slime-ball gutter-snipe named Jack Stone.'

'Now look here—' he began.

'So you are the shitehawk I was looking for!'

His mates were all grinning, and he was beginning to suspect he was losing this encounter.

'I think you should be very careful what you—' he began.

'You're a coward and a loser,' I interrupted him. 'Every other feller in this room would take rejection by a woman like a proper man should. But then you're not a man at all, are you – because you have to lash out at someone weaker than you? You're beneath contempt.'

His mates were looking at him – still amused, but mainly wondering what he would do next.

For a second or two, I was afraid that he'd do nothing at all, which would have been humiliating for him, true, but nowhere near humiliating enough to fulfil my purposes.

Then I realized that it was not so much a question of his responding as it was of working out what particular form that response should take.

Verbal fencing just wouldn't cut it, because that would bestow on me an equality he wasn't ready to concede. Besides, I was clearly a bright girl, and with a few well-chosen thrusts and parries, I might even win.

So it had to be something physical. But what form should that physicality take?

If I'd been a man, he would have hit me, but I was seven inches shorter and four stone lighter than he was, and even *his* bunch of creepy friends would consider it an awfully bad show.

Then a complacent smile spread across his face.

'You can't speak to me like that,' he said. 'Do you know what I'm going to do? I'm going to teach you a lesson.'

'If you're the teacher then it must be a very simple lesson indeed,' I said, just in case there was even a slight chance of him backing away from a confrontation at the last moment.

'I'm going to put you over my knee, and tan your bare arse till it's as red as your hair,' he said.

His friends roared with laughter at this witticism, and elbowed one another in the ribs. This was classic Jack, they told each other.

I think he was half-expecting me to run away, which would have served his purposes well enough, since it would have left him clearly the winner.

But I stood my ground, which was even better from his point of view, because what he was about to do now, he believed, was going to make him a rugby club legend.

Just looking at him, I could tell he could see the whole thing clearly in his head.

Me – bent over his knee, red hair dusting the ground, skirt raised and knickers down.

Him – raising his ham-like hand and striking my backside, leaving a red imprint on my white skin, while all his mates cheered and banged their pint pots on the table.

Perhaps his imagination took him even further than that. Perhaps the treatment I had received would captivate me, and I would become his willing slave – it being well known that all women dream of being dominated by a caveman just like him.

He stood up. 'Well, you asked for it,' he said.

Two seconds later, he was lying on the floor. It seemed to have come as a complete surprise to him.

'What . . .?' he moaned. 'How did you . . .?'

How did I learn to flip him over so easily?

It's really very simple, my friend, I thought, and it goes right back to my childhood.

When you're a redhead called Redhead, you see, you're the ideal target for playground bullies who are always on the lookout for an excuse to pick on someone, which was why, as soon as I was old enough, I enrolled in a course of mixed martial arts – and turned out to be rather good at it.

He struggled to his feet.

'Even a moron like you should know when you're outclassed,

so why don't you just quit,' I advised him, knowing he wouldn't take my warning seriously – and not wanting him to.

He roared with rage, and when he came at me again, all thoughts of my femininity had been pushed aside. He intended to attack me as if I were a man, and hurt me badly.

This time I was not so gentle, and inflicted a few injuries which would probably trouble him for several days.

When he hit the floor for a second time, I knelt down beside him.

'You leave Elaine alone, or I'll come back and really give you something to moan about,' I said softly. 'If you've understood, nod your head.'

He just lay there.

'If you've not understood, maybe we should continue the lesson,' I suggested. 'So before I begin again, I'll give you one last chance. Did you understand me or didn't you?'

This time, his head did move a little, though the effort obviously hurt.

I stood up, and surveyed the table.

'Would anyone like to buy me a drink while we wait for the police to arrive?' I asked.

All Jack's mates had their heads down and were studying the table, but now one of them looked up and said, 'Nobody's called the police . . .'

'Oh well, I expect it's only a matter of time before they do.'

'. . . and nobody's going to.'

Of course they wouldn't. I knew that. Jack had attacked me, rather than the other way around. And even if they could persuade the police to arrest me, all that would mean was that I would go to trial, and Jack would be even more humiliated – this time in open court.

'I still fancy a drink, but I can't get it myself, because I'm not a member of this club,' I said. 'So would anyone like to be a gentleman and buy me a gin and tonic?'

This was their chance to show they had a bit of style, but none of them availed themselves of it, so I left.

When Elaine asked me what had happened, I told her Jack and I had had a serious discussion and he'd seen the error of his ways, which was (if you're interpreting the incident generously) what actually happened.

It would have been impossible for Jack to continue living in an area where everyone knew he had been humiliated by a woman – and a *ginger* woman, at that. I was told that he applied for a transfer the very next day, and within a week he had been moved to a fire station somewhere on the south-east coast.

I don't think anybody really missed him.

'How's life, Elaine,' I whisper to my old client.

By way of an answer, she points to the badge pinned just above her right breast, which says 'Library Assistant of the Year 1974'.

Second time, hey? Pretty good!

'And I'm getting married next year,' she says. 'You must come to the wedding.'

'I'd love to,' I enthuse.

And already my mind is working on how I can get out of it without hurting her feelings, because a wedding reception seems to me a bit like the wake at a funeral – a celebration of a life now at an end – which just shows you what a sick puppy I really am.

But though I hate to admit it, I do get a bit of a warm glow over the thought that Elaine seems very happy, and that I have played my part in it.

In a way, I'm a little like the Lone Ranger, except that I don't have any silver bullets.

Or a horse!

Or a faithful Indian companion!

OK, bad example.

'I'm going down into the newspaper stacks,' I say. And then, Captain Oates-like, I add, 'I might be some time.'

'I'll bring you a coffee in about an hour,' Elaine says.

Good girl!

British newspapers come in all shapes and sizes. The *Telegraph* and *The Times* are broadsheets, which makes them almost impossible to read on the train or bus, unless, that is, you were born into the world of men who wear bowler hats and pinstriped trousers, where such a skill seems inherent. The *Mail* and the *Express* pretend to be broadsheets, but are slightly smaller and much less weighty. They are traditionally read by men who wear trilbies, often with a feather in the hatband. The *Sun* and the *Mirror* are tabloids, the fodder of the working class. They often feature pictures of semi-naked young women, and make less of an effort to hide their irrational prejudices than the more respectable tomes take to hide theirs.

Down here in the archives, all newspapers are equal – even the *Financial Times*, which is not only a broadsheet but pink – because they have been captured on microfilm, and are thus reduced, each and every one of them, to black shiny plastic.

I feed the first newspaper into the reader, and get to work.

April 1972 was, it appears, a very busy time. Jack Nicklaus triumphed at the US Masters, and Jane Fonda and Gene Hackman both won Oscars, Fonda for *Klute* and Hackman for *The French Connection*. The USSR performed an underground nuclear test, and the Provisional Irish Republican Army exploded twenty-four overground bombs in towns and cities across Northern Ireland. Apollo 16 astronauts landed on the moon, which was rapidly becoming NASA's favourite picnic spot. And for American fans still mourning the break-up of the Beatles there was some good news – John Lindsay, the young and dynamic mayor of New York City, had made a personal appeal to the US immigration department not to deport John Lennon.

There was news of a more parochial nature, too. A new link road to the M6 motorway had been completed, a boom in the sale of colour televisions was expected soon, and there was a man in Swindon who ate sandwiches which had cigarettes as their filling.

After three hours of intense microfilm reading – and three coffees kindly provided by Elaine – I have a splitting headache and the room seems be swimming before my eyes, but I haven't found a single mention of Dr Grace Stockton, anthropologist and murder victim of this parish.

That's how it goes sometimes.

# TWENTY

The trick was not to be overly ambitious, Grace reminded herself, as, on her knees, she scrubbed and scrubbed away at the ingrained dirt on the kitchen floor of the house on Bombay Street. And what that meant, in purely practical terms, was that she should not attempt to achieve too much herself, nor – more importantly – should she try to push Jane too hard.

For example, Jane should not stay in this house. It was unhealthy for her baby, not just because of the damp and the crumbling walls, but because it had no running water, and the nearest tap was a hundred yards away, which can seem like a huge distance when you're carrying two heavy pails.

But while all that was true, Jane refused to leave because of her fear that the authorities would take her baby from her.

Very well, then, if she wouldn't move, the house needed to be sanitized from top to bottom.

But that wasn't possible, either. It would take a small army of workers to get the whole place reasonably clean, and a smaller – but still significant – army to *keep* it clean.

So what you had to do was scale back – abandon the idea of attaining the perfect, and work towards what could be done.

And what could be done was to establish this one room as an island of hygiene, floating above the sea of filth which surrounded it.

She had already begun this process, with the cleaning, and Jane – bless her heart – was doing her best to help, even though it was obvious that she had never been taught how to tackle housework.

Once they had the room thoroughly clean, Grace intended to replace all the furniture (most of it currently in the back yard) with some basic – but good – second-hand furniture.

She looked up from her task. Jane was conscientiously working away in the far corner.

'That's it,' Grace called out encouragingly. 'We'll soon have this place so clean you could eat your food off the floor.'

And that was another thing, she thought, she needed to teach Jane how to eat properly, because while the rations provided by the government weren't very tasty (now that was an understatement!), they did contain all the nourishment that a woman with a baby growing inside her needed.

She stopped scrubbing, and stood up.

'I think we've earned a brew,' she said.

She had brought a spirit stove and kettle with her, and having spent a good fifteen minutes cleaning the cups she'd found in Jane's cupboard, she had everything she needed.

It was awkward pouring water from the bucket to the kettle – she should bring a jug with her the next time she came, she thought – but she managed that too, and they sat on the floor, waiting for the kettle to come to the boil.

'I'm going to love my little baby, and my little baby will love me,' Jane said. A look of anguished uncertainty suddenly crossed her face. 'He *will* love me, won't he, Grace?'

Grace laughed. 'Of course he will. But you do know that it might be a girl, don't you?'

Jane shook her head. 'He'll be a boy. I know he will.'

Oh dear, Grace thought.

'Does that mean that if the baby's a girl, you won't love her?' she asked, anxiously.

It was Jane's turn to laugh.

'Of course not! I'll love her – I'll love her to pieces. I'm going to be the best mum there ever was.'

'That's good,' Grace said.

But as she poured the boiling water into the teapot, she found herself worrying that however willing she was to reform, Jane might yet give in to her weaknesses.

'You're worried I'll start drinking again, aren't you?' Jane asked, reading her mind.

'A little,' Grace admitted, cautiously.

'You've no need to be. I haven't had a drink since we met last night. It's been very hard, but I haven't.'

'It'll get harder yet,' Grace cautioned.

'I know that – but my little boy deserves the best.'

Grace poured the tea, and they sat drinking it in companionable silence.

Then Grace decided the time had come to take another gamble, and reached into her handbag.

'Here's a pound,' she said. 'I'll be giving you some money every week, but I don't want you to spend it. What I do want you to do is to save it, because when the baby's born, you'll need to buy him things.'

'Wouldn't it be better if you saved it for me?' Jane asked.

'No,' Grace said firmly. 'By giving it to you, I'm saying I trust you, and I know you won't let me down.'

'I won't. I won't,' said Jane, with tears in her eyes. She took the pound carefully, as if it were some holy relic. 'Nobody's ever trusted me before.'

'Now the next thing we need to discuss is getting you the care you need,' Grace said.

Jane put down her cup. The cheerful, intimate atmosphere evaporated, to be replaced by a chill of fear and suspicion.

'What do you mean, "getting me the care I need"?' Jane asked.

'Well, we'll have to arrange for a qualified midwife to come and see you regularly and—'

'No!' Jane interrupted.

'What do you mean?'

'I'm not seeing anybody but you.'

'Be reasonable,' Grace pleaded. 'You'll have to see a midwife eventually, because you'll need her to help you give birth.'

'You can help me.'

'But I'm not qualified.'

'You can do anything you put your mind to,' Jane said. 'I know you can. You're just marvellous.'

'I'm not marvellous, but even if I was, I simply don't have the training a midwife has.'

'If you won't help me, I'll do it on my own,' Jane said stubbornly.

She would, too, Grace thought. Such was her terror of the authorities that she'd risk her baby's life – and her own – rather than have anything at all to do with them.

'*Will* you help me?' Jane asked.

She had watched babies being born in Papua New Guinea, Grace reminded herself. She had even assisted in a couple of the births. But she had never done it alone.

Yet what choice did she have? If she refused to help, it was possible that Jane, in return, would refuse to see her again. Even worse, the girl might begin to see her as just one more enemy, and, in a panic, run away, only to die unloved and uncared for in some anonymous alley.

'Yes, I'll help you,' she said. 'You can always rely on me.'

Jane looked at the hair bracelet on her wrist, and then the one on Grace's wrist.

'You're the best sister a girl could ever have,' she said, with tears forming in her eyes.

# TWENTY-ONE

It is late afternoon, darkness has begun to cast its heavy cloak over the ancient city of Oxford, and the air temperature has already started to drop. I have dined, in some style, on one of the Bulldog's excellent prawn sandwiches, and washed it down with a gin and tonic. Now, I'm back at St Aldate's police station, this time in one of the less impressive conference rooms (and accompanied by one of the less impressive representatives of law and order).

The reason I am here is that, having drawn a blank with all the national newspapers I viewed in the Oxford Central Library, there seem to me to be only two courses of action that are still open to me.

The first is that I can visit the public libraries of every town and city in the whole country, and check through the local news-papers in their stacks, in order to see if I can find any reference to Grace Stockton. At a conservative estimate – and working flat out – that should take me at least a year.

Thus, I have chosen to go with the second option, which is to examine Grace Stockton's papers (currently held by the Thames Valley Police, as part of their cold case investigation) in the hope I'll find something there that will point me in the right direction.

Last time I was here (God, was it only this morning!), I had DS George Hobson – old friend and ex-lover – riding shotgun on me, but it would appear that George's talents are in demand elsewhere, so this time my companion on my journey of discovery goes by the name of Detective Constable Bentley.

Bentley is around twenty-three, I would guess, which is rather young to be in the CID. He has vague, hazel-coloured eyes, a nose which is only remarkable in its lack of remarkableness, and a mouth edged by unexceptional lips. In other words, his is the sort of face you forget the moment he has walked out of the room.

As I suggested earlier, he does not seem to be the brightest new star in the CID firmament, which is probably why he has been assigned to watch me, rather than devoting his talents to tracking down serial killers or gangs of international jewel thieves.

The conference room contains a table and six foldable chairs, and on the table sit the evidence boxes and personal documents which relate to the murder of Grace Stockton, and which have just been delivered by a middle-aged female clerical officer with a bad cold and rampant dandruff.

The document that I am most interested in is Grace's diary from 1972, which is listed as being in Evidence Box 2.

The list does not lie, and the diary is just where it is supposed to be. It is about the size of a paperback novel, though nowhere near as thick. And (it soon becomes apparent), it is not, as so many diaries are, a place in which hopes, aspirations and fears are recorded, but instead contains nothing more than a list of appointments and dates she needs to remember.

I quickly flick through the pages covering the relevant period before the murder, which (according to the police theory) took place shortly after the arrival of Red Duffle Coat Woman on the 13th of April.

*10th April:*
*Dentist 10.30.*
*Hairdresser 2.30.*

I feel nothing but admiration – with perhaps a stab of jealousy thrown in – for any woman who could face up to two of the things that I hate most in the world on a single day.

Under the entry for the next day, I discover the probable reason for her visit to the hairdresser's.

*11th April:*
*Talk. Southwark. 2.00 pm. The work of an anthropologist.*

Southwark is a borough of London. I do not know London well myself – we northerners have a distrust of the capital city handed out to us with our rattles and teething rings – so I have no idea how many institutions there are in Southwark which are important enough to host a lecture by a world-famous anthropologist. Still, that obviously narrows down my search a little.

I move on.

*12th April:*
*Reception at Master's Lodge, St Luke's.*

Oh yes, Oxford dons do love a good reception, and not, as the naive outsider might think, because it provides a forum for fine minds to discuss weighty matters. Rather it provides an opportunity or excuse (call it what you will), to raid the college cellars for fine wines that were laid down twenty or thirty years previously by some epicurean bursar.

The 13th to the 15th have the same two words written in them: *Research/Article.*

Or to put it another way, the darker side of my brain suggests: Research/Article/Decapitation.

I think about the relative isolation of the manor house, and what a perfect location it is for anyone who wanted to be left alone to finish a scholarly article. It is also, of course, the perfect place to commit a murder and escape from the scene of the crime without anyone noticing.

The entry for the 16th reads: *Pick up Derek from airport.*

She's got that wrong, I tell myself, because he arrived back at Heathrow on the fifteenth.

There is a phone at the end of the table – one of the old-fashioned ones made from chunky black Bakelite which used to feature prominently in 1950s films about newspaper offices.

'Would it be all right if I used that phone?' I ask DC Bentley.

A dubious look comes to his face and is almost instantaneously replaced by a worried one.

'I don't know if you can,' he says. 'I'm not sure whether the regulations cover civilian use of police telephones.'

'But I really need to use it,' I tell him.

'I'd have to check,' he says, 'and I couldn't do that without leaving you alone with the evidence.'

Heaven forbid he should leave me alone with something I have permission to see! And if it needs someone's permission, why doesn't he use the bloody phone to ask for it?

'I'll tell you what – why don't you arrest me?' I suggest.

'Arrest you?' the Einstein of St Aldate's nick repeats. 'Why would I want to do that?'

'Ah well, you see, DC Bentley, if you arrested me, I'd be entitled – by law – to make one phone call.'

'But you haven't done anything wrong, Miss Redhead,' he says, sounding puzzled.

I sigh. I love working with people with no sense of humour – it brings that extra little zing to an otherwise mundane existence.

'How would it be if you made the call, and then handed the phone to me once you've been connected?' I say.

He still looks uncertain.

'If you're ever going to climb your way to the top of your chosen profession, you're going to have to learn to be decisive,' I tell him. 'Do you think DCI Macintosh would ever have hesitated like you are now?'

That seems to do the trick.

He picks up the phone. 'Who would you like to talk to?' he asks.

My first impulse is to tell him I'd like to speak to Slasher McVicious or any other member of the Cornmarket Mad Dog Cutthroats, but there's always a danger he'll take me seriously, and write me up as someone with known criminal associates who is well worth keeping an eye on.

So what I actually say is, 'I'd like to talk to Dr Derek Stockton. You'll probably find him either at his home number, or in his study in St Luke's College.'

DC Bentley (or rather, the woman manning the police switchboard) tries the college first, but eventually finds Dr Stockton at home.

'What is it now, Miss Redhead?' he asks, when DC Bentley – gingerly and unsurely – hands me the phone.

Does his voice sound weary or wary?

It's possible that it's both.

'Your wife wrote in her diary that she was expecting you on the 16th of April,' I say. 'Was that a mistake on her part?'

'No,' he replies. 'Originally, I was coming back on the 16th, because I was meant to debate Oliver Keanan in Boston on the 15th.'

'Oliver Keanan?' I hear myself repeat.

'Yes,' he replies in a voice which indicates that he's surprised I don't seem to know who he's talking about. Then, realizing that not everyone is as wrapped up in his subject as he is himself, he adds, 'Oliver Keanan is a famous – though some might say infamous – American atheist. I was supposed to be debating him at Harvard, but he pulled out at the last minute. I saw no point in kicking my heels in Boston, so I decided to catch an earlier flight.'

'Did you tell your wife?'

'I thought I did at the time.'

He *thought* he did?

'What exactly do you mean by that?' I ask.

'When I rang her, all I got was the answering machine, and so I left her a message.'

'How many times did you ring her?'

'Just the once.'

If I wanted someone to pick me up, I'd make bloody certain they'd got the message, I think, so why didn't Stockton?

'Are you still there?' he asks, and I realize I've been pondering in silence for maybe ten seconds.

'Yes, sorry, I'm still here,' I say. 'I was just wondering . . .'

'You were wondering why I didn't ring her up again, to make sure she'd got the first message.'

'Well, yes.'

'You wouldn't wonder if you'd known Grace. She was one of those people who – however busy they are – religiously check the answerphone every two hours. When I rang her on Friday, I was confident that she would get the message and be there to meet me on Saturday, but as we now know' – his voices drops to almost a whisper – 'when my call was being recorded on the answerphone, she was already dead.'

I feel a sudden wave of guilt at having put him through all this for what must be the hundredth time.

'I'm sorry to have bothered you,' I say.

'My daughter has asked me to co-operate with you, and that is what I'm doing,' he tells me.

And then he hangs up.

I suppose he could have been more gracious about it, but I can't help feeling that I have got off lightly.

If the police know their job, they will have listened to the answerphone, and there should be a transcript of what was on it, I tell myself as I search through the list of evidence.

It's not that I doubt Dr Stockton, you understand – he's up to his neck in solid alibis – but in this job you quickly learn to trust no one, not even God (unless he can produce a library card or some other form of identification).

There *is* a transcript, but there is also the answerphone itself. I plug it in, hoping it has not seized up in the three years it has remained dormant, and I am in luck, because the lights come on and there is a slight static hiss.

I rewind the tape, and then press play.

'Hello, this is Martha,' the caller says. 'I was hoping to catch you at home, but it's nothing important – I just felt like a chat.' A pause. 'To be honest with you, I'd like some reassurance that I wasn't being the least beastly to Charles at the St Luke's reception last night.' Another pause, and then, sounding very disappointed, Martha continues, 'Well, I suppose if you're not there, you're not there.'

I press the pause button to give myself thinking time. The reception was held on Wednesday the 12th, which meant this call was made on Thursday the 13th, the day the police believe Grace was murdered, and since it is the first call on the tape, she must have rubbed off all the previous ones.

I press play again, and this time the speaker has a rich baritone voice and an obvious air of self-importance.

'Grace, my dear it's Geoffrey Markham here,' he intones. 'It's Thursday afternoon and I have the most wonderful news for you. You're very much in the running to be one of the principal speakers at the World Anthropological Society's conference in Vienna next year, but before the final selection is made on Monday, I need you to commit to appearing if chosen, and I'd like you to make a decision right now, in order to give the committee the mental space to mull it over.'

The next call is also from Geoffrey Markham.

'Grace, it's Friday morning. I'm rather disappointed you've not got back to me yet, because in matters of this nature, as you know yourself, timing is crucial.' He gave a sigh and then continued, 'I'll ring you again tomorrow, Grace. You really don't want to lose this opportunity, you know.'

The next call was from Derek Stockton, who sounded very cross.

'Hello, darling. It's just after noon on Friday here, which, if I've got my calculations right, means it's late afternoon there. You remember I was supposed to be debating Oliver Keanan tomorrow night? Well, the little shit has cancelled on me, and since I've had just about enough of America for this trip, I've changed my flight. I'll be arriving at the time you expected me, but it will be Saturday rather than Sunday. If you can't pick me up, could you ring me at the hotel and let me know?'

There were no calls after that. I wonder what had prevented Geoffrey Markham – who seemed to require an answer so urgently – from ringing again.

As I reach into my bag for my notebook, DC Bentley says, 'What are you doing?'

'Since I'm not supposed to take anything from this room, I'm making some notes,' I say.

He frowns. 'I'm not sure you're allowed to do that,' he says.

Oh, come on now!

'Tell me, DC Bentley; are you Chief Inspector Bentley's son by any chance?' I ask, taking a stab in the dark.

'No, I'm *Superintendent* Bentley's son,' he says.

Ah, that explains a lot.

'So if I'm not allowed to take notes, am I allowed to memorize everything?' I ask him.

His frown deepens. 'I don't know,' he admits.

'Because if I'm not, we have a problem, since some of the material is already in my head. Do you have a machine at this station for removing memories – or will you have to send to headquarters for one?'

His perplexity deepens. 'I didn't know . . . didn't know . . .'

'You didn't know that such a machine existed?'

'Yes.'

'Of course you didn't – it's not until you're promoted to sergeant that they let you in on the secret.'

If Bentley were a lot smarter, he'd tell me I'm talking sci-fi rubbish. If he were just a *little* smarter, he'd ask me how it is that I know the secret myself. Neither of these things occurs to him. Instead, he just sits there like a goldfish – mouth wide open, mind grappling with his dilemma. If this were a cartoon, smoke would appear from his ears and the top of his head might possibly blow like a volcano. As it is, he only looks set for a heart attack.

'Let me take the notes now, then I'll hand them over to DCI Macintosh and let him decide whether I should have them or not,' I suggest.

'You *will* hand them over, won't you?' he asks.

'Of course.'

'Then go ahead,' he says, sounding relieved – although we both know I'll do no such thing.

I jot down the name of Geoffrey Markham – the man who wanted Grace to address the important meeting in Vienna – and the time and date of her lecture in Southwark.

They say the first forty-eight hours are vital in a murder investigation, which means that I am three years, six months, fifteen days and – I check my watch – three and a half hours behind schedule.

It's a good job I'm an optimist.

I am back in my office and on the phone to the University of Cambridge Anthropology Department, where (according to my faithful researcher Elaine, in the Central Library) Geoffrey Markham is in gainful employment.

I am put through to his secretary. 'A word of warning,' she says, in a voice which proclaims she is long-suffering, 'if you don't want to get off on the wrong foot with him, remember to call him Sir Geoffrey, rather than Dr Markham.'

'It's a recent honour, is it?' I guess.

'Last year,' she replies, 'but the novelty still shows no sign of wearing off. I can only pray he never gets made a lord.'

'Miss Redhead?' Markham says when I'm put through to him.

His tone suggests it is an impertinence for anyone to actually have such a name, and his timbre is even more self-important than it sounded on the answerphone, because, when all is said and done, he is now a knight of the realm.

'Yes, I'm Jennifer Redhead, Sir Geoffrey,' I say, humbly.

'And you're working for my colleague Julia Pemberton?'

'That's right. I'm investigating the death of her mother, Grace Stockton.'

'Ah, dear Grace,' he says. 'Her death was a great loss to the world of anthropology – indeed, to the world in general. The average person in the street little appreciates what a valuable glue anthropology provides for a society which is increasingly divergent and—'

'The thing is, Sir Geoffrey . . .' I interrupt, aware that I'm risking offending him, but also aware that if I listen to him much longer, pulling my own head off will become an increasingly attractive alternative, 'what I really want to know about is the phone calls you made to her just before she was murdered. Do you remember them?'

'Of course I remember them,' he says haughtily. 'I wanted her to be a keynote speaker at the Vienna conference.'

'You called her on the Thursday and Friday, and you said it was very important you got an answer and you were going to call again on the Saturday. But you never did. Can I ask you why you didn't make that third call?'

'I did make it,' he says.

'Are you sure of that?'

'Remind me what year it was.'

'1972.'

'Hettie, can you find my diary for 1972?' Markham says.

His voice sounds a little distant, because he's talking to his secretary, rather than to me.

There is a pause of perhaps a minute and a half, then he comes back on the line and says, 'I did ring her – first thing in the morning, before I set out for my game of squash. She was dead by then, wasn't she?'

'Yes, she was,' I agree. 'There's no record of that third phone call on the answerphone. How do you explain that?'

'Are you accusing me of being mistaken?' he blusters. 'Are you saying I never made the call?'

'No, of course not,' I say, hastily. 'The problem is, as I told you, that there's no record of that call on the tape. I can't work it out, but you're much smarter than I am, so I thought there was just a chance you might come up with an explanation.'

There is an even longer pause on the other end this time, but finally, he says, 'No, I can't explain it. I must have heard the recorded message, otherwise I would have made a note of it, and if the message was there, then my third call should be there too.'

'Thank you for your time, Sir Geoffrey,' I say, and hang up.

Markham has convinced me that he left a message, but that message is not on the tape. There is only one conclusion to be drawn from that, which is that someone erased the message.

But who would have done it?

And, more importantly, *why* would they have done it?

# TWENTY-TWO

I force myself to ring my widowed mother once a week.

It's hard to say exactly *why* I do it so often, because we have nothing to say to each other.

Not really.

It's true that words do pass between us, but they are either the replay of old arguments or resentments (in which the script never varies) or – worse – phrases as lifeless as plaster of Paris, which are inserted into our so-called conversation solely to fill the gaps.

Tonight is no exception.

'How are you, Mother?' I ask.

(It's been a long while since I felt I could call her Mum.)

'Oh,' she says, 'you know . . .'

And I can picture the forlorn shrug of the perpetual martyr she thinks of herself as.

'Your cousin Enid's got another promotion,' she says.

Ah, my cousin Enid! The family paragon!

Enid didn't run away to Oxford University to study English Literature, did she? No, Enid went to a new university, much nearer home, which is, of course, just as good (if not better) than a crumbling pile like Oxford – and anyone who says it isn't is just being jealous. Nor did Enid read for an airy-fairy degree. She took a practical business studies course, and when she graduated, she moved right back to Whitebridge, which is exactly what any intelligent, *normal* human being would have done.

'Good for Enid,' I say, trying – and failing – to sound impressed. 'How's the weather up there?'

'How do you think it is?' she counters scathingly. 'This is Lancashire. It's raining.'

My mother has never really shown me any maternal affection, and I wonder – periodically – if she ever had any to show, or if she gave birth to me simply because that was what you did when you got married.

'Have you made any plans to move back home yet, our Jennifer?' she asks me.

Note the *yet*, as if we both know it's only a matter of time before I give in to the inevitable.

'No,' I say. 'For the moment, I'm quite happy here.'

Why do I play along with her game? And that *is* what I'm doing, because my 'for the moment' just seems to confirm the implicit assumption of her 'yet'. Why can't I come right out with it and tell her that, come hell or high water, I'm never going back to Whitebridge?

'So you're quite happy there,' she says, and she sniffs, as if she considers happiness to be quite reprehensible.

'I have to go,' I say.

'I thought you might. You're never on the phone for long,' she says triumphantly, as she wins – in her own mind – a competition that I haven't even entered.

As I hang up, a single thought keeps flashing through my mind like a neon sign on the blink.

You need a G&T . . . You need a G&T . . . You need a G&T . . .

I'll drink to that.

\* \* \*

I was hoping to come across Charlie – my perpetual source of comfort and reassurance – in the Eagle and Child, but he isn't there. In fact, there's not a single person in the pub that I recognize, with the exception of Father Jim O'Brien, who is propping up the bar.

'Do you need company?' I ask hopefully.

'Why not?' he asks, and then adds, 'as long as you don't try to convert me to heathenism.'

I order my G&T.

'Why do we drink so much?' I wonder, as the barman slides the glass across to me.

'I can't speak for you, Jennie, but I do it to deaden the pain,' Father Jim replies.

'What pain?' I ask.

'The pain I carry with me every day after confession,' he says.

'I thought priests were trained to be above all that,' I reply, knowing I shouldn't be saying this to him, yet somehow unable to stop myself. 'I thought you accepted whatever happened as part of God's great unknowable purpose.'

'Father James O'Brien SJ does accept it,' he tells me. 'He accepts it readily and gladly. It's little Jimmy O'Brien, the barefoot boy from a dirt-poor farm in the Republic of Ireland who has difficulties dealing with it.' He pauses. 'Have you ever had a murderer confess to you, Jennie?'

'Twice,' I say.

'And what happened to them?'

'One gave himself up to the police, the other hanged himself.'

'I've had three people confess to me over the years, and they're all still walking around,' he says.

'And did you forgive them after they confessed?'

A grill-like mask slides over his face, as if my words have inadvertently pushed a secret button.

'I can't discuss that with you,' he says, and it's clear that Jim O'Brien has gone, and Father O'Brien is back.

'The Church has its weaknesses and its failings,' he says, 'but in a shifting world where good and evil seem to have become no more than a matter of personal preference, it is a rock to which I can chain myself, and I thank the Lord God daily for providing it for me. He provides it for you, too, Jennie, and one day you will feel the need of that rock, and you will come and ask me where to find it.'

'Over my dead body,' I say.

'Oh, I wouldn't leave it that long if I were you,' he says, with just a hint of Jim O'Brien.

And then he winks.

# PART THREE
## Wednesday 29th October, 1975

# TWENTY-THREE

The London Borough of Southwark is on the south bank of the River Thames, and in the golden age of Queen Elizabeth I, it served as a sort of Tudor Las Vegas for the people who lived on the other, more puritanical, side of the river.

(Perhaps, back in those days, there was a common saying that ran something along the lines of, 'What happeneth in Southwark, stayeth in Southwark!' – but I somehow doubt it.)

There were any number of pleasures to be sampled. The borough had a profusion of taverns in which the reckless could lose a fortune at dice or cards. Bear baiting was popular, as were bull baiting and cock fighting. And for the young man who was feeling an unbearable pressure on his codpiece, there were more brothels than you could shake an erect organ at. It was here that the first British theatre, called the Rose, was built, with Bill Shakespeare as one of its resident playwrights. Shakespeare was a provincial – some considered him a mere country bumpkin – and unlike most of the other hacks who churned out plays to order, he did not have the benefits of a university education. He did, however, have a burning ambition, and when the next theatre, the Globe, was constructed, he was one of the main shareholders.

In the nineteenth century and earlier part of the twentieth, it was through Southwark's docks that Britain conducted much of its trade with its empire (an empire which, at its height, encompassed a quarter of the world), and it was for that reason that it was bombed so heavily during the Blitz.

Southwark thus had had more than its fair share of history, and, as a minor footnote to that history, it is also possible that it was here, three years ago, that Grace Stockton's fate was sealed.

I emerge from the tube (or to give it its proper name, the Underground Metropolitan Railway) at the Borough High Street station in Southwark, and head straight for the local library. The place is called the John Harvard Library, and is named after a local clergyman who emigrated to Massachusetts sometime in the seventeenth century, and while he was there, founded a university. (The name of the university slips my mind – maybe it was Yale!)

Once down in the library archives, I select a microfilm of the *Southwark Gazette* for March/April 1972, fit it into the reader, and begin to scroll down.

It does not take me very long at all to find exactly what I am looking for.

Famous anthropologist gives exciting talk at local girls' school

The pupils of the Lady Margaret School for Girls were today treated to a fascinating lecture by the famous anthropologist Dr Grace Stockton. The subject of the lecture was the life of an anthropologist, and it has led to a number of the girls wanting to follow in Dr Stockton's footsteps.

Grace Stockton once lived in the Borough, and for a while, near the end of the war, taught English and Geography at Lady Margaret's. She now lives in a converted farmhouse just outside Oxford, and teaches at the university.

Accompanying the article is a photograph of Grace, standing in front of some nondescript building.

This simply has to be the newspaper photograph that Red Duffle Coat Woman showed around Oxford railway station, and it proves not only that RDCW lives here now – or at least did until three years ago – but also that she was living here thirty years ago, as the Second World War drew to a close.

My only difficulty now is to locate her in an area where there are a quarter of a million other people living.

Needles and haystacks come instantly to mind.

The Lady Margaret School for Girls is just off Great Suffolk Street. It is a large nineteenth-century, mock Gothic building constructed of red brick, with gargoyles aplenty, grinning wickedly down. It is the sort of worthy edifice that respectable, civic-minded gentlemen of the Victorian era would consider building after a jolly evening spent in a brothel which specialized in children. The whole structure positively aches of fake piety and self-indulgent seriousness, and despite my usual respect for historic buildings, I feel an almost overwhelming urge to attack it with a sledgehammer.

The headmistress of the school projects a self-image which is in marked contrast to the building itself. She is in her late thirties and wearing a pale lemon trouser suit, and though the polished brass plate on the door of her light and airy study announces she is Mrs Horner, we have only just gone through the preliminaries of shaking hands when she asks me to call her Sue.

'It was really very good of you to find the time to see me at such short notice, Sue,' I say, ingratiatingly.

'If it hadn't been for what it said on your business card, I probably wouldn't have, because I really am very busy,' she admits. 'But when all's said and done, you are a fellow Oxonian.'

Which of your many business cards is this one? I hear you ask.

It is the one that reads:

Jennifer Redhead MA (Oxon)
Confidential Research Consultant

(The MA, I should explain, isn't something we graduates of Oxford and Cambridge have actually earned, it's more a top-up on the BA, which we're entitled to apply for four years after graduating, providing we've managed to stay out of debt and out of prison until then.)

Most of my business cards are outright lies, and this is no more than the truth, so you might imagine I should be quite happy using it.

I'm not!

The problem with this particular card is that it deliberately plays on a snobbery that I personally despise, and thus, when using it, I despise myself a little. Having said that, of course, I wouldn't be here in this office, talking to my new friend Sue, without that snobbery.

'So what do you think of my school?' Mrs Horner – Sue – asks.

*My* school!

A warning message lights up inside my head, and scrolls its way across my brain.

'Play it carefully with this bugger, Jennie,' the sign says, 'because she's just the sort of woman who'll withdraw her cooperation at even the slightest hint of criticism.'

'So what do you think?' she asks again, with just a touch of impatience in her voice.

'It reminds me of some Oxford colleges,' I answer, cleverly.

Why is that clever?

Because it means whatever you choose it to mean.

And what my friend Sue chooses it to mean is that I think this a fabulously top-hole place.

'The Board of Governors appointed me to my post specifically because they wanted someone who was dynamic enough to sweep away all the cobwebs that have been allowed to accumulate since I-don't-know-when,' she says. 'Their expectation is that I will drag the school, kicking and screaming if necessary, into the second half of the twentieth century.'

And did they also hire you to speak in clichés? I wonder.

But I say nothing – which, as it turns out, is exactly what she requires. Because she doesn't really care what I want to contribute to the conversation – all she wants is a captive audience.

And she plays to that audience for the next fifteen minutes. She tells me of her battles with the conservative elements in the school – battles which would have broken a lesser woman – and how she has emerged from the fray triumphant. She offers me a vision of the future, in which the school's brilliance will inspire others, and folk will come from far and wide to study it and marvel.

At least, I assume that's what she says, because after the first couple of minutes, I switch off completely.

Finally, she remembers I'm not just there to be an unwilling witness to her fantastical bragging.

'So what was it that you wanted to see me about, Jennie?' she asks.

'Dr Grace Stockton,' I tell her.

'Doctor Grace Stockton.' She repeats the words carefully, because anyone with the word 'doctor' in front of her name must merit serious consideration. 'It's before my time,' (she makes it seem like the Dark Ages – and she probably considers that that's exactly what it was), 'but didn't Dr Stockton give a lecture here three or four years ago?'

'Yes, she did.'

'I seem to have the vague impression from somewhere or other that something unpleasant happened to her.'

'Yes, it was quite unpleasant – she was murdered.'

Mrs Horner grimaces. The kudos that Grace Stockton had gained in her eyes as an academic has been quite drained away with the knowledge that she was stupid enough to get herself killed. After all, no one admires a victim, do they?

'I don't really see how I can help you, then,' Mrs Horner says, having already gained what she wanted from our encounter, and now ostentatiously glancing at the door. 'If she was only here for the one afternoon . . .'

'She wasn't. She taught here in 1944.'

Mrs Horner favours me with another frown.

'There may be some record of Dr Stockton's time here as a teacher,' she says, 'though I wouldn't hold my breath, because until I took over, the whole attitude to paperwork was quite lamentable.'

'I'd be grateful for anything you've got,' I say humbly.

The conversation, having reached its zenith – the dazzling career of Mrs Sue Horner MA – it is now, as far as she is concerned, in free fall, and is beginning to bore and irritate her in about equal measure.

'When she can find the time, I'll get my secretary to . . .' she begins airily. 'No, I've a better idea. You can have a talk with Miss Benton. She was here in 1944.' She sighs, theatrically. 'It sometimes feels as if she's *always* been here.'

'When can I see her?' I ask.

'Oh, anytime, I imagine.'

'I don't want to interrupt her teaching.'

'Oh, good heavens, I don't let her actually *teach*. Education has moved on somewhat since she was trained. She just couldn't cope. So I've given her an office of her own, and she counsels any girl who feels the need of counselling. She'll probably be free right now. She usually is.'

'It's very kind of you – positively generous, in fact – to give her so much consideration,' I say – though it's not so much a case of complimenting her on her thoughtful act as it is poking her with a metaphorical stick, just to see how she'll react to it.

She looks slightly uncomfortable. 'One or two of the governors asked me to see what I could do for her, and were more than pleased when I assigned her this new role,' she says.

Translation: I wanted to get rid of her, but a couple of members of the board had a strong enough sense of decency to make sure it didn't happen.

'Thank you for your time, Sue,' I say.

'My pleasure, lady,' she replies in a truly cringeworthy American accent. 'If I ever need the services of a private eye, I'll be sure to look you up.'

And I'll be the one hiding behind the filing cabinet until you get tired of waiting and bugger off, I think.

As I walk down the corridor in the wake of Mrs Horner's secretary (who, like her boss, makes a positive virtue out of being brisk) I'm building up a mental picture of Miss Benton. She will be close to retirement (obviously), with white hair which has been lightly permed. Chances are, she will be wearing a floral dress, and may – or may not – have a string of artificial pearls around her aging neck.

Her office, I should think, will be in marked contrast to the modern science labs I glance at as we pass them, and will probably bear a close resemblance to a broom cupboard.

We reach the end of the corridor.

'That's it,' says the secretary, pointing to a door which, unlike all the others on this corridor, has no sign on it to identify it. 'You can introduce yourself to her, can't you?'

There is contempt in her tone – contempt for Miss Benton which is more than evident in the way she says 'her' and contempt for me because, by asking to visit Miss Benton, I have painted myself with the same brush.

'Thank you,' I say humbly. Then I add, 'I do hope they catch the Southwark office rapist soon.'

'What!' she says.

'Haven't you heard?' I ask. 'He always targets office workers. Actually, now I stop to think about it, he always targets *school secretaries*.' I paused for a second. 'Still, if you go straight home after school and lock all your doors, you'll probably be all right.'

She rushes off down the corridor, heading, no doubt, straight for her boss's office, where she will demand to know why she hasn't been informed of the danger she is in.

You couldn't have said that to her if you'd been Detective Constable Redhead, could you? I ask myself. In fact, you couldn't have said it even if you'd been *DCI* Redhead.

Ah, the joys of freedom!

I chuckle to myself, and knock on Miss Benton's door.

The door opens, and a girl comes out.

'Thanks a lot, miss,' she says over her shoulder, then she smiles at me, and is gone.

'Come in, whoever you are,' says an obviously aging woman's voice.

I step inside, and immediately award myself full marks for imagination. Miss Benton does indeed have white hair, lightly waved. She is wearing a floral dress. True, there are no artificial pearls, but then I always postulated them as no more than a possibility.

I was right about the office, too. It is just about large enough for a small table and two chairs, and the only light enters through a skylight. This set-up says, more clearly than words ever could, that the occupant of the office is not to be taken seriously.

'What can I do for you, my dear?' she asks.

'Mrs Horner thought you might be able to help me,' I begin. 'I'm a private detective, and I've—'

'Oh, how exciting,' she interrupts me. 'Do sit down.'

It is no mean feat to squeeze my legs under the tiny table, and I have only just accomplished it when there is a knock on the door, and another girl appears.

Two girls in two minutes! It would appear that Miss Benton's counselling is not quite as obsolete and unwanted as Mrs Headmistress Horner would like to think it is.

'Not now, Linda,' Miss Benton says to the girl. 'In fact, it would be better if we didn't do this in school at all.'

The girl instinctively glances over her shoulder, and says, 'You're probably right, miss.'

Miss Benton opens her appointments diary. For a dinosaur's date book, it seems pretty well filled up.

'I'll tell you what,' she says, 'I'll see you in the car park behind the Bull and Bush, at six o'clock. Then we can really get down to cases.'

The girl grins. 'Right you are, miss,' she says, and departs.

'You probably wonder why I've arranged to meet her in the car park,' she says to me.

'I wouldn't be much of a private eye if I wasn't at least a little bit curious,' I reply.

'I assure you, I have no carnal thoughts about Linda,' Miss Benton says. 'If I have a sexual encounter – and they are, alas, few and far apart these days – I much prefer my partners to have something meaty hanging between their legs. No, the reason we are meeting in the car park of the Bull and Bush is to avoid the green-eyed monster.'

She looks at me expectantly.

'Jealousy,' I say. 'It is the green-eyed monster that doth mock the meat it feeds on.'

Miss Benton claps her hands together – carefully and delicately, but with obvious delight.

'Oh, you are well-read,' she says. 'The problem with Linda is that she's the head prefect and the captain of hockey. And to cap it all, she's likely to win a scholarship to Cambridge next year.'

'I see,' I say.

'No, you don't,' she contradicts me.

'No, I don't,' I agree.

'The headmistress doesn't want me here, but she will admit that I perform a useful function, which is to give guidance to what she thinks of as the deadwood in the school – and who I prefer to think of as the academically and physically challenged. I keep them out of her hair, leaving her more time to concentrate on what really matters.'

'But Linda is a winner,' I say, catching on.

'But Linda is a winner,' Miss Benton agrees. 'Winners belong – body and soul – to Mrs Horner. She sees their success as almost entirely her doing, and she demands complete loyalty from them. Cross her, and she'll find a way to get back at you. Suddenly, you've been dropped from the netball team. Or your offers from universities are not quite as good as expected, which makes you think – quite correctly – that your reference from the school has been lukewarm. What I'm really saying, I suppose, is that our beloved headmistress is nothing but a complacent and vindictive bitch.' She pauses. 'You've met her, so you'll have seen that for yourself, won't you?'

I hesitate for a moment, then say, 'I wasn't with her long enough to establish that she's vindictive.'

Miss Benton favours me with another little clap.

'Was that a test?' I ask.

'Yes.'

'And did I pass?'

'With flying colours. So what do you want to know?'

'I'd like you to tell me whatever you can about Grace Stockton,' I say

'In a moment,' Miss Benton replies. She reaches into her drawer and produces a large can of air freshener. 'Could you bolt the door, please?'

I struggle out of my chair, slide the bolt, and struggle back in. While I have been doing that, she's reached into her drawer again, and produced a joint.

'It's purely medical – for my arthritis,' she explains.

She lights up, inhales deeply, and offers the joint to me.

I shake my head. 'My pot days are over. I'm now slave to quite another drug,' I tell her.

She nods. 'Each to her own. Why do you want to know about Grace?'

'She was murdered . . .'

'I know.'

'. . . and her daughter wants me to track down her killer.'

'Do you think you can?' Miss Benton asks.

'Not really – but I'm giving it my best shot.'

Miss Benton nods again. 'Grace came to work here in '43. It wasn't that she needed the job – she was already employed by some ministry or other, besides which she was doing some independent social work – but she'd heard we were short-handed, and wanted to help.'

'She wasn't qualified,' I say, remembering that when her university had moved to Cambridge, she hadn't gone with it.

'No, she wasn't qualified,' Miss Benton agrees, taking another pull on her joint. 'But the headmistress back then was what I'd call a *real* headmistress – she didn't judge people on certificates, she judged them on how they did the job – and Grace was a superb teacher.'

'She must have got married and pregnant while she was here.'

'She did.'

'How did she feel about being pregnant?'

'Why do you ask?' Miss Benton says, suddenly suspicious.

'To tell you the truth, I don't know,' I admit, and I wonder why the question should get such a reaction. 'It's more of a gut feeling than anything else. That's how I work.'

Miss Benton seems satisfied. 'Grace was very excited about being pregnant,' she says. 'But it seemed to me at the time she was excited for the all the wrong reasons.'

'All the wrong reasons?'

'Oh, I don't mean she didn't want the baby. Please, don't think that for a minute. I saw them together, once Julia was born, and it was obvious she adored the little mite. But she still saw Julia more as a gift for her husband than as a person in her own right. I'd go further – presenting him with this gift was the only thing that made her worthy of him, as far as she was concerned.'

'Really?' I say, noncommittally.

She grins. 'You're patronizing me, aren't you? "Poor old bag," you're thinking. "Not only has age melted her brain, but now there's the pot she's just smoked in there, kicking around in the slush".'

'I didn't mean to . . .' I begin.

'Don't worry about it,' she says cheerfully. 'I've been patronized by experts in my time – and you don't even come close. But if I were you, I wouldn't dismiss what I've said completely out of hand. You have to remember that Grace was brought up in Papua New Guinea among the natives, and it's the lessons we learn earliest in life that are the most difficult to dislodge.'

'So you're saying it's possible to be a strong, high flying, independent woman – which she obviously was – and a tribal wife at the same time?' I suggest.

'Exactly! We're all capable of contradictions. I'd be willing to bet that there are times when you're at a sophisticated cocktail party, talking ever so smartly, and you suddenly feel like no more than a snotty-nosed kid from the north.'

She's not quite right there. My mother would never have allowed me to have a snotty nose, because that wasn't 'respectable', and therefore the worst crime imaginable. But I can still see what she's getting at.

'So Grace worked here until her husband returned from the war, did she?' I ask.

'No. One day towards the end of 1944, she simply didn't turn up. She sent the headmistress a letter of apology, but that was some time later. She said in it that she'd nearly been killed by a flying bomb, and that made her realize that her first duty was to her baby, which was why she was getting out of London.'

'Can you remember anyone from that time who might have wanted to kill her?' I ask.

'Hitler had it in for her – I do know that,' Miss Benton says. She grins again. 'Seriously, everyone liked her – and with good reason. She was hard working, and she was kind. It's impossible to believe she could have done something which would make anyone want to hurt her.'

'What was she like when she came back three years ago?'

'Older, wiser, with a little more natural authority (though she always had plenty of that) but otherwise pretty much the same. She was still the marvellous teacher I remembered, and she had all the time in the world to listen to the girls after she'd finished her talk.'

Miss Benton suddenly frowns.

'What's the matter?' I ask.

'There was one girl – I say "girl", but what I mean is "old girl" – who she was really rather abrupt with, which was strange, because the girl in question, Annie Tobin, had been one of her favourites when she was teaching here. I believe Annie did a lot of babysitting for her, while she was out doing her good deeds, which makes it all the stranger that she should choose to treat her unkindly.'

I feel a shiver run through me, as if death has just blown on the back of my neck. It may mean nothing – often, in the past, similar feelings have turned out to be a false alarm – but I don't dare ignore it.

'Do you have this Annie Tobin's address?' I ask.

'No,' Miss Benton says. 'But I can tell you where she works.'

# TWENTY-FOUR

*September, 1944*

Grace looked across the table at Jane, who was cradling her baby in her arms, and she felt a wave of pride and happiness sweep over her.

They had done it, she told herself.

Against all the odds, they had bloody well done it!

Who would have been willing to bet, a few months earlier, that Jane could have given up alcohol completely?

No one.

But she had!

Who would ever have imagined that a woman like herself, with very little formal education, and virtually no medical training at all, could have delivered a baby – a beautiful healthy baby – right here on this table?

Again, absolutely no one.

Yet she had done just that.

They were still not out of the woods. She fully realized that. The Germans seemed to be sending over more flying bombs every day, and because there was no precision to the attacks (someone had said it was like an angry blind man firing a pistol into the darkness) you could never guess where they were going to land. All you *did* know was that you could hear them coming (the drone of their engines growing louder and louder as they approached) and that you could do nothing but stand there and wait for the engine noise to begin to fade again, which meant the bomb had passed over you, and would soon be imperilling someone else.

But if that didn't happen – if, instead of fading into the distance, the sound just suddenly stopped – then you knew, as sure as eggs were eggs, that you were about to die.

Not that that was the only thing she had to worry about.

The allied forces had landed in Normandy nearly three months earlier, and though it might take time for the Third Reich to finally fall, everyone knew that, to all intents and purposes, Hitler was finished. Yes, the war would be over, but there was no guarantee that Derek – the love of her life, the whole purpose of her existence – would survive.

He might even be dead already.

And then there was her unborn baby. The doctor had assured her that everything was going very well, but she still couldn't help worrying.

She rubbed her stomach gently, to communicate to the baby that it hadn't been forgotten.

'This will be my last visit for a while,' she said to Jane. 'But Annie will visit you every day, won't you, Annie?' she continued, looking towards the girl who was standing quietly in the corner.

'Yes, Mrs Stockton,' Annie replied.

She had made the right choice in selecting Annie for this job, Grace thought. The girl wasn't the brightest of her pupils, and she wouldn't win any prizes for personality, but she was conscientious and caring, and – perhaps most important of all – her obvious meekness would put Jane at her ease.

Jane looked far from at ease at that moment.

'Your last visit?' she repeated.

'For a while.'

'But you can't . . . you promised . . .'

'Would you mind stepping out into the corridor for a moment, Annie?' Grace asked the girl.

Annie nodded obediently. 'Yes, Mrs Stockton.'

'We talked about all this before, didn't we?' Grace asked Jane, when Annie had gone.

'Yes, but . . .'

'The doctor says if I don't get more rest, I'll be putting my baby at risk, and you don't want that, do you?'

'No, of course I don't,' Jane said. 'It's just that I get so frightened without you. You're so strong and I'm so—'

'You're much stronger than you realize,' Grace interrupted her. 'You were a real alcoholic, and managed to stop drinking. In your place, I'm not sure I could have done it.'

'Really?' Jane asked.

'Really,' Grace said. 'Anyway, Annie will be looking after you, but I am relying on you to look after her, too.'

'How could I look after her?'

'Annie hasn't got much self-confidence. I think that's her mother's fault. The bloody woman is deliberately undermining her, so she can keep her tied to her apron strings forever. But if we can show her that she can do things on her own – if we let her know that we value and respect her – well, maybe she'll learn to stand up for herself.'

Jane smiled. She couldn't remember smiling much before, but now she was doing it all the time, and this particular smile was a mixture of amusement and admiration.

'That's what you do, isn't it?' she asked.

'I don't know what you mean,' Grace said, looking slightly embarrassed.

'You go around trying to change everybody's life for the better.'

'Oh, I don't know about that,' Grace said, and she really was sounding flustered. 'I'd never have enough energy to make everybody's life better. But I do try to help the people I care about, whenever I can.'

'Like me,' Jane said with pride.

'Like you, my dear little sister,' Grace agreed. She reached into her pocket and took out an envelope. 'The school's just paid me my last wages, so here's another pound.'

'But you'll need it for your baby,' Jane protested.

'I've got everything I need for my baby,' Grace told her. 'And when my husband comes back from the war, I'll have even more.' She held the envelope out. 'Go on, have it.'

Jane took the envelope from her.

'I haven't spent a penny of the money you've given me,' she said. 'It's all for my baby.'

'I know it is,' Grace said. 'And I'm so proud of you.'

'You will be coming back, won't you?' Jane asked, as a new wave of anxiety hit her.

'Of course I'll be coming back,' Grace said. 'Give me a week or so to get over giving birth and you won't be able to keep me away.'

# TWENTY-FIVE

T he woman leaving the offices of Campion, Campion and Blaine (Solicitors and Commissioners for Oaths) is somewhere in her mid-forties, and if I were to disguise myself as a solicitor's secretary during the course of an investigation (and such things have been known to happen!) I would probably dress myself in a tweed suit and sensible shoes similar to the ones she's wearing now.

Her face reveals her to be a kindly, sensible person (which only serves to confirm the thumbnail sketch given to me earlier by the admirable Miss Benton), but there is something about the way she moves – a heaviness, a tired acceptance – which also suggests that she is a woman who has been constantly disappointed by what life has had to offer.

My experience of ambushing people tells me that they tend to get jumpy if your first approach is when they're walking along, so I stay close to her, but keep silent, until she reaches the pelican crossing and comes to halt, just as the red light instructs her to.

Then I say, 'Miss Tobin, my name is Jennie Redhead, and I'm investigating the murder of Grace Stockton.'

She looks very perplexed. I would have been surprised if she hadn't, because women like her never get stopped by women like me.

'Are you from the police?' she asks, tremulously.

'I'm working with them,' I reply, neatly side-stepping the truth, without actually lying. 'Do you think you could you spare me a few minutes to answer one or two questions?'

The crossing light changes to green. Her instinct tells her she should cross the road, but she does not want to appear rude.

'My mother's expecting me at home,' she says, keeping her eye firmly on the light.

She speaks in a dull, flat tone which suggests that though she knows that going home is as inevitable as the sun setting in the evening, it is not a prospect she looks forward to with relish.

She would be greatly relieved, I suspect, if I could find a way to talk her out of doing her duty, at least for a little while.

'It really would be most useful to me – and to the murder investigation – if you could spare me a few minutes,' I say.

The light has changed to red again, temporarily cutting off her escape.

'Well, I . . . you see, my mother gets worried if I'm late,' she says, almost pathetically.

I want to grab hold of her and shake her till her teeth rattle, while all the time screaming things like, 'For God's sake, Annie, you're not a kid – you're a middle-aged woman. You're too old to be rushing home to Mum.'

I don't do that, of course, because I've learned from experience that such a course of action tends to put a potential witness into a particularly uncooperative frame of mind.

But I need to do something quickly, because when the light changes again, she'll be off like a greyhound out of its trap.

I decide it is time to bring out the big guns.

'Miss Benton was hoping that you could grant me just a few minutes of your time,' I say.

Her face lights up, as if I've just said the magic word – which, in fact, I probably have.

'You've talked to Miss Benton?' she asks.

'Yes.'

'And she mentioned *me*?'

There's a hint of incredulity in her voice, because she really can't see why anyone – especially someone as marvellous as Miss Benton – would even bother to mention an insignificant worm like her.

'Miss Benton didn't just mention you,' I tell her. 'She spoke of you very warmly.'

The light has changed again, but the crisis has been averted.

'Well, I suppose giving you a few minutes would be all right,' Annie says, trying her best to disguise the fact that she is inordinately pleased.

'I noticed earlier that there was a café just down the road,' I tell her.

'Yes, there is.'

'I think we'd be much more comfortable having our little talk there, don't you, Annie?' I ask.

'Yes, I suppose so,' she says uncertainly.

The café is called the Cosy Tea (tea cosy – get it!). There is a hand-printed notice on the wall which proclaims that as well as nine different and distinct blends of tea, it also offers scones and cakes.

I order a pot of Darjeeling from the smiling young waitress, and ask Annie if she would like scones or cakes to go with it. I see her mouth watering, then she shakes her head, regretfully.

'No, thank you. They look very nice, but I don't want to spoil my appetite. Mother will be cooking dinner, you see, and . . .' She looks around her worriedly, as if she expects to see her mother there, censoring her for her recklessness. 'Are you married?' she asks me.

'No, I'm not,' I reply.

'Are your parents still alive?'

'My mother is. My father died a couple of years ago.'

'Do you live with her – your mother, I mean?'

'No, I don't.'

'But you live close to her, don't you?'

'Not really. She lives in Lancashire, and I live in Oxford.'

She looks at me as strangely as she might have done had I announced that I was a transvestite tightrope walker and amateur chicken sexer from Outer Mongolia. I am living a life, it seems, which is not only outside her experience, but beyond *any* normal person's experience.

And then enlightenment dawns – or, at least, she thinks it has.

'You have brothers and sisters in Lancashire who take care of your mother,' she says.

I shake my head. 'I'm an only child.'

So, it would seem, the world really had gone mad.

'Didn't your mother want you to move back home when your father died?' she asks, wonderingly.

Oh yes, she most certainly did, because it would have been a great comfort to her – in her bereavement – to have made my life thoroughly miserable.

'Yes, she asked me to move back,' I say aloud. 'And I made her a counter-offer.'

'A counter-offer?'

'Yes, I said she could come and live with me.'

The offer had been sincere (honestly it had!), but – thank God – she hadn't accepted it.

'So what happened then?' she asks, with a hint of amazement in her voice, as if what I'm telling her could only happen in a Hollywood picture, because it had no place in the real world.

'Nothing happened,' I say. 'Neither of us wanted to move, so we both stayed as we were.' All this is really very depressing. I take a sip of tea and find myself wishing it was gin and tonic. 'Could you tell me about the old days, when you were Mrs Stockton's babysitter?' I continue.

'Yes, of course. What do you want to know?'

'How did you get the job in the first place?'

Annie giggled. 'It was silly, really. It all began with the pram.'

'The pram?'

'I was in the park, sitting on a bench. I was feeling a bit miserable that day. To tell you the truth, I might even have been crying a little. Anyway, I looked up, and there was Mrs Stockton standing there. She didn't ask me what the matter was – that would have been awful.'

'So what *did* she say?'

'She said she was going to look at a second-hand pram, and, if I could possibly spare her the time, she'd really appreciate a second opinion. So we both went to see the pram.'

'Did she buy it?'

'Yes, she did. It was a blue Silver Cross pram. They were the best, you know. King George VI had ordered one for Princess Elizabeth. This one was in beautiful condition. The chrome gleamed. The rubber on the handle was hardly worn at all. And best of all, it didn't squeak. A lot of prams do squeak, but this one was as quiet and as smooth as a . . . well, as a perfect pram.'

'You seem to know a great deal about it,' I say.

'Oh yes, I used to love prams. I'd spend hours and hours looking at them in the shops.'

'But you don't do that now?'

'There's not much point now, is there?' Annie asks bitterly. She takes a deep breath. 'Anyway, Mrs Stockton asked me if I'd do her a favour. She was helping this friend of hers on the other side of the river, who'd just had a baby herself, but she knew she wouldn't be able to do it for a while after her own baby was born, so she wondered if I'd step in and fill the gap. She said she wouldn't ask just anybody, but she knew how trustworthy and responsible I was.'

She glows with the memory, and then her face clouds over as she remembers how the story ended.

Was this the point at which someone learned to hate Grace so much that they would store that hatred for thirty years, I wonder.

'Tell me about this other woman.'

'She lived in Bombay Street in Camden Town, and her name was Jane.'

'What was her surname?'

'I don't know. She never told me what her surname was, and neither did Mrs Stockton.' Annie looks anguished. 'I'm sorry. Maybe I should have asked, but I didn't really think.'

Jesus, this is a delicate soul!

'It's not important,' I assure her. 'Tell me some more about this Jane, if you can.'

She smiles happily, because she knows that this time she is not going to disappoint me.

'She wasn't very educated,' Annie says. 'She asked me once if I could read something to her because her eyes were hurting, but I think that the truth is, she didn't know how to read. But she was one of the nicest people I've ever met and she was very, very fond of Mrs Stockton.'

She doesn't sound much like an assassin, I think.

'Was there any other woman in the house?' I ask Annie.

'No, there was just Jane.'

'And did she have any female visitors apart from you and Mrs Stockton?'

'No, not while I was there. To be honest, I don't think Jane had any other friends.'

This is looking increasingly like a dead end, but I'm here now, so I might as well run with it until I hit the wall.

'So after Mrs Stockton's baby was born, you stopped going to Jane's house, and looked after Julia instead?' I ask.

'That's right. I don't think Mrs Stockton liked leaving Julia so often, but she knew that Jane really depended on her.'

'I expect that extra pocket money must have come in useful,' I say.

Annie looks horrified at the very idea. 'Oh, I didn't get any money for it,' she says. 'Mrs Stockton tried to pay me, but I wouldn't accept it.' She smiles, sadly. 'If I'd had to, I would have paid to look after Julia. I loved babies. I was going to train to be a nursery nurse.'

'Why didn't you?'

'Mother said training to be a secretary would be much more sensible, and after that night, I just didn't have the strength to fight her.'

'What night?'

'The 25th of November 1944.' A single tear runs down Annie's cheek. 'The day before my birthday.'

'What happened?'

It was a cold dark night, Annie tells me. The wind had been blowing in from the river, and the rain had been coming down in buckets for hours, so it was hardly surprising that there was no one else out on the street as Annie made her way towards the three-storey house where Grace had her flat.

Once she got there, she rang the bell and waited outside on the pavement for Grace to come downstairs and let her in.

No one came.

The rain had found its way under her collar, and she felt its icy fingers crawling slowly down her back.

She rang again.

This time, the door opened, but it was not Mrs Stockton, it was Mrs Jurewitz, the Polish refugee who lived on the ground floor.

The old woman peered into the darkness.

'Yes?'

'It's me, Mrs Jurewitz. Annie.'

'Come in, you poor child,' the old woman said. 'Come in quickly, before you drown.'

There was only a dim light in the hallway, but it was bright enough for the Polish woman to examine the new arrival.

'How terrible is your state,' she said. 'Come to my room and I will give you a hot blackcurrant drink – with perhaps a little Polish vodka.'

Annie felt the kind of embarrassment she always experienced when someone was being nice to her.

'No thanks,' she said. 'I . . . I have to go and see Mrs Stockton.'

'I ran up the stairs to the top floor, which is where Mrs Stockton lived,' Annie tells me. 'I suppose what I was really doing was running away from Mrs Jurewitz. We . . . I . . . I wasn't used to being so intimate with people I hardly knew.'

'What did you do when you reached Mrs Stockton's door?'

'I knocked. And from inside, I heard the sound of Julia crying. It was terrible. It was much stronger and louder than I'd ever heard her cry before.' She pauses. 'I'm not lying.'

'I never thought you were.'

'No one came to the door, but I wasn't surprised, because I'd no doubt in my mind that Mrs Stockton was comforting the baby, which was much more important than finding out who was outside.'

'Go on,' I encourage her.

'But a minute passed, and then another minute. Julia was still crying. It was getting worse and worse, and Mrs Stockton still hadn't come to the door. I banged harder, and there was still nothing, just the baby breaking her heart. I began to think about all the terrible things that could have happened. Mrs Stockton could have fallen over and been knocked unconscious. She could have had a heart attack, and died. There was a pay phone downstairs, and I decided the best thing that I could do would be to call the police.'

'And did you?'

'No, because just then I heard the front door open. Whoever it was started walking up the stairs, and – you know how you can recognize some people's footsteps, even if they are climbing stairs . . .?'

'Yes.'

'Well, I knew it was Mrs Stockton. So I stayed where I was. She didn't see me until she reached her landing. She looked shocked that I was there, even though we'd made the arrangement several days earlier. I said, "Julia is crying. Is there anyone with her?" Mrs Stockton shook her head as if it was really none of my business, then she must have felt guilty, because she said, "I only popped out for a minute or two." But it wasn't true.'

'Are you sure of that?'

'I'm sure. Her mackintosh was soaked through, so she must have been out for at least half an hour – and she stank of paraffin.'

I am instantly suspicious of the statement.

'When you fill a paraffin heater, you do sometimes smell of it for a while, but surely the rain would have washed that away,' I say.

'I said she *stank* of it – as if she'd spilled it all over herself.'

If tentative little Annie was so sure of herself, she must be telling the truth, I think.

'Julia was still crying,' Annie continues, 'and I said, "We'd better go inside and settle her down." But Mrs Stockton barred my way.'

'She did *what*?'

'She stood with her back to the door, as if she thought I was going to force my way in. And maybe I would have done, because the crying was so terrible it was almost breaking my heart, but there was this wild – frightening – look in her eyes, like nothing I'd ever seen before, and I thought that if I didn't back off, she'd grab me and throw me down the stairs.'

'You can't really have believed that,' I say.

'I did,' she insists. 'And you would have too, if you'd been there.'

'Fair enough,' I concede. 'Carry on.'

'The madness was only there for a few seconds, but what replaced it was even worse. Her eyes were as cold as ice, and she said, "I'll deal with Julia. You can go home now." She didn't apologize for bringing me out on a wet night for nothing. She didn't even offer me a cup of tea. And that wasn't like her, because usually she was the kindest, most considerate person you could ever hope to meet.'

I feel a prickling at the back of my neck and an excitement welling up deep inside me, but I say nothing yet, for fear of spoiling the magic.

'"I don't mind coming in and looking after Julia just while you get out of those wet clothes," I told her,' Annie says. 'And she looked at me as if she hated me. "I don't need you now, and I won't need you ever again – because we're moving out of London tomorrow," she said.' Annie's eyes filled with a remembered fear. 'I got this sudden pain in my chest, and for a few seconds I thought I'd forgotten how to breathe. Do you know what I mean?'

'Oh yes,' I say, 'it's one of the classic symptoms of shock.'

'I said to Mrs Stockton, "You're . . . you're leaving?" and she said, "Yes. Didn't you hear what I said – or are you just stupid?" The words sounded awful, but they just didn't match the look in her eyes.'

'And what was that look?'

Annie shrugs. 'I probably shouldn't have mentioned it. You'll say I'm only being fanciful.'

'I promise I won't.'

'The iciness had gone, just like the madness had, and she was just looking hurt. It was as if . . . as if she really didn't want to be nasty to me, but she had no choice.'

'And why might she have had no choice?'

Annie waves her hands helplessly in the air, drawing ever and ever tightening circles.

'I don't know. I told you I was being fanciful.'

I'm pushing her too much, I tell myself.

'Have a cake,' I say.

'I really shouldn't.'

'Look, I'm dying for one,' I lie, 'but I'll feel really awkward eating it on my own.'

'I don't . . .'

'Why don't you have one, and eat only half of it?'

'Mother says I shouldn't.'

'Your mother isn't here.'

For a second it looks as if she wants to claw my eyes out in defence of the spectre she lives with, then she smiles and says, 'No, she isn't, is she? I'll have one of those with cream in the middle.'

I order a whole plate of assorted cakes. She doesn't object.

'So there you were standing on the landing and Mrs Stockton told you to leave,' I say. 'I imagine that after what you'd just been through you did just that, didn't you?'

'No, I didn't,' Annie says. 'I wanted to, because I was frightened and I was hurt, but if I was never going to see Julia again, I wanted to say goodbye to her, so I asked Mrs Stockton if I could see her one last time. "The child's disturbed," she said. "You can hear that for yourself. The last thing she wants is to have someone like you bothering her." I couldn't believe I'd heard it. I went down on my knees in front of her – begging. Could you believe that anyone would be willing to humiliate themselves like that?'

'You weren't humiliating yourself,' I tell her.

'If it wasn't humiliating, then what was it?' she asks.

'It was tragic,' I say. 'Tell me what happened next.'

'I grabbed hold of the hem of her coat. I said, "Please, Mrs Stockton, let me see her – just for a few minutes." I was looking up at her, searching for some little sign of pity, I suppose, but she wasn't looking back at me. She was gazing at the ceiling, instead, and she said, "Now you listen to me, you foolish girl – if you don't leave this house now, I'm calling the police."'

We private eyes quickly learn to be hardened and objective, so it must be the cake itself, rather than her words, which makes what's in my mouth suddenly taste like sawdust. Annie is having the opposite reaction. The cakes appear to be sustaining her, and she's almost ready for her third.

'You went home, then?' I say.

'Yes,' she answers, miserably. 'I went home. Home to Mother.'

It's cruel to carry on, but I don't see I have any choice.

'You saw Mrs Stockton again, didn't you?' I force myself to say. 'You went back to your old school when she gave a lecture, three years ago?'

'Yes.'

'What made you go?'

'Several of the girls who were taught by Mrs Stockton went,' Annie says evasively.

'What made *you* go?' I repeat.

Annie shrugs helplessly. 'I don't really know. I suppose I just wanted to find out what I'd done wrong all that time ago.'

I'm so exasperated that I feel the urge return to shake her until her teeth rattle. But it wouldn't do any good.

'Nothing that happened was your fault. You must remember that,' I insist. 'Tell me about the lecture.'

'Most of the audience were current pupils at the school, but, like I said, quite a few old girls turned up. They had fond memories of Dr Stockton, you see, just as I would have done if it hadn't been for that night.'

'Nothing that happened was your fault,' I repeat, almost as if it were a Buddhist chant. 'Nothing that happened was your fault.'

'We old girls sat at the back of the hall,' Annie continues. 'But when Mrs Stockton – Dr Stockton – had finished her lecture, she invited anyone who was interested to come up on stage, and continue the discussion. Four or five of us went down, but when we got to the actual stage, I . . . I held back.'

'You were nervous,' I say reassuringly. 'That's only natural.'

'I don't think Dr Stockton actually remembered any of the other girls – such a long time had passed, and so much had happened since they last met – but she pretended to recognize them, because she was such a nice woman. And even though she didn't do a particularly good job of pretending, they all believed her, because they wanted to believe her – because who wouldn't want to be remembered by someone like her?'

You poor woman, I think. You poor, poor bloody woman!

'And then my turn came,' Annie says. 'Dr Stockton shook hands with me, and said, "You're another of my old pupils, aren't you?" And when I agreed that I was, she said, "How you've all changed. How big and strong and confident you've become. And when you tell me your name, I'm sure I'll be amazed when I remember the little thing you once were." So I told her my name. With the others, she'd smiled, and said something like, "Of course you are." But it was different with me.'

I sodding well bet it was!

'Her face froze, and for a moment I thought she'd had some kind of attack. Then she said, "Good God, are you still here? I'd have thought you'd have left the area long ago." I still didn't get it – despite all the signals, I conned myself into thinking we were having a normal conversation, and I said, "I probably would have left if it hadn't been for Mother, but she needs—" "I really don't want to talk to you," she interrupted me. "I trusted you with my baby – and you neglected her so badly that she nearly died." It wasn't true, and I wanted to tell her it wasn't true, but I got this stabbing pain in my stomach and I had to rush to the toilets. I seemed to be throwing up forever, and when I got back to the hall, she was gone. But the thing is, the look in her eyes was exactly the same as the look in her eyes on that terrible night the day before my birthday.'

'What do you mean?'

'The eyes were telling me she really didn't want to hurt me, but she had no choice in the matter.'

'Why did she have no choice?'

'I can't explain it, but I believe it.'

'Even so, when you came back from the bogs and she was gone, you must have really hated her.'

'No, I didn't. Maybe I should have, but I didn't. I just wished I understood why she acted like she did. I still wish that.'

'Were you glad when you read in the paper, a few days later, that she'd been murdered?' I ask.

'No.'

'Are you sure?'

'The only thing I thought was that it was going to be very hard on little Julia. That's how I think of her, you see – little Julia – though I know she's a grown woman now.'

'Did you recognize the woman whose picture appeared in the papers – the woman who probably killed her?'

'No, I didn't.'

I take the picture out and lay it next to the nearly empty cake plate. 'Take another look.'

'It's a lot clearer than it was in the paper,' she says.

'So do you recognize her?'

'I'm not so sure any more. She looks vaguely familiar, but I don't think I could put a name to the face.'

'Have you seen her around here recently?'

'I don't think so.'

'Imagine her twenty or thirty years younger.'

She closes her eyes in concentration, then opens them again.

'No, that doesn't help.'

A suspicion which has never occurred to me before begins to grow inside me like a cancer.

Annie loved Grace Stockton (I don't think that's too strong a word for it) and Grace not only let her down, but in doing so virtually condemned her to a life of misery.

Then, when Annie gave her a chance to redeem herself, Grace all but spat in her face.

And now we have a situation in which Annie claims to be unable to recognize the face of another woman who, in all probability, has lived in the area all her life, (as Annie has), and who must have known Grace when Annie did.

Unless . . .

Unless Red Duffle Coat Woman didn't know Grace at all, but

had been hired as a hitman by a spinster lady who had no idea how to go about contacting a professional killer.

'Are you saying you really don't know her?' I persist. 'Or are you holding out on me?'

I am being more transparent than I thought I was, because the look that comes to her face now tells me she has worked out what I'm thinking.

'Do you think *I* killed Mrs Stockton?' she asks angrily.

'No, I think the woman in the photograph did.'

'But you think that I might have been the one who hired her?'

I could deny it, but there would be very little point.

'That's a possibility I can't entirely rule out,' I confess.

With a speed which catches me completely off guard, she reaches across the table and grabs the lapels of my jacket.

'Listen,' she says, dragging me across the table so our faces are almost touching, 'if I'd paid her to kill anybody, I'd have paid her to kill . . .'

She stops suddenly, as a look of horror crosses her face. She lets go of my jacket and slumps back in her chair.

She's not my killer – not even by proxy – I think. She couldn't possibly be.

'That felt good, didn't it?' I ask her.

'What?' she asks, pretending not to know what it is that I'm talking about.

'It felt good getting angry!' I say. 'It felt good to be fighting back, instead of just lying there and getting trampled on!'

'I completely lost control of myself,' she says primly. 'I behaved in a most undignified manner, and I'm very sorry for it. Even pigs have more manners than to act like that.'

I grin.

'Have I said something funny?' she demands.

'In some ways, you're quite right about the pigs,' I say. 'I can't remember a pig ever grabbing me by the lapels and hauling me across the table. On the other hand, they do screw in the open air, regardless of who's looking. And they almost never apologize for anything.' I grin again. 'When you say they've got more manners, you're quoting your mother, aren't you?'

She blushes. 'Mother may have said something similar,' she admits.

'I've two things I have to say to you,' I tell her. 'The first – and

this may come as something of a relief to you – is that it's obvious
to me now that you played no part in Grace Stockton's murder.'

She is expecting me to say more – but I don't.

We sit there in silence for maybe twenty seconds before Annie
cracks and says, 'What's the second thing?'

'You don't have to hire a hitman to be free of your mother,' I
tell her. 'All you have to do is show her that you are your own
woman.'

# TWENTY-SIX

*25th November, 1944*

I n an effort to make life as difficult as possible for any future
Luftwaffe bombing raids, the British government had imposed
a blackout over the whole country in September 1939.

What that had meant, in practical terms, was that all the street
lighting was turned off for the duration of the war, and it became
an offence (punishable by a fine, or even imprisonment) for people
to leave a gap in their living room or bedroom curtains which
allowed the light to leak out onto the street. Cars – of which, as
a result of petrol rationing, there were fewer and fewer around –
were only permitted to drive on sidelights, and pedestrians were
instructed to ensure that the torches they used to find their way
had their reflectors covered with tissue paper.

There were, of course, unintended consequences of this newly
imposed darkness. In the early months of the war, for example,
six hundred people a month were run over by motor cars, but the
powers-that-be in Whitehall considered this a reasonable price to
pay for stopping the Germans from pinpointing exactly where they
should drop their bombs.

Thus it was that the great city of London – which in peacetime
had cast a light into the sky that could be clearly seen from at
least thirty miles away – had fallen into darkness.

PC Turnbull disliked the blackout even more than most people
did, and with – so he considered – very good reason. The rest of

London didn't have to go out in the dark if it didn't want to. It could relax behind its blackout shades, snuggled down in cosy armchairs, sipping from bottles of beer, and listening to any number of cheery morale-boosting variety shows on the wireless.

But not PC Clive Reginald Turnbull!

Oh no!

It was PC Turnbull's duty to pound out his beat along Bankside each and every night (save for his day off).

And not only was it a lonely task, but it was also a pointless one, because when there was no moon, any number of murders, robberies or burglaries could have been perpetrated within fifty yards of him, and unless the murderers, burglars or robbers went about their work in a particularly noisy manner, he would have remained in blissful ignorance of it.

And what about the bright nights, when there was a full moon? Well, as far as he was concerned, that was an even worse situation.

'I mean, what's going to happen if I come across some villain whilst he's in the process of committing a criminal act?' he'd asked his old mate, Edgar Swann, over a pint of bitter (one of the few things that was not on the ration) in the Dog and Whistle.

'I don't know,' Edgar had replied. 'What is going to happen?'

'Well, he's going to scarper – make his getaway, like – isn't he?'

'You'd better hope he does, because if he decides to stay and slug it out with you, you're in real trouble,' Edgar had said.

'I can give as good as I get if it comes to a punch up,' replied Turnbull, though he convinced nobody (himself included). 'What I can't do is match him for speed. I mean to say, the chances are he's one of them fit young men what's recently deserted from the army. And what am I?'

'A knackered old bugger who's been dragged back into the force out of retirement?' his friend suggested.

'I wouldn't have put it quite like that,' said Turnbull, somewhat offended. 'But, given the circumstances, it would be unreasonable to expect me to catch him, now wouldn't it?'

It was his 'so-called' friend's comment that Turnbull was musing over as he walked along the embankment.

*A knackered old bugger who's been dragged out of retirement!*

The more he thought about it, the more unfair the comment

seemed. True, his stomach was more rounded than it had been
(and growing daily, his wife complained, when she had to let his
trousers out yet again), and true, he had a variety of aches when
he woke up in the morning which had been totally absent a year
or two earlier, and yes, he had given up running to catch a bus
that was just pulling off, because that brought on his chest pains.

But even so . . .

It was while he was fully dissecting the complete unfairness of
his friend Edgar's description of him that he noticed the river
was on fire.

Not that it was the whole river on fire, of course, but there was
definitely a spot in the middle of it that was blazing away.

Slowly his eyes adjusted to the sudden increase in light, and
now he could see it was not the river at all that was burning, but
a rowing boat which was floating on the current.

Not that it would be floating for long, he thought, because the
fire was hungrily – and rapidly – devouring it.

PC Turnbull trotted, at a gentle pace, towards the nearest police
phone box, which was a hundred yards away. He was not sure what
the burning boat signified, or how important it was, but he knew
that he had better report it to the duty sergeant as soon as possible.

*26th November, 1944*

Detective Inspector Clem Bannister sat in his office, wishing his
leg would stop itching. It was the shell fragments that were causing
the problem, he told himself. He knew, of course, that there *were* no
longer any shell fragments in his leg, because he had seen the X-rays
for himself, but though his mind had accepted the truth, the rest of
his body seemed to be taking a long time to get the message.

When the German tank shell had burst uncomfortably close to
him in 1942, Bannister had been a major in Field Marshall
Montgomery's Eighth Army, serving in North Africa. He had spent
nearly a year in hospital, in the course of which he had undergone
several operations. After the last of these, a physiotherapist – who
probably wasn't, in fact, quite the sadist that he sometimes appeared
to be – had subjected Bannister to a programme of rehabilitation,
at the end of which he announced he had done all he could, and
recommended the major be discharged.

The leg was mended, but nowhere near as good as new, and there had been no prospect of him re-joining the army. There would probably have been no prospect of returning to the police force (his peacetime occupation) either, under normal circumstances. But circumstances were not normal – the Met had been very understaffed and had welcomed him with open arms.

So now he was Inspector Bannister once more, charged not so much with investigating crime as finding a way to keep a lid on it.

He had not been expecting his office door to suddenly burst open that morning, but when it did, he knew, without even raising his head from the report he was reading, who his caller had to be.

Bannister looked up at Assistant Commissioner Horrocks – a man as stupid as he was discourteous.

'Did you know there was a rowing boat on fire in the middle of the Thames last night?' Horrocks asked, in a voice that sounded like a malfunctioning traction engine.

'Yes, sir, I did,' Bannister said mildly.

'Well, give me the details, man! I need the details.'

'The rowing boat belonged to a chap called Harry Driver, and he's a waterman,' Bannister told him. 'If you'd asked me yesterday, I'd have said that the trade of waterman died out years ago, but Harry says that even in this day and age, there's enough people wanting him to ferry them across the river to make it just about worthwhile.'

'And what have you done about Mr Driver's boat?' Horrocks wanted to know.

'Not a lot. You see, by the time the fire brigade got there, it had already gone under.'

'So you are not treating it as a serious incident?'

'No, sir.'

'And may I ask why not?'

'Because it was either an act of revenge against Harry – and he was honest enough to admit to me that he's made a few enemies in his time – or it was the act of some hooligan. In either case, investigating it would be a waste of our valuable time and meagre resources.'

Horrocks sneered. 'I don't suppose it even occurred to you that it was the work of a German spy, did it?' he asked.

'No, sir, it did not,' Bannister agreed. 'Is there any particular reason why it should have occurred to me?'

Horrocks sighed theatrically, which he probably thought was showing the natural exasperation of a very clever man who was having to deal with a much inferior mind.

'You had a fire burning in the river – pinpointing the location of the docks – and you don't think it was the work of a German spy?' he asked.

'Good God, no!'

He was handling this all wrong, he realized. When you were speaking to an arrogant idiot who was also your boss, it was wise to talk like a *subservient* idiot. Well, to hell with that. He'd faced death in the Western Desert, and there was only so much crap he was prepared to take now he was back home again.

'You do realize that we haven't been bombed for nearly four years, don't you, sir?' he asked.

For a moment, Horrocks was lost for words, and he just stood gazing at the wall. And then an answer came to him.

'If there's no danger of being bombed, then why is the blackout still being enforced?' he asked, triumphantly.

The blackout was still in force for psychological rather than practical reasons, Bannister thought. It was there to remind the civilian population that though the war had finally turned the corner, it was far from over, and they could not afford to relax their efforts.

Did Horrocks really not realize that obvious fact? From the way he was talking, it would seem not.

'The blackout's just a precaution, sir,' Bannister explained. 'The German Luftwaffe is smashed. That's why Hitler has resorted to using these V-2 rockets. No one in authority over here actually believes Germany has the power to launch a proper bombing campaign against London again.'

'I believe it,' Horrocks said, 'especially after what this spy did last night. I want him caught. Make it your top priority.' He gave Bannister a weak man's hard stare. 'And I'll be watching you, Detective Inspector, to make sure my orders are obeyed.'

Then he turned and stormed out.

Napoleon once said that the English were a nation of shopkeepers. He had meant it as an insult, Inspector Bannister thought, but as the former emperor rotted in exile on St Helena, far away from the Europe he was once master of, he must have cursed those English shopkeepers' spirit.

The local shop occupied a central part in English daily life, although – in a strictly geographical sense – it was located on edges rather than in centres. The average local shop, in fact, usually occupied one end terrace of a row of houses – the other end being, almost invariably, a pub.

In peacetime, these corner shops – which sold almost everything most people could ever want – were open all the hours that anyone could reasonably be expected to be awake. The owners all wore long brown khaki jackets, and appeared to be middle aged. Indeed, they gave the impression of having been born middle aged – of emerging from the womb with quick, calculating eyes and furrowed brows. They knew all their customers' likes and dislikes, and catered for them, because the customer was the lifeblood of the business – and if they were not careful, those customers might transfer their loyalty to another corner shop.

The war had changed all that, as it had changed so many other things. Almost everything was rationed now, so there was little scope for initiative for the wily shopkeeper. It was impossible for him to make a clever purchase and earn an extra few shillings, and he could no longer tempt customers by catering to their weaknesses, because he didn't have the stock to do it with.

Ration cards were the great equalizer. The shopkeeper would be allowed a limited amount of stock, and, because there was a shortage of almost everything, he would sell it all, almost without effort. There was nothing he could do to improve his position, so he might as well not try.

That was probably why the owner of this small corner shop, just off Bankside, was not even there, Bannister thought, but had instead left the business in the hands of a pimply youth who would probably never even have been allowed through the door in the old days.

Bannister looked around the shop's shelves, his sweeping glance taking in cigarettes, candles, tins of corned beef and packets of powdered egg. He sniffed, and inhaled the smell of carbolic soap, chicory and furniture wax. Things simply didn't get more English than this, he thought.

'You want something?' the youth asked, his voice devoid of any interest in the answer to his question.

'I expect a lot of people round here use paraffin heaters, don't they?' Bannister asked.

The boy was not interested in being drawn into conversation. 'Is that what you want?' he asked. 'Paraffin?'

'Yes, that is what I want,' Bannister agreed. 'Have you got a couple of gallons of it to spare?'

'If you've got the coupons for a couple of gallons, then we've got the paraffin,' the boy said, smirking because he knew that this customer – or any customer, for that matter – couldn't possibly have that many coupons.

'There was a rowing boat set on fire in the river last night,' Inspector Bannister mused. 'It must have taken a fair amount of paraffin to get that burning, don't you think?'

The youth shifted uneasily behind the counter. 'I wouldn't know anything about that,' he said, in little more than a mumble.

Bannister smiled to himself. He had figured out that the paraffin must have been acquired from somewhere near the point at which the boat had been stolen – because no one would want to run the risk of walking very far with that much illegal fuel – and in coming to this particular shop, he seemed to have hit the jackpot first time out.

He produced his warrant card. The youth examined it, and looked instantly miserable.

'I'd like to see how much paraffin you have in stock, and then check it against the records to see how much you *should* have,' Bannister said.

'The governor's got all the paperwork,' the youth replied, clearly in a panic now.

'When will the governor be back?'

'I don't know.'

'Does he always take his big bulky sales' ledgers with him when he goes out?'

'Yeah.'

'I don't believe you,' Bannister said. 'Step aside so I can get behind the counter, and I'll soon find what I'm looking for.'

The youth didn't move. 'Look, inspector,' he said, 'I'm not a thief. I swear I'm not.'

'So the books will balance, will they?'

The boy looked down. 'No.'

'Then tell me what happened.'

'There was this young lady – real good looking – came in. She said she'd lost her coupons, but she really needed the paraffin because her granny was freezing to death.'

'And did you believe her?'

'Yes.'

'Did you really?'

The boy looked down again. 'No.'

'So why did you give her the paraffin, when you must have known you were almost certain to get caught?'

'I don't know.'

Bannister slammed his hand down on the counter. 'That's really not good enough!' he roared.

'She . . . she said if I gave her the paraffin, she'd do something for me,' the boy admitted, reddening.

# TWENTY-SEVEN

My working theory is as follows:

(i) Grace Stockton's killer (Red Duffle Coat Woman) was living in London at the time of the murder, since she arrived in Oxford on the London train, and left the same way.

(ii) Grace must have known her killer, which means they met during the time she spent in London during the war.

(iii) The motive for the murder lay in something unusual or disturbing that happened on or around the 25th of November 1944, which was when, according to Annie Tobin, Grace behaved monstrously to her and then suddenly and dramatically left London.

I imagine you're thinking to yourselves that the theory, as it stands, is somewhat flawed.

*Somewhat* flawed!

I want to hold onto it because it's all I've got, but even I can see that there are holes in it big enough to drive a steam train through!

For a start, the killer might live in Cornwall or Kent, or any of a score of other locations that do not have a direct connection to Oxford, so it was not so much a case of her coming from London as it was of her *changing trains* in London. She might not have known Grace at all – the victim could have been no more than a symbol, as Sharon Tate was in the Manson family murders. And Grace might have left London so suddenly for any number of reasons, not the least being the one she stated – a fear that it was not a safe place to bring up her baby.

Given all that, however, I've got to have something as a basis from which to work, which is why I'm now in Camden Town, because it was here, sometime in 1944, that Grace delivered the baby of a young woman who, for the moment, I know only as Jane.

Bombay Street is clearly marked in my A to Z, and the road is indeed still there. What is missing is the actual terrace of houses that Jane used to live in and Grace used to visit. Instead, there is a children's playground and a tall steel-and-concrete tower block (which, according to the sign in front of it is called Queen Elizabeth II House).

Gazing up at the windows on some of the lower floors, I note that most of the curtains are light and modern. Examining the washing lines on the balconies, it seems to me that a lot of the underwear hanging from them is skimpy and lacy, and would have scandalized most women back in the 1940s. And looking around at street level, I see that most of the people out and about are either women in their thirties or kids in their early teens.

Conclusion? I'm going to be hard pressed to find anyone who lived here in 1944.

I should have been expecting this, I suppose. After the war, the government moved the population out of the heavily bombed areas, in order to completely redevelop them, and by the time the work was completed (at least two or three years later – and often much longer than that), many of those evacuees were either happily settled somewhere else or dead, and so the neighbourhood was repopulated by an entirely new set of people.

But all is not yet lost, because just up the road I've spotted a pub called the King's Head, and it is not beyond the realms of possibility that someone in there will remember the old days.

Beyond the realms of possibility?

*Beyond the realms of possibility!*

Who – in God's name – talks like that?

I do, apparently – when I'm really desperate.

The King's Head is one of those late-Victorian pubs built of red-glazed brick, with big frosted windows and ostentatiously arched doorways. There are three of these doorways, leading to three different bars – the working men's public bar, the saloon bar (for men who wear ties, and do not leave their wives and girlfriends at home when they go out boozing); and the lounge bar (normally the province of passing solicitors' clerks, travelling salesmen and doctors working as locums).

Approaching any pub, my natural inclination is to choose the public bar, where there will almost inevitably be a dartboard – I'm a real killer with the arrows – and where I can swear without scandalizing any of the other drinkers. On this occasion, however, the confidential enquiry agent in me vetoes the public bar, and steers me towards the saloon.

There is no one else in the saloon bar, but there is an old-fashioned bell on the counter, and when I hit it with the palm of my hand – ding, ding, ding – a man appears almost immediately.

He is around sixty, I guess. He is slightly plump and has a roundish face, topped off with a shiny bald head which reflects the overhead light back at itself. He is wearing a shiny waistcoat (perhaps to go with his dome) and this waistcoat is struggling valiantly to contain a pot belly of some proportion.

'How can I help you, madam?' he asks.

Whenever anyone calls me 'madam', I instinctively want to turn round to see who else is there, but, over time, I've learned to restrain myself, and I say, 'I'd like a gin and tonic, please – Gordon's, if you've got it.'

'Gordon's it is, madam.'

'And have one yourself.'

'That's very kind of you.'

He serves my drink, and as he pulls himself a half of bitter, he says, 'First one of the day.'

Yeah, right – if it's your first of the day, my friend, I'm Snow White's illegitimate love child.

With the drink I've just bought him in his hand, he can't very well abandon me (all part of my cunning plan, you see) and feels obliged to make some conversation.

'I haven't seen you round here before, have I?' he asks.

'No,' I agree. 'I'm here with a task to fulfil.'

It would be churlish of him to say nothing, and I've already assessed him as too nice a man for that, so it does not surprise me at all when he repeats, 'A task to fulfil, eh?' as if that explains it all.

'Have you been in this pub a while?' I ask.

'Yes, I suppose you could say I have,' he responds, with a smile. 'My dear old dad – God rest his soul – was the landlord here before me, and I was born just upstairs,' he continues pointing his thumb at the ceiling.

'Did the pub stay open throughout the whole of the war?' I ask, crossing my fingers.

'It most certainly did,' he replies.

I breathe a sigh of relief.

'And is there anyone who worked here back then who is still . . .' I begin. Then I stop and search my brain for some word slightly more tactful and sensitive than *alive*, 'who is still living in the area?' I continue.

'*I* worked here,' he says, and then, before I have time to ask him why he wasn't in the army, he quickly adds, 'I signed up, right at the start of the war, but I had poor eyesight and flat feet. The doctor told me he might just have passed me with one of them, but . . .' He shrugs. 'Anyway, if I couldn't fight abroad, I was determined to do what I could on the home front to keep up morale, and that's why we never closed, not even when all the streets around us were having the shit bombed out of them.' He stops, and reddens. 'Sorry about the language, miss.'

'From the pictures I've seen, there's no other word you could have used,' I reassure him.

He looks relieved. 'Well, there you are then. We were just like the Windmill Theatre – we never closed.'

'You should have got a medal,' I say, ingratiatingly.

'Get away with you,' he says, embarrassed. 'You don't expect a medal for just doing your job.'

I reach into my handbag and take out a card from the collection I store in there. This one says:

Jennifer Redhead
OXFORD MAIL

'I'm doing a series on the Blitz,' I say, 'and my editor specially wanted me to include Bombay Street, because a relative of his lived there in 1944.'

The landlord gives me a look which hangs somewhere between puzzlement and suspicion.

'Are you sure you've got the year right?' he asks.

'Yes, I am.'

'And what's your editor's name?'

'George Hobson. Why?'

'The reason I'm asking is that Bombay Terrace – that's the row of houses that ran most of the length of Bombay *Street* – was bombed out in 1941. There were only a couple of houses left standing by 1944, and only one of them had anybody living in it – and that was a woman called Jane.'

'That's her,' I say.

His look is now definitely more suspicion than surprise.

'And she was a relative of your editor, was she?' he asks.

'A distant relative,' I tell him. And, because I'm in danger of losing him, I decide to take a gamble, and add, 'She was pretty much the black sheep of the family, if you want the truth.'

He nods. 'I can't say I'm exactly surprised about that. She used to stand on the corner opposite the pub and sell herself to any man who had a few shillings in his pocket. This was when she was pregnant. It was really disgusting.' And his disgust has been showing on his face, but now it melts away into a smile. 'Then Grace came along.'

'Grace?'

'She was a real lady, was Grace. You'd have thought she had enough on her hands with her own pregnancy, but she decided to take Jane in hand. The first thing she did was to stop my customers giving Jane any money.'

'And how did she do that?'

'She threatened them with some kind of voodoo.'

'And they believed it?'

'Yes, she was very convincing – so convincing that every time they saw her after that, they put their hands in their pockets and checked that their balls were still there.' The landlord blushes again. 'Sorry, miss, I don't know what's got into me today.'

'There's no harm at all in a bit of plain speaking,' I say. 'What else did Grace do?'

'She got Jane off drinking, and occasionally she'd come in here and make a collection for her. Most of my customers paid up, maybe because they were afraid of her, but mostly, I think, they did it because they were a little bit in love with her.' He sighed. 'I know I was.'

'Did she stop coming once her own baby was born?' I ask.

'Yes, but she sent a girl in her place. I can't for the life of me remember her name.'

Poor Annie Tobin, I think, so bloody diffident that she drifts through life leaving barely a trace of herself behind.

'Grace was killed a few years back,' the landlord says, with a hint of sadness. 'They had a picture of her murderer in the paper.'

'And did you recognize him?' I ask, avoiding falling into the trap of seeming to know too much.

'It wasn't a him, it was a her,' the landlord says. 'And she did seem vaguely familiar, but I just couldn't put my finger on it.' He takes a sip of his half of bitter. 'Anyway, I was telling you about what happened in 1944.'

'You were,' I agree.

'Grace started coming back about a month after her own baby was born, and that went on for three or four weeks. And then, of course, it happened.'

'What happened?'

'The terrace was hit by a doodlebug. Do you know what that is, Miss?'

'A V-1,' I say. 'A German flying bomb.'

'That's right, only we always called them doodlebugs – maybe because that made them sound less frightening. You could see them streaking through the sky, and people said that as long as you could hear the engine, you were safe. Anyway, this doodlebug hit what was left of Bombay Terrace, and it was gone. Boom! Just like that! Bricks and pieces of slate were flying everywhere. One of the bricks smashed through the window of the public bar, and we had to keep it boarded up until after the war, when there was fresh glass available. Anyway, the next day, when they were combing through the wreckage . . .'

'Did you say *the next day*?'

'That's right.'

'Why did they leave it so long?' I ask, horrified. 'There could have been people lying injured under all that rubble.'

The landlord shakes his head in a gesture that seems to signify both pity and contempt.

'You youngsters,' he says. 'You've absolutely no idea what things were like during the war. For a start, if you'd seen the mess left behind after a flying bomb struck, it would never have occurred to you that anyone could have survived it. Secondly, you have to understand just how stretched our resources were. On the same day that the V-1 hit Bombay Terrace, a V-2 rocket hit the Woolworths store in New Cross, killing *a hundred and sixty people* and injuring over a hundred more. All those people, who'd just stepped out to do a bit of shopping, ended up dead or mutilated. Let me tell you, that was enough to keep the civil defence teams busy, and any bodies lying under the rubble in Bombay Terrace just had to wait.'

'You're right, I shouldn't go making assumptions when I know nothing about how things were,' I say, humbly. 'I'm sorry.'

The landlord looks embarrassed for a second time. 'No, girl, I'm sorry,' he says. 'I shouldn't have flown off the handle like that.'

'They did clear the rubble eventually,' I say, carefully.

'They did,' he agrees. 'But Jane and her baby weren't there, so they must have been out of the house when the bomb landed, which is a bit of a miracle in itself, because she hardly ever left home.'

'So what happened to Jane after that?'

The landlord shrugs. 'We never saw her again.'

'Didn't you wonder about her?'

'Not really. That was one of the things about wartime – people drifted into your life, and when you turned around again, they were gone.'

Someone calls, 'Hey, Jack, there's no chance of a bit of liquid refreshment back here, is there?'

'Coming right now,' the landlord calls back. He turns to me. 'Have you finished with your questions?'

'I've just one more,' I tell him. 'What date did this flying bomb land on Bombay Terrace?'

'It was sometime before Christmas 1944,' he says, turning to go to his new customer. 'I can't be more precise than that. But if you look it up in the library, I expect you'll find it easily enough.'

Yes, I suspect I will. And I'll be very surprised if it wasn't the 25th of November – the day before Annie Tobin's birthday.

Once I am back in the John Harvard Library, I test my theory on the date of the flying bomb by going directly to the 26th of November 1944 microfilm edition of the *Southwark Record*.

And there it is – an extensive account of the V-2 which landed on the Woolworths store and killed so many people, and a second article, which is barely more than a footnote to the first, on the destruction of what little remained of Bombay Terrace.

I am on the point of returning the microfilm to the stacks when another article catches my eye.

The Mystery of the Burning Boat.

Late last night, while PC Clive Turnbull was following his customary beat along Bankside, he noticed something on fire in the river. He soon ascertained that it was a rowing boat. It took him no time at all to call the Fire Brigade, and the Brigade responded with the speed and efficiency which has made us Londoners justly proud of it, but even so, by the time they arrived on the scene, the boat had sunk without trace in the middle of the river.

The rowing boat belonged to Mr Harry Driver, a well-known local character who claims to be London's last waterman. He talked exclusively to the *Record*. 'I keep the boat moored on the river,' he told us. 'Everybody in the area knows it belongs to me. I don't see why anybody would want to steal it, and even less why they would set it on fire. It seems a terrible shame.'

We at the *Record* agree with you wholeheartedly, Harry.
It is a terrible shame, and we cannot even imagine why
anybody would want to do such a despicable thing.

It could be a coincidence that the boat was set ablaze – for no
apparent reason – on the same night that Grace Stockton arrived
at her lodgings smelling of paraffin, but even if I hadn't read some
of Grace Stockton's writings when I was an undergraduate, I
wouldn't have let it pass unchecked.

I go back to the central library hall, and consult the book cata-
logue. The library has a copy of one of Grace's books. It is called
*Anthropology for the Layman*, and I'm almost certain it's the one
I dipped into all those years ago.

I take it down from the shelves (it was purchased by the library
eleven years ago, but there is only one stamp to show it was ever
borrowed) and quickly find the relevant page.

The Trinka culture of death seemingly has echoes in it of
both the Zoroastrian culture of ancient Persia and the Viking
culture of Scandinavia. Both the Zoroastrians and the Trinka
revere the earth, and would consider it polluting (and actually
sacrilegious) to bury their dead in the ground. It is here,
however, that the belief systems diverge.

Zoroastrians also worship the other elements – air, water
and fire – and do not employ any of them in the disposal of
their corpses. Instead, they build towers – known as Towers
of Silence – on which they lay the bodies to be picked at
and eventually devoured by carrion birds.

The Trinka, on the other hand, worship river gods, who
they believe would welcome the dead, and here we have an
overlap with the Vikings. The bodies of the Trinka are placed
in boats which are set on fire and then pushed adrift.
Important Trinka personages – tribal chiefs and their wives,
for example, are placed in elaborately carved war canoes,
while more humble members (including children) are laid
in much simpler craft, some of them barely river-worthy.
However, the ceremony is essentially the same whatever the
deceased's position in society.

The investigation is suddenly moving in ways I had not anticipated, and consequently there are new people I am more than eager to talk to. But it is far too late to set off in an entirely fresh direction today, I counsel myself, and my best plan would be to go home for the night.

Once I am sitting on the train back to Oxford, I am surprised to discover that I am exhausted. How can that be, I wonder? I am a young woman – well, youngish, anyway, and though I may drink too many gin and tonics (which is, at the very least, debatable), I compensate for that by working out in the gym three times a week.

The ticket collector, who is bow-legged and looks as if he is approaching retirement, inspects my ticket, clips it, and leaves me in peace.

There is no reason in the world why a day's investigating in London should leave me shagged out, I think. In fact, I should be ready and eager, once I'm back on home ground, to indulge in one of my favourite recreational activities, which is to hunt down a willing – and reasonably attractive – man and abandon myself to a night of wild, meaningless sex.

I'll be fine after five minutes' rest, I tell myself, as the train pulls out of the station.

The next thing I know, the ticket collector is shaking my shoulders.

'Your ticket is to Oxford,' he says.

'Wake me up when we get there,' I mumble.

'We're there now,' he tells me. 'And if you don't get off the train soon, you'll be going to Didcot.'

And I wouldn't want that, would I? I struggle to my feet, and get off the train just in time.

My bike is parked – amongst hundreds of others – in the car park, but the thought of pedalling down the Iffley Road is just too much.

I hail a taxi.

Why not?

I'm on expenses!

Let's live a little!

# PART FOUR
## Thursday 30th October, 1975

# TWENTY-EIGHT

t is morning. The birds are singing and the sun is shining. I should be feeling fresh and revitalized after my night's sleep, but I don't. I'm tired and listless and even the excited explosions coming from my cereal bowl (snap-crackle-pop, snap-crackle-pop) fail to make me feel any better.

But at least I've worked out *why* I feel this way, I tell myself, as I sip my third black coffee of the morning. The problem is that I've done something I always promise I won't do, which is to become personally involved in the case.

I feel for Grace Stockton, who stayed in London out of a sense of duty when there would have been no shame in leaving, and who took Jane under her wing despite her own pregnancy.

I feel for Jane herself, who, with Grace's help, managed to turn her life around.

And I feel for Annie Tobin, who only ever wanted to be helpful (and perhaps, if there was any to spare, a little love).

All of them have done things that make me want to admire them, but it is unlikely that there was a happy ending for any of them, and I have this dread feeling – deep down in my gut – that one of them is going to let me down badly.

I force myself through my toughest cycle of exercises, and then – with my muscles still aching – I make two phone calls. The first of these calls is to the police station in Southwark, and the second is to a private number that I've talked the desk sergeant into providing me with.

That task completed, I decide that even though my body still hurts, I'll walk all the way to the railway station.

Sometimes, I'm a glutton for punishment.

It is eleven thirty in the morning, and I'm back again in Southwark, sitting at a table in the lounge bar of a pub called the Green Dragon. I'm sipping at an orange juice, because it's too early in the day (even by my flexible standards) to start hitting the hard stuff.

The door opens, and a man steps inside. I assume he's the one I'm waiting for, since he's around the right age (late sixties), and, as I've been led to expect, drags his left leg slightly.

'Have you ever heard of Hopalong Cassidy, Miss Redhead?' he'd asked me over the phone.

'Was he a television cowboy?' I asked, dredging up distant memories from my childhood. Unbidden, another detail comes to me from the dark recesses of mind. 'Didn't he wear a black hat, whereas most heroes wore a white one?'

'Yes, he did,' Inspector Bannister chuckled delightedly. 'Cassidy always was an unconventional righter of wrongs. That's how I saw myself, too – an unconventional righter of wrongs – Hopalong Bannister!'

I wave to him, and he acknowledges the wave with a slight nod of his head, then makes his way carefully over to my table.

'Miss Redhead?' he asks.

I stand up and hold out my hand. 'DCI Bannister?'

'Not any more,' he says, shaking my hand and sitting down. 'They tell me you used to be a copper yourself.'

'That's right.'

'Were you any good?'

'Yes. I was *very* good.'

'So why did they make you resign?'

I grin. 'You've been checking up on me, haven't you?'

'I certainly have,' he agrees.

'You seem to have found out a great deal about me in a very short time,' I say.

He smiles. 'Like you, I was very good at my job – and I wanted to know exactly who I was dealing with. So why *did* they make you resign?'

'I was carrying out my own investigation into a high-ranking member of the Thames Valley police. It made him feel very uncomfortable.'

'Bent, was he?'

'As a corkscrew.'

'And where is he now?'

'He's behind bars. They finally caught up with him last year.'

Bannister smiles again. 'I do like a story with a happy ending,' he says. He slaps the table top with the palm of his hand. 'Right, now that we've established that we like each other, and, more importantly, we trust each other . . .' He pauses, and a look of mock concern crosses his face. 'We do like each other and trust each other, don't we?'

'Definitely,' I say – and I mean it.

'Then let's get down to business,' he suggests.

'All right.'

'And the first order of business is for you to call the waiter and get me a rum and peppermint.'

When the waiter brings his drink, Bannister licks his lips and then takes a sip. 'I used to look down on rum and pep as an old man's drink,' he says, 'but somehow, when I wasn't looking, I became an old man myself, and now it really hits the spot.' He takes another sip. 'So you want to hear about the case of the burning rowing boat, do you?'

'That's right.'

'Why?'

'Because I think I might know who set it on fire.'

He chortles. 'So you've solved a case that the combined resources of the Met failed to solve thirty years ago.'

'Yes, I think I have.'

'Tell me about it.'

'No,' I say, 'you tell me, first.'

'Fair enough,' he agrees. 'Actually, there's not a great deal to tell. I estimated it would have taken at least a couple of gallons of paraffin to set the boat ablaze, and I tracked down the source of that paraffin to a general store on Bankside. The owner had left a callow youth in charge, and the woman . . .' He pauses again, and examines my face. 'I'm guessing you already knew it was a woman. Am I right?'

I nod. 'My whole theory's based on it being a woman,' I admit.

'So this woman must have known that the owner wasn't there – and the boy was – before she ever entered the shop.'

'What makes you say that?'

'She couldn't have had enough ration coupons for that much paraffin. No single individual did. And she must have known that no shopkeeper would risk breaking the law, even if she was prepared to pay well over the odds, because things were very tightly regulated back then, and he'd have been bound to get caught and probably faced prison. But suppose financial gain is not your main concern, and your driving force is your raging hormones.'

'The callow youth behind the counter,' I say.

'The callow youth behind the counter,' he agrees. 'He sees an attractive woman enter the shop, and those hormones go into overdrive.' Bannister pauses. 'Look, you're a young lady . . .'

'No, I'm bloody not.'

'. . . and I'm an old-fashioned man,' he continues, ignoring the comment, 'so I'm not sure how I'm going to phrase this.' He takes a deep breath. 'She told him that if he gave her the paraffin she needed, she would pleasure him manually.'

'She agreed to toss him off?'

He grimaces. 'No.'

'But I thought you said . . .'

'She didn't *agree* to it – it was her idea in the first place. The lad knew it was a mistake right from the beginning. He knew that he'd be caught in the end. But he just couldn't resist. And that must have been part of her calculation.'

'Did he tell you anything else?'

'Yes, she'd brought a pram with her – one of those big solid ones they used to make before the war.'

Of course she had.

A Silver Cross.

The Rolls Royce of perambulators.

'Did he see what was in the pram?' I ask.

'No, he only looked in its direction once, but she screamed at him not to do that.'

'Would that kind of pram have been big enough to carry a small woman, do you think?'

'I suppose it's just possible, but it would have been very uncomfortable for her.'

'Not if she was dead.'

'No, not then.'

'I think that what she had in the pram was an alcoholic called Jane and her baby,' I say. 'I think she dug them out of the rubble in Bombay Street, and pushed them out into the river on a burning boat.'

And then she went back to her own flat, where her own baby was crying, and Annie Tobin was waiting outside the front door.

No wonder Grace had looked wild, and had spoken roughly to her.

'Why did she do it?' Bannister asked.

'As a mark of respect,' I say, and tell him about the traditions in which Grace's Trinka nannies brought her up.

'That all sounds a bit far-fetched, but then the truth often is,' Bannister says. 'Oh, by the way, there's a postscript to the story.'

'Yes?'

'Just after the war, someone sent an envelope to the local nick with twenty pounds and a letter in it. The letter was printed in block capitals, and it said something along the lines of: "Please give this to Harry Driver, and tell him I'm sorry I had to burn his boat." I thought at first that meant she must have known Harry, but, of course, it didn't.'

'No, she could simply have got his name from the newspaper.'

'Exactly.'

I suppose I should be feeling triumphant, because I have solved a thirty-year-old mystery all on my own. The problem is that, by being proved right in this one part of the puzzle, I have effectively demolished my main theory.

According to that theory, Grace had to leave London in a hurry, and her reason for that was directly connected with the reason for her murder, nearly thirty years later. If I could find the motive for the former, I could deduce the motive for the latter, I'd told myself. But now I think I know the real reason she left, I can find no way to tie that in with the murder at all – because the only other person involved had already been dead for twenty-seven years by the time Grace was killed.

And it isn't as if I've now freed myself to follow one of my other lines of inquiry, because there are no other lines. I have no idea why Grace Stockton was killed, and I have no idea where to even begin looking.

My best plan – my only plan – is to travel to Cambridge later today and tell my client that the situation is hopeless.

It's not a meeting I'm looking forward to.


In many ways, Cambridge is similar to Oxford. It, too, has a river running through it, on which college rowing teams practice energetically at ungodly hours of the morning, and where young men punt young women up and down, in the belief that a dash of romance is the gateway to their knickers. It, too, has monumental buildings dating back seven hundred years, and bicycle thieves who work on an industrial scale. But there are differences, too. If you plan to be a comedian in later life, then Cambridge is the place for you. It certainly worked for Peter Cook, John Cleese and Eric Idle. If, on the other hand, you plan a life in politics, then you should probably choose Oxford – certainly our last five prime ministers seemed to think so!

All these thoughts flit through my mind as I wait for my client in the bar of the University Arms, one of Cambridge's finest hotels.

Julia walks in. Her entrance causes heads to turn and conversations to be suspended mid-sentence. It is hardly surprising, because she is wearing an expensive blue suit in which she looks sensational, and strides across the room as if she were the mistress of the galaxy.

What woman wouldn't want to be her? What man would consider it anything but a great honour to be selected as her devoted slave?

It is only when she sits down opposite me that I can see the uncertainty in her eyes.

A waiter is instantly hovering in attendance, and she immediately orders a double scotch.

She knows what I'm going to say, I think, or at least believes there's a possibility I might say it – and she's dreading that.

'Did you see the Archaeology and Anthropology Museum when you were coming here?' she asks.

'Yes,' I reply. 'It's just down the road, isn't it?'

'That's right. I would sometimes catch myself thinking that the main reason my mother came to Cambridge was not to see me at all, but to visit that museum.' Her scotch has arrived, and Julia lifts it from the tray and takes a deep slug before putting it on the table. 'And at times like those, I wondered if it was all my fault – if I had tried hard enough to make her love and respect me.'

This is a new Julia I am seeing. Gone is the confident Dr Pemberton, and in her place is a worried little girl – which is going to make what I have to say all that much harder.

'It was foolish of me, of course,' Julia continues. 'She did love me – deeply – but she couldn't show it.'

I know I shouldn't ask her why she didn't show it – I don't even want to know the answer – but I hear myself saying it, anyway.

'The Trinka woman has two duties,' she explains. 'The first is to give her husband whatever he wants, because, as her protector, that is no more than his due. The second is to educate her children, from an early age, to rely on no one but themselves until they marry, because life is hard and there might come a point at which they have to manage on their own. So while it is permissible to show interest and affection to other people's children, your duty to your own is to prepare them for the difficulties that could lie ahead.'

'I can see that,' I say, 'but England isn't Papua New Guinea, and your mother wasn't a Trinka.'

It was a stupid comment to make, and I regret it the moment it has left my mouth. But Julia does not look offended or hurt in any way. Instead, she merely seems eager to explain.

'You're right, my mother wasn't a Trinka in the true ethnic sense,' she agrees. 'But her parents were so busy trying to convert the natives to Christianity that they left most of her upbringing to her Trinka nannies. I think it would be fair to say that my grandparents' labours only resulted in one real convert – and that conversion, in their terms, was in totally the wrong direction.'

'We need to talk about what I've found out,' I say.

She nods, reluctantly, and takes another swig of her whisky.

I describe the course of my investigation, and when I reach the part about setting the rowing boat on fire, she nods again.

'Was this girl Jane my mother's *kimpum*?' Julia asked.

'Her what?'

'Her *kimpum*. It's a sort of spiritual sister. They both wear bracelets out of their intertwined hair.'

'And did your mother have one of these bracelets?'

'No, but if you're right about what happened, she wouldn't have, because once your *kimpum* dies, the bracelet must be destroyed.'

'I'm sorry, I can't help you there,' I say.

'I think this Jane must have been her *kimpum*,' Julia says, reflectively. 'After all, she rescued her from the gutter, and showed her all the proper respect when she died.'

'I think you're right,' I agree.

'The proper respect,' she repeats. She smiles – a little sadly. 'Throughout my childhood, whenever one of our family pets died, my mother would build a small raft, fasten the animal to it, set it on fire, and push it out into the river. We had to stand on the bank and watch, until it sank. Sometimes, if the wind was blowing in the wrong direction, we could smell the burning flesh, but my mother refused to let me leave until it had disappeared below the water line. I haven't had a pet since I left home – I've wanted to, but I know that if I had one and it died, I'd have to perform the ritual. It's not logical, but I wouldn't be able to stop myself.'

We're all screwed up by our parents, I think, but Julia Stockton's mother seems to have done a particularly professional job on her.

'I'm a scientist,' Julia says. 'I don't believe in the Trinka gods or any other gods, but if I'm entering a building I've never been to before, I have to walk around it once in a clockwise direction and once anticlockwise. And that's only a ritual I recognize! I'm sure there must be half a dozen more I don't even know that I'm enacting.'

'How did you get on with your father?' I ask – knowing it's none of my business, but once more unable to stop myself.

She smiles, and – for just a moment – her face is at peace. 'My father gave me – and my mother – his uncritical, unreserved love,' she says. 'He is a truly wonderful man.'

We're still putting off the inevitable. Well, here goes.

'I've gone as far as I can with the investigation,' I say.

She should have been expecting something like this, but she still rocks in her seat as if she's been punched in the stomach by an invisible hand.

'I sometimes find, in my line of work, that if you try looking at the problem from an entirely new angle . . .' she begins, with a hint of desperation.

'There are no other angles,' I say firmly. 'I have absolutely no idea at all where to look next.'

'Perhaps if you went back to the school where she worked . . . What was it called?'

'The Lady Margaret School.'

'Perhaps if you went back to the Lady Margaret School—'

'I'm sorry,' I interrupt her. 'I know you're desperate to track down your mother's killer – maybe to prove to yourself that you love her, maybe because it's a Trinka thing – but there's nothing more I can do.'

She smiles sadly again. 'I think it may be both those things driving me – or perhaps they're just two different sides of the same thing,' she says, 'but if you say there's nothing more to be done, well, you're the expert, and I just have to take your word for it.' Another smile from her – and this time, a creditable attempt at a brave one. 'We all reach a point when we have to accept that the experiment is never going to work.'

She reaches into her handbag, and takes out her cheque book.

'I haven't had time to itemize my bill yet,' I tell her.

'It doesn't matter,' she says, uncapping her fountain pen and filling out the cheque. 'I just want it over with.'

She rips out the cheque, and hands it to me.

I quickly scan it.

'This is at least two hundred and fifty pounds too much,' I protest.

'You've worked very hard, and if you've failed, it's only because I've set you an impossible task.'

'I still can't accept it,' I say firmly.

She stands up. 'Please take it – if only for me. And if you don't want it, donate it to your favourite charity.'

She doesn't shake hands, but turns and walks quickly away. I can tell from the way her shoulders are heaving that she's sobbing her heart out.

I catch the train home weighed down by my own defeat.

The buffet car is closed – 'We just couldn't get the staff today,' the ticket collector tells me, without an ounce of sympathy – so I don't even have the consolation of a gin and tonic.

I slouch in my seat, feeling thoroughly miserable. I want to tear up Julia Pemberton's cheque, but I can't do that because I'm owed – and need! – some part of it. But what should I do with the rest?

Tell my bank to keep it?

No, the bank's rich enough already.

Hand the cash over to the first person I meet on the street?

No, I've never been big on making dramatic gestures.

And suddenly, I have a great idea – a world class of an idea.

True, it will involve poking my nose into someone else's

business, and attempting to change – uninvited and probably unwelcomed – the course of a fairly miserable life, but what the hell.

I definitely shouldn't do it – I know that – but nothing's going to stop me now.

# PART FIVE
## Friday 31st October, 1975

# TWENTY-NINE

'd swear that when I was a kid, shops didn't start filling their
display windows with Christmas decorations until well into
December, yet here we are, on the last day of October, and
already some of the shops on Borough High Street have cotton
wool snow stuck to their windows, and stuffed reindeers vying for
space with unconvincing snowmen.

Dear God!

And yet, I suppose, it is in some ways fitting for the occasion,
since my own mission of the day is to act as a kind of Santa Claus,
albeit one that (possibly) will not be welcomed at all.

I am standing outside the building which houses the offices of
Campion, Campion and Blaine (Solicitors and Commissioners for
Oaths), and in my hand I'm holding a ticket-sized envelope which
looks, on the face of it, perfectly harmless, but in fact contains
what could turn out to be a veritable bombshell for its intended
recipient – and for those connected to her.

I glance down at my watch. It has just gone twelve o'clock,
which – on this routine-driven island of ours – means that for
ninety-nine per cent of office workers, it is the start of the lunch
break.

The revolving door of the building turns, and disgorges two
young men wearing suits which won't have cost them an arm
and leg, but are still smart enough and confirm them as members
of the reasonably well-paid clerical class. They turn sharp right,
and I'd bet good money that they're heading straight for the pub,
which is located four doors up.

Their appearance is followed by that of three young women,
who are already in deep conversation when they hit the street.
The women cross the road, still chattering, and I guess they are
heading for the Cosy Tea, which, I noticed when I was passing
it, offers a lunchtime special.

Two more women, slightly older than the first three, come
out next. They look first across the street and then down it, as if

weighing the merits of a pint and a pasty against those of a bacon sandwich and a cup of tea. In the end, they plump for the pint and pasty, which I personally consider a wise choice.

And, finally, Annie Tobin leaves the building – a mouse, emerging cautiously from its hole. She is alone – which does not surprise me in the least – and is carrying a large paper bag in her hand. She sits down at a bench no more than ten yards from the office. She opens the bag – clumsily, because she's wearing home-knitted gloves – and extracts a sandwich which seems, on first inspection, to be rather heavy on thick-sliced bread and very light on interesting filling.

I sit down beside her, and say, 'It's a bit of a chilly day to be eating outside, isn't it, Annie?'

She jumps, startled.

'Oh, it's you,' she says. 'Young Mr Campion's made it quite plain to all the staff that he doesn't want any of us eating our food in the office, so there's not much choice, is there?'

'There's no choice about leaving the office, but you could go to the pub or the café with your mates,' I say.

She shrugs, helplessly. 'I suppose I could, but they're not really my mates. Besides, my mother made me these sandwiches.'

Oh, well that explains everything. Her mother made it, and the only way she can show her gratitude for this almost unbelievable act of kindness is by chomping her way through the unappetizing parcel of starch she is holding in her hands.

I pass her a leaflet. 'Look at this.'

She scans it. 'It's a brochure for a singles' cruise of the Mediterranean,' she says.

'That's right.'

She looks at it again.

'It's exclusively for people between the ages of forty and sixty, and it says there will be an equal number of men and women on the cruise.'

'Yes, that is what it says,' I agree.

'But you can't be more than thirty.'

When you're thirteen years old, you resent the hell out of someone knocking a year off your age, but if you're thirty-one when it happens, it's a different story entirely, and, despite knowing it means nothing at all, I experience a momentary flush of well-being.

'I'm older than I look,' I tell her, 'but, you're right, I'm not old enough for that.'

'So it's no good to you, is it?'

'No, it isn't,' I agree, 'but then it's not my name on the ticket.'

I hand her the envelope.

She looks down at it.

'Open it,' I say.

She takes off her glove, opens the envelope and extracts the ticket. As she reads what it says, her eyes widen.

'It's in my name!' she says.

'That's right.'

'I can't possibly accept this. I really can't,' she says, holding the ticket out to me.

'You can please yourself,' I tell her, folding my arms, 'but the ticket's already paid for, and the money's non-refundable.'

'But . . . but I can't just go on a cruise,' she moans.

'Why not? Have you used up all your available holiday time?'

'No, no, it's not that. As a matter of fact, I haven't used any of it at all, because my mother doesn't like to go—'

'Well, then, if you're owed the time, just what is stopping you?' I interrupt her.

'Could my mother come along?' she asks.

'Certainly,' I reply, 'as long as she pays her own way, there are still places available, and she's under sixty.'

'But she isn't . . .' Annie says. She pauses for a second, then continues, 'You're laughing at me, aren't you?'

'No,' I say, 'I promise I'm not.'

And then I feel a little bit guilty, because a small, unworthy part of me has been doing just that.

'My mother's over sixty,' she says. 'You must know that.'

I nod. 'I can do the maths.'

'Well, then?'

'In my own awkward way, I was trying to make a point. You need to be doing things that women of your age do, Annie – not things that women of your mother's age do. Can you understand that?'

'But I can't just leave her on her own for a whole two weeks, can I?' Annie asks.

'Can't you?'

'Well, no.'

'Well, I've bought the ticket, and that's the end of it as far as I'm concerned,' I say. 'What happens next is up to you.'

She shivers. 'I'm not sure I'd have the nerve,' she says. 'Even the thought of it frightens me.'

'Most things that are worth doing in this life are a little bit frightening,' I reply.

'But do you think I *could* do it?' she asks, almost pleadingly.

'I'm sure you could,' I tell her.

And then, looking over her shoulder, I see someone in a bright red duffle coat walking up the street.

'I have to go,' I tell Annie.

'Couldn't you just . . .?'

'No, I really have to go.'

'But I haven't decided . . .'

'You'll have to make your own decisions, Annie,' I call to her, over my shoulder.

I sprint up the street, but I soon discover there'd been no need to hurry, because the figure in the red duffle coat has stopped to look at the televisions on display in an electrical store's shop window.

I tap her lightly on the shoulder and she turns to look at me. She is probably the same age as the suspected killer, but her face is much thinner, and her nose considerably larger.

She looks terrified.

'There's no need to be alarmed, madam,' I say soothingly. 'I'd just like to know where you bought that duffle coat from.'

Her thin lips move up and down, but for several seconds, no sound comes out of her mouth. Then she rasps, 'We're not supposed to talk to anybody on our first few times out.'

'What do you mean, "your first few times out"?' I ask.

But instead of answering the question, she hunches her shoulders and scurries away.

I notice one of the shop's employees standing in the doorway. He is disguised as Santa, though the grey flannel trousers and black shoes which project from beneath his robe sort of give him away. He has stepped out of the shop to smoke a cigarette – which would have been much easier and safer if he hadn't been wearing a cotton wool beard and whiskers – and I can tell he has enjoyed the unexpected entertainment he has just witnessed, because his fluffy beard does nothing to hide the superior smirk which has spread across his face.

'My function is nought if not to amuse you, good sir,' I say – remembering I'm in Shakespeare's Southwark, and accompanying the words with an elaborate stage bow.

'You what?' he says, proving – though no such proof is necessary – that he is not a man of wit and erudition.

'The woman I was just talking to – does she belong to some sort of order of nuns?' I ask.

There seems to be no end to my ability to entertain him, and he laughs so much that it brings on a cough.

'An order of nuns?' he says, when he's recovered himself. 'That's a good one.'

'So she isn't?'

'Nah, she's not a penguin.'

Get it? He's pointing out that nuns look like penguins! What a joker he really is.

'So if she's not a nun, what is she?' I ask, wondering how well his beard is glued on, and how much it will hurt if I decide to yank it off.

'She's one of the loonies from up at St Dims,' he says.

The building has a high brick wall all around it, and two massive iron gates set in the middle of that wall. Next to the gates is a small brass plaque which reads St Dymphna's Institute. There is nothing on the plaque stating the nature of the institute, and if you do not already know that St Dymphna is the patron saint of mental illness, you might well conclude it is a scientific research centre or some kind of financial organization.

When I ring the bell, a large square porter with a bushy beard and a blue uniform appears, looks me up and down through the gap in the ironwork, and says, 'We're not buying anything.'

'Then that's fortunate, because I'm not selling anything,' I reply, a little miffed to be taken for a travelling salesman.

I hand him one of the business cards on which I've promoted myself from reporter on the *Oxford Mail* to special correspondent for the famous – and notoriously muck-raking – national Sunday newspaper that goes by the name of the *News of the World*.

'I'm writing an article on the more enlightened of our mental institutes,' I say, 'and I'd like to talk to your director.'

He retreats into his little lodge by the gate and emerges again a minute later. 'The director doesn't give interviews,' he says, with a superior sneer. 'And he especially doesn't want to talk to anybody from a scandal sheet like the *News of the World*.'

'How interesting,' I reply. 'Then try this: tell him if he doesn't talk to me immediately, I'm ringing the police about this institute's involvement in the murder of Grace Stockton.'

Behind the beard the porter pales, which instantly removes from my mind any possible concern that I'm on the wrong track.

'I can't tell the director something like *that*,' he says, trying – and failing – to sound as decisive as he did just a few moments ago.

'Oh, you can't, can't you?' I ask. 'Well, I suppose you must please yourself – after all, it's *your* job that's on the line here.'

And I turn and start to walk away.

'Wait!' he calls urgently after me. 'Wait just a minute.'

I wait.

He is inside his lodge for considerably more than a minute this time, but when he comes back out he presses a button which opens a side gate and says, 'You're to follow me.'

There is a driveway running along the wall on the right-hand side of the building (I'm guessing it probably leads to the trades-men's entrance) but most of the area in front of the institute is occupied by an unexpectedly pretty garden, which has a path snaking through it towards the impressive front door.

I'm half-expecting my bearded minder to escort me down the driveway to the tradesmen's entrance, but instead he gestures – with a lack of grace he must have been working on – that I should follow him up the path.

The garden is nothing like stately home-sized, but for somewhere in a built-up area like Southwark it is impressively large. There is a lily pond, though there are no lilies to provide cover at this time of year, and the brightly coloured fish which I see darting back and forth are dangerously exposed to any passing heron. There are flower beds and a rose garden, carefully trimmed hedges and a small copse of trees. And there are wood and metal benches, on which inmates of the institution, lured out by the recently emerged sun, sit basking alone or in pairs.

The men, I note, are all dressed in blue jeans and blue shirts, the women in sapphire blue dresses with pockets just below the waistline.

I have had an uncomfortable feeling in my stomach for the last half hour – a feeling initially set off by my learning about the very existence of St Dymphna's Institute – but now that I see the women's blue uniforms, it is all I can do to avoid throwing up.

The institute is housed in a large Victorian building which might once have been the home of a prosperous merchant. It looks forbidding from the outside, but once through the door, I see that an attempt has been made to brighten it up with pastel walls and brightly patterned carpets. Still, whatever they do, nothing can hide the stern dignity of the high ceilings and gothic staircases.

My mind is racing as we climb the steps to the first floor, and by the time we reach the director's office, I have a pretty clear idea of what must have happened, though I have no way – as yet – of proving any of it.

The porter knocks and the director calls, 'Come in!' The porter opens the door and then steps back – and I enter the lion's den.

The director is not a very scary lion. He is in his fifties, with a receding chin and a disappearing hairline. He is wearing an expensive suit to show that he is in charge, and a white coat to remind us that he is still a doctor. I would be prepared to thoroughly dislike him, were it not for his eyes. They are kind and caring, and give the impression that he does not let his patients suffer alone, but goes through the agony with them.

Nevertheless, he's undoubtedly the enemy at the moment, and must be treated accordingly.

'Take a seat,' he says, ignoring the comfortable armchairs in the corner of the room and pointing to the straight-backed chair in front of his desk.

I sit, and he takes up his commanding position *behind* the desk.

'I have rung the *News of the World*, and talked to the editor himself,' he says. 'No one there has ever heard of you. You are nothing but a fraud, Miss Redhead – a delusional fraud.'

'So why have you agreed to see me?' I ask.

We both already know the answer to that. I am here so he can assess just how much I know, and thus, how much of a danger I am to the institute.

But he can't come right out and say that, can he?

'You are here because I think that you probably don't quite appreciate the damage you can do to this wonderful institution by spreading these wild stories of yours, and I'd like to take this opportunity to explain it to you.'

'If they're so wild, I don't see why you're worried,' I say. 'And you are worried, aren't you?'

'I will not deny it,' he admits. 'I am worried because there are some people who are always willing to jump on anything which will discredit our work, however incredible that anything may be.'

'I saw one of your inmates out walking on Borough High Street today,' I tell him.

'One of our patients,' he corrects me censoriously. 'Patients is a much less degrading term than inmates to apply to these unfortunate people, don't you think?'

'I stand corrected,' I say – because he is right, and I am a little ashamed of myself.

He looks down at the notes on his desk.

'It would be Edna that you saw on the High Street. It was her third time out.'

'What do you mean by that?' I ask, knowing he's trying to distract me, and – for the moment – quite content to let him.

'It is our policy, once the patient shows signs of being ready for it, to reintegrate him or her into the community. On the first two or three occasions, they have a medical orderly by their side, and then the orderly keeps his distance, until, eventually, there is no orderly at all. It is one of the ways we have of building up our patients' confidence, and I have to tell you that it has proved to be remarkably effective.'

'So there was an orderly watching Edna today?'

'Yes, and he reported back to me that she handled your intrusion into her privacy very well indeed.'

Intrusion into her privacy! That makes me look like the bad guy, you see. Clever!

'And that's why you dress them up in bright red duffle coats, is it?' I ask. 'So it's easier for your orderlies to maintain visual contact?'

'Yes, it seemed like no more than a sensible precaution.'

'The police couldn't find a single company which sold bright red duffle coats,' I say.

'How do you know that?' he asks, suddenly sounding more worried.

'So since none are available commercially, what did you do?' I ask him, ignoring the question. 'Do you dye them yourself?'

'We *have them* dyed,' he says. 'We hand them over to people who are professional within their sphere, and leave them alone to get on with it, just as we hope that other people will allow us to get on with the tasks that we are professionally trained to deal with.'

This is another dig at me. This man is not half-bad at defending his little kingdom, but we have reached a stage in the investigation where half-bad simply isn't good enough.

'So one day, one of your patients does a runner,' I say. 'She travels to Oxford and kills Grace Stockton. There are CCTV pictures of her on the television and in the newspapers, but no one in Southwark – that is to say no one in Southwark outside *this* institution – recognized her. But that's hardly surprising, is it, because she was probably locked away in this place for years. And as for her distinctive duffle coat – well, CCTV is in black-and-white, and if you see a black-and-white image of a bright red duffle coat, it loses its distinctiveness and there's nothing to distinguish it from every other duffle coat.'

The director stands up. 'I'd like you to leave now, Miss Redhead,' he says shakily.

I stay firmly in my seat. 'Throw me out now, and I'll go straight to the nearest police station,' I say. 'They'll be here within the hour, checking through your records, and they'll soon discover that one of your patients is missing. And how will you explain that to them?'

'That's really none of your concern,' he says, and I can see the sweat forming on his forehead. 'Please go.'

'On the other hand,' I continue, more soothingly and reassuringly, 'if you tell me everything I want to know, I just might be able to keep you and your institution out of it.'

'How could you possibly do that?' he asks, incredulously. 'Molly killed that woman, and . . .' A look of horror fills his face. 'I didn't mean . . .' he splutters. 'I wasn't suggesting . . .'

'The reason I can probably keep you out of it because I don't believe Molly *did* kill Grace Stockton,' I say. 'And because I'm almost certain she's dead herself.'

And that's no bluff – no line of bullshit to keep him talking. There are so many things that I still don't know – the main one being that I still have no idea why Molly should have wanted to kill Grace – but I do know that the woman found in the shallow grave in the bluebell wood was wearing the same dress as the women I saw earlier, in the institute garden.

The doctor is still standing there, hesitant.

'Please sit down,' I say. 'Just looking at you hovering there is making me tired.'

He flops back into his seat, exhausted.

'Why didn't you inform the police at the time when Molly went missing?' I ask.

'I called a full staff meeting and we discussed it for hours, but in the end, we decided the consequences of reporting it were just too awful to contemplate. This institute pioneered the idea of releasing patients into the community for limited periods, you see, and the results have been little short of miraculous. But once we came out and admitted Molly was one of our patients, the experiment would be over – not just for us, but for all those other hospitals which had taken us as a model. And the doctor who authorized her limited excursions – a brilliant, caring young man – would have his career destroyed. The authorities might even have closed the place down. So we said nothing.'

'But you must have known it would all come out in the end.'

The doctor shrugs. 'Perhaps, but by keeping silent, we bought ourselves three more years, didn't we? And we've accomplished remarkable things in that time. Besides' – suddenly he's sounding very uncomfortable – 'we thought there was always a chance that she'd drown herself.'

'She was *suicidal*?' I demand, outraged. 'You let her out, knowing that she was suicidal?'

'No, no, of course not,' he says, holding up his hands to pacify me. 'She had been suicidal in the past, it's true, but she hadn't talked about drowning herself for years. Everyone agreed she'd got past that stage in her recovery.'

'How many times had she been allowed out on excursions before she went missing?' I ask.

'She'd been out twice before.'

'So there was still someone watching her?'

'Yes, but she managed to lose him in Borough Market.'

'She needed money to buy a train ticket to Oxford. Do you know where she got that from?'

'There's a petty cash box in the office,' the doctor says. 'We didn't keep it locked back then, though we do now.'

'Well, that was very careless of you, wasn't it?'

'Leaving it open made it easier for the staff to access it, and there seemed no danger of a patient taking it, because some of them had forgotten what money was, and even those who hadn't, felt no need for it in here.'

'Until Molly,' I say.

'Until Molly,' he agrees.

I know where she came from, and how she got to Oxford, but I still have no bloody idea why she desperately needed to see Grace Stockton.

'Tell me more about her,' I say.

The director opens a desk drawer, and pulls out a file which must have been sitting there since shortly after the porter informed him that I was at the gate.

'For her first few months here, she just sat there, staring at the wall. Then, for no discernible reason, she became manic, and rushed around the institute screaming that she had to find her child.'

'Did she say where she thought the child was?'

'No, at that stage she was nowhere near articulate enough. But she wasn't being entirely delusional, because there was clear medical evidence that she had given birth sometime in the past. At any rate, the institute simply couldn't tolerate that kind of behaviour – it would have unsettled all the others – so she was kept sedated for nearly a year.' He consults the file again. 'Then one of the doctors came up with the idea of giving her a doll, and apparently it worked like magic. She calmed down almost immediately, and became a model patient. Over the years, she grew less and less dependent on the doll, but even so, the sight of a baby on television was more likely than not to bring tears to her eyes.'

My gut is telling me that it was a mistake to ever come here, but it's still not too late to back out.

And now my brain is getting in on the act, reminding me that I don't work for Julia Pemberton any more, and that I can probably save myself a considerable amount of emotional wear and tear by telling the local police everything I've found out, and then walking away.

And do you know what? I simply can't bring myself to do that!

'The way you've been talking about Molly, you make it seem as if all this happened before your time,' I say. 'Did it?'

The doctor laughs with what seems like genuine amusement.

'Oh, good heavens, yes,' he says. 'I know I'm nothing like those handsome young doctors you see in the television dramas, but I'm not *that* old. In fact, when Molly was admitted here, I was still in medical school.'

My stomach is revolving like a tumble dryer.

'How long was she a patient here?' I ask.

'Nearly thirty years. The police found her wandering up and down the Borough High Street in the winter of 1944. When they questioned her, she didn't seem to know who she was, or where she'd come from. Her clothes were in rags, and she had cuts and bruises all over her body. The doctors who first examined her thought the most likely explanation was that she'd been caught in a bomb blast – there were a lot of doodlebugs being aimed at London around that time – and that all her problems stemmed from that trauma.'

My stomach has switched from tumble dryer to loaded cement mixer gone berserk.

The winter of 1944!

It couldn't be!

It couldn't possibly be!

'It wasn't the 25th of November when all this happened, was it?' I ask, dreading the answer.

The doctor consults his file again.

'As a matter of fact, it was. How could you possibly have known that?'

Oh my God!

'But you said her name was Molly,' I gasp.

'Yes, that's right. Or rather, that's what she was called here. She seemed to have no idea what her real name was, you see, and the staff had to call her something, didn't they? She acted as if she was quite happy to be known by that name – and why wouldn't she be, it's a perfectly reasonable name – but then the day before she disappeared, she told me that she'd remembered that her real name was Jane.'

But Jane is dead, I tell myself.

Jane was pulled from the rubble of Bombay Terrace by Grace, taken away in a pram, and put on a burning rowing boat in the river.

Except that that had never happened. Jane wasn't dead – she'd only been sleeping inside Molly – and the article in the local newspaper about Grace Stockton's visit to the school had brought her back to life.

So why did neither Annie Tobin nor the landlord of the King's Head recognize her from the photograph taken at Oxford railway station?

Simple! The Jane who was living in Bombay Terrace was an undernourished eighteen- or nineteen-year-old alcoholic, and she bore no resemblance to the Jane who had lived on a balanced diet and under constant medical supervision for twenty-eight years, and who, if she hadn't been mad for all that time, was, at the very least, hugely emotionally disturbed by the photograph she saw in the local paper.

I have been wrong before during the course of this investigation – so very, very wrong – but now I think that I have finally got it right.

I know who was in the rowing boat that Grace drenched in paraffin, set on fire, and then pushed out into the river.

I know why Geoffrey Markham's phone call was erased from Grace's answering machine – and I know who erased it.

And lastly, I know how Jane – who hadn't left the confines of the institute for nearly thirty years – found the strength to enter an alien world and make the journey to Oxford. It had been a tremendous achievement – the equivalent, perhaps, of a blind man skiing down a mountain – but that really must have been stretching her ability to its maximum. It was unrealistic, almost criminally stupid, to ascribe anything else to her, to imagine – even for a second – that she would have the skill to decapitate her victim, or the forethought to bury her victim's body, once the terrible act had been carried out.

\*    \*    \*

I cannot get out of St Dymphna's Institute fast enough, but on the way back to the underground station, I force myself to make time to pay a final visit to the library, because there is something else I need to look up in Grace's book.

I take the book from the shelf, and there it is in black and white – the section of the text which might provide me with the confirmation that I need. I could stop and read it here, but I don't want to. My brain tells me that London holds nothing that is threatening to me, and I know that to be true – but I *feel* threatened, and I need the security of my poky little flat back in Oxford.

I photocopy the relevant section of Grace's book, stuff it into my pocket – and flee.

Last night, I was so exhausted that I fell asleep minutes after the train pulled out of the station. There is no danger of that now. My nerves are stretched on the rack of my recent discoveries, and I doubt if I will sleep at all until I have brought this terrible business to its tragic, untidy conclusion.

As we leave the big city behind us, I take the photocopy from my pocket, smooth it out, and read what is written there.

> The Trinka attitude to dead enemies is also illuminating. A slit is made at the back of the head of the dead enemy, and the skin is peeled free of the skull. The skin is turned inside out, and the spare fat cleared out. The skin is boiled for half an hour (any longer, and the hair would start to fall out) then further fat cleaning occurs, this time using heated stones and hot sand (for the more inaccessible areas). This process is repeated for up to six days, until the skin has shrunk by the required amount.
>
> Some anthropologists have viewed this as an act of triumph – the final humiliation of the enemy – but I do not believe this to be the case.
>
> And why do I not believe it?
>
> Because it is an essential part of the ritual that the eyelids of the dead man be sewn up, so that his soul cannot see out, and his lips likewise fastened together, so that he cannot ask that his death be avenged.

In other words, the whole process should be seen as no more than a defensive act by the killer, who believes that the battle goes on even after death.

But no one will have your head, will they, Grace, I think. Wherever you are, it will still be firmly attached to your shoulders, because your killer doesn't believe in that sort of thing.

# PART SIX
## Saturday 1st November, 1975

# THIRTY

I was wrong to think that I wouldn't sleep last night. I did sleep, but it would have been better – much better – if I hadn't.

As I tossed and turned in my narrow bed, the faces of the now-dead – all of them as pale and unnaturally elongated as the faces in an El Greco painting – floated back and forth across my unconscious mind. They mocked me for my incredible stupidity. They challenged me to do the right thing, when the time came for the right thing to be done. And when I finally awoke, at just after a quarter past eight, the feeling of dread which had cocooned me through that long terrible night still clung to me like a second skin.

I breakfast on a bowl of Rice Krispies, but though they do their best to cheer me up with their usual 'snap, crackle and pop' routine, I stop eating halfway through, run the bowl under the tap, and abandon it in the sink.

I brew myself a strong cup of coffee, and when I take a sip of it, I discover that it tastes like mud.

If only I smoked, I would have something to do with my hands, but I know that in my present state, the tobacco would carry with it the delicate flavour of dried cow dung.

I pace my flat – no mean feat in a flat that size – asking myself what is wrong with me.

No woman in her right mind would have paid that visit to the institute, instead of going to the police and handing the problem over to them, I tell myself.

Any investigator with even half a brain in her head would have pulled out of the whole case while she had the chance.

I am right about that – I know I am right – but I also know that if I was facing the same dilemma again, I would act in exactly the same way.

I check my watch.

Nine o'clock.

Time to go.

\*   \*   \*

It is five days to Bonfire Night, and the air on the street is crisp and clear. On my way to my borrowed car, I pass three small children, standing next to a dummy dressed in a pair of old trousers and a tatty shirt, stuffed with newspaper. Unlike the corpse discovered in the bluebell wood, this figure has a head – a large cabbage to which a grotesque mask has been affixed. This is Guy Fawkes, who once tried to blow up the Houses of Parliament, and has been burned in effigy, across the whole country, every 5th of November since then.

One of the children boldly steps forward, effectively blocking my way.

'Penny for the guy, miss?' he asks.

I smile. As a kid, I too was heavily involved in an extortion racket aimed at raising money to buy fireworks, except that back then, a penny really did mean a penny, which was enough to buy a banger. Now, the fireworks have got more elaborate and more expensive, and when the boy thanks me politely for my fifty pence, it is plain from his lack of excitement that he regards this as no more than a standard contribution.

As I walk towards my borrowed car, I find myself thinking about other people's childhoods.

The young Grace Stockton probably never knew about Bonfire Night, and even if she had, it would have seemed a strange and exotic ritual to a girl brought up amongst river gods and spirits of the forest.

Annie Tobin, I imagine, would never have experienced the joys of Bonfire Night, because that would have involved mixing freely with other children, and thus jeopardizing the hold her mother had over her.

And what about Jane? I know so little about her – even her second name is an unknown, and will probably always remain an unknown – but I suspect that she had an unhappy childhood in which the pleasures of Guy Fawkes Day were reserved for the kids who had parents who loved them.

I drive to Oxford Railway Station, leave my car in the car park, and walk up the main concourse. Given the day I have ahead of me, this might seem to some people like a deliberate diversion – a way of postponing, for the moment, an encounter I am dreading.

It isn't.

I am here searching for the spirit of Jane, in the hope that I can somehow tap into it and purloin for myself a little of her strength.

At the top of the concourse I turn around, and gaze down on the city as she must have gazed down at it, three years ago.

I try to see what lies before me as she must have seen it – with the eyes (and the mind) of a middle-aged woman who had been shut off from normal life since she was a teenager.

Her tentative, monitored expeditions onto Borough High Street might have taken a little of the edge off the shock, I think, but it will still have been a frightening prospect to her.

There will have been so very much to get used to. When she'd been growing up, the roads had been populated by clumsy, clunky cars like the Morris 8 and Austin 10, so the sleek aerodynamic vehicles which were zooming along the Botley Road below her must have seemed like something out of a science fiction magazine. Then there were the shops – no longer dingy little establishments, displaying only the limited stock that wartime rationing allowed, but bright shining temples of unlimited consumption.

And the people! No uniforms in evidence now, as there had been during the war. Instead there were women dressed like fashion models, and girls dressed like tramps (in carefully torn designer jeans). Men had always worn hats before the war, but now they were in a small minority. And just when, she must have wondered, did boys stop wearing short trousers?

Yes, it must all have been both fascinating and frightening. She will have been torn between running away, and lingering to savour this strange and wonderful new reality. But she hadn't done either of these things. Determined to be neither seduced nor frightened off, she had set out on her quest – and I was about to follow in her footsteps.

I drive to the manor, and park by the dolphin fountain. The ancient Greeks admired dolphins, and if Greek mariners saw the creatures following in the wake of their ships, they took it as a sign of good luck. But the dolphins certainly hadn't brought this place much good luck in the last few years, I think, as I climb out of the car and ring the front doorbell.

Derek Stockton answers the door, and I note that he is old-fashioned enough to be wearing a tie, even though he is in the house alone.

Stockton does not look at all pleased to see me, and in case his facial expression is not enough to communicate his feeling, he underlines it with the tone of his voice.

'Look, Miss Redhead,' he says, 'I've tried to be reasonable with you for my daughter's sake, but enough simply has to be enough. Don't you realize how painful it is for me to talk about Grace's death?'

Hypocrite! I think instinctively.

Yet perhaps I'm wrong about that. Grace's death was – I am almost sure – unintended, and the fact that he tried to conceal it does not necessarily mean that he didn't love her.

But whatever his motives – whatever his true feelings – I need to find some way to weaken his resolve if we are to conduct our necessary business.

'"I've tried to be reasonable for my *daughter's* sake!"' I repeat back at him. '"Reasonable for *my* daughter's sake!"'

I'm not exactly taking a leap in the dark here, because Jane's actions that fateful morning three years ago (and Grace's later that same day) would already seem to confirm my theory, but until I see the look of hurt come into Derek Stockton's eyes, I don't know for sure that I'm right.

'I've no idea what you're talking about,' he says.

But he has – and he knows that I know he has.

'I think I'd better come inside, Dr Stockton,' I say.

He sighs. 'Yes, I suppose you better had.'

Last time, he took me to the kitchen with its cosy family atmosphere. This time, he leads me into a much more formal reception room, and indicates I should sit down on one of the leather armchairs.

'Would you like a drink?' he asks once I have done as instructed.

Yes, a voice within me screams, I'll have a double gin and tonic. No, better make that a treble.

'No, thank you,' I hear myself say. 'I think it would be best to get this over with as soon as possible.' I take a deep breath, then continue, 'Killing your wife was an accident, I presume.'

'What!' he exclaims.

'Killing your wife was an accident, I presume,' I repeat.

'What makes you think I killed my wife?' he asks, in a voice which suggests he will not go down without a fight. 'I was in America when she died.'

'No,' I contradict him. 'You were in America when the woman found in the shallow grave was killed.'

'And that was Grace.'

I shake my head. 'No, it wasn't. And you knew as you were identifying her that it wasn't.'

'Let's say for a second that you're right,' he proposes. 'It won't make any difference, because that body has been cremated. So even if it wasn't Grace, you can't prove that now, can you?'

'No, I can't,' I agree, 'but I can certainly make a very strong circumstantial case for it.'

'Then by all means go ahead and try.'

'The person who, until now, was presumed to have killed her, was called Jane. She'd been in a mental institution in Southwark for twenty-seven years. The woman who was disinterred in the bluebell wood was wearing the sapphire blue dress which was the uniform of that institution, and on her wrist she had a hair bracelet which you identified, so the police tell me, as being something that Grace habitually wore.'

'And so she did,' Stockton says.

I shake my head. 'No, she didn't. But I can see why you lied about the bracelet.'

'Can you?'

'Oh yes. It was all part of making a positive identification. You wanted to establish an alibi for yourself, and if this body was Grace's, then you couldn't possibly have killed her, because, as you've already been at pains to point out, you were in Boston at the time she died.' I pause. 'Shall I go on?'

'If it makes you happy.'

'It makes me anything but happy,' I tell him, 'but it still has to be done. The bracelet was Jane's. It's made from the entwined hair of two women who consider themselves to be spiritual sisters or *kimpums*. When one of the *kimpums* dies, the other one burns her bracelet. Grace burned hers, because she thought Jane had died in an explosion in Bombay Terrace back in 1944, but Jane knew Grace wasn't dead, and she wore hers until the end.'

'It's still all just a theory,' he says. 'A theory, furthermore, that has a lot of gaps.'

'Then consider this,' I say. 'Given her background, it would never have occurred to Jane to decapitate Grace, because it's simply not something that girls like her could ever imagine doing. And even if we accept – against all the odds – that that is something she might do, she would have used an axe or a knife, and made a complete hash of it. What she wouldn't have done was recognize that the best weapon for the job – the weapon designed specifically for that purpose – was hanging on the wall in Grace's study. Then, once the bloody deed was done, she'd never have thought to bury the body in the nearby woods – woods that she, as a stranger to the area, didn't even know existed.'

'Is that it?' Stockton asks.

'No,' I tell him. 'On her way here, Jane was photographed by all the cameras on Oxford Station. Why didn't she try to avoid them, considering the fact that she was already on the run?'

'I've no idea.'

'She didn't avoid them when she arrived because she'd been cut off from the world for so long that she had no idea that such things existed. Yet when she supposedly returned to the station, she not only knew that she should avoid the cameras, but she knew exactly where they were located. How did she acquire that knowledge in such a short space of time?'

'I don't know.'

'The answer is that she didn't!'

'Then how do you explain her behaviour?'

'I was puzzled right from the beginning about the timing,' I say. 'There were only four hours between Jane arriving here and her returning to Oxford Station. Given that killing and burying Grace would take her at least two hours, how did she get back to the station so quickly? She didn't take a bus, she didn't call a taxi, and she didn't hitchhike. She might have stolen Grace's car, I suppose . . .'

'Exactly.'

'. . . but she didn't, firstly, because she'd never learned to drive, and secondly because if she had, the police would have found the car at the railway station, not in your garage.'

'So you're saying it wasn't this Jane at all who was picked up by the station cameras?' he asks.

'You know it wasn't. It was *Grace*, wearing Jane's red duffle coat. If there was ever an investigation into Jane's disappearance, Grace wanted it on tape that she had left Oxford again.' I pause, because this really is taking it out of me. 'And finally,' I continue, 'even if we choose to disregard everything I've just said, are we expected to believe that this woman – who had no experience of the world and no resources to draw on – could evade capture for over three years, even after an extensive manhunt during which her image had been flashed all over the television and the newspapers? Of course we can't believe it – because it's impossible!'

'Why would my wife decapitate her?' Stockton asks, tactically shifting his ground.

'Because that's how you have to go about killing your enemies. Once they're dead, you see, you need to have their heads in your possession, since that's the only way you can keep control of their souls.'

'But what was her *motive*?' Stockton persists.

'There was nothing else she *could* do, after Jane confronted her and accused her of stealing her life,' I say.

# THIRTY-ONE

*25th November, 1944*

For once, little Julia had allowed her the privilege of a few hours' sleep, Grace thought, as she dragged her still-tired body out of bed, but now the baby really needed to be fed, even if it meant waking her up.

She knew that something was wrong the moment she lifted Julia from her cot. Her little body seemed both too heavy and too unyielding.

She laid the baby on the table, and felt first for a heartbeat and then for a pulse. She could find neither.

She realized just how cold the baby's skin was, and how her little arms seemed to have no flexibility at all.

She tried to force Julia's mouth open, so that she could breathe a little air into the tiny lungs, but her jaw was locked solid.

The baby was *dead*!

Julia was *dead*!

What would she tell Derek? How could she ever confess to him that she had let him down so badly?

She wanted to run headlong against the wall, crushing the brain which was responsible for these feelings of loss and failure, paying for her sins by baptizing the wall with her blood.

But she didn't.

Instead, she forced herself to calm down, and consider what the proper thing to do was in the circumstances.

The consideration did not take her long. It required her only to draw from the reservoir of ancient Trinka wisdom which was stored deep inside her.

She pulled her suitcase from under the bed, and took out the jar of sacred cream that one of the tribal elders had given to her as a parting gift when she abandoned her home in the rainforest and journeyed overseas. She unscrewed the jar, and, after she had undressed the baby, began to gently rub the ointment on Julia's tiny legs. She worked tenderly and slowly, singing, as she worked, an ancient Trinka chant that she was not even aware she knew. She worked steadily – occasionally stopping to wipe the tears from her eyes – and finally it was done.

Later, she would lay her hands on a boat somehow, and push her darling baby out into the middle of the river. But for the moment, she had no role to play, because it was ordained that the baby be left alone, so it could make its peace with the world it was about to leave.

The hammering on the front door was unexpected and frightening, and Jane's first reaction was to freeze.

Who could it possibly be? her panicked brain screamed.

Apart from Grace and Annie, nobody ever came to visit her.

Nobody!

And both Grace and Annie had their own keys.

The hammering continued.

Bang, bang, bang; bang, bang, bang.

It was growing louder with every knock, but even in her nervous state, she recognized that it didn't sound like the police, because when they came calling, there was something confident and authoritative about the way they announced their presence, whereas this knocking merely sounded desperate.

She wished Grace were there with her, because she would know how to handle this, as she seemed to know how to handle everything. But Grace wasn't there, so it was up to her.

She wondered if she could just sit it out, but she was worried all the noise would wake the baby, and so she rose reluctantly to her feet, forced herself to walk down the hallway, and opened the front door.

The man standing there was around twenty-four or twenty-five. He had a pinched, poverty-lined face, and was wearing a cheap suit which must have looked pretty good the first two or three times he wore it.

'You've had new locks fitted,' he complained.

But she scarcely heard his words.

'Archie,' she said in a voice which was almost a whisper, 'you've come back to me.'

He looked nervously over his shoulder, then pushed past her into the hallway. She followed him into the back room.

'New furniture,' he said.

'It's not new,' she told him. 'It's only second-hand.'

'Still, it's a bloody sight better than what was here before,' he said.

She pointed to the cot standing in the corner. 'Look, Archie, that's your little baby daughter. Her name's Ellen.'

He barely gave the baby a glance. 'Very nice,' he said. 'Listen, Jane, they told me in the pub that you've got a new friend – a posh one.'

She herself had once thought of Grace as posh, but that had been a long time ago, and now it was strange to hear her described in that way.

'She's been very good to me,' she said.

'Yeah,' Archie said. He licked his lips. 'Was it her who bought the new furniture?'

'Yes, it was.'

'And has she given you any money?'

'I don't know what you mean,' Jane told him.

'Bloody hell, girl, I should have thought it was a simple enough question. Has this rich friend of yours given you any money?'

'Yes, but it's not for me, it's for our baby,' Jane said.

'How much is it?'

'I don't know,' Jane said, wishing she'd lied.

'You don't know how much it is?'

'I forget. I haven't counted it recently.'

'But it must be a few quid, then.'

'Yes,' Jane agreed, reluctantly, 'it's a few quid.'

'The thing is, I'm in a bit of trouble with some lads from Mile End Road,' Archie said.

'What do you mean by a bit of trouble?' Jane asked.

'I mean I owe them money. And believe me, you really don't want to owe that particular bunch of lads any money, because they can turn very nasty if you don't pay them back.'

'You're not having the baby's money,' Jane said firmly.

'Come on, girl, it would only be a loan. I'd pay you back as soon as I could,' Archie wheedled.

'No,' Jane said firmly.

'I could make you, you know,' Archie threatened.

'Whatever you do to me, you're not having the money,' Jane said firmly.

For a moment, it looked as if Archie would start hitting her, then he smiled, reached into his pocket, and produced a half-bottle of cheap whisky.

'Let's sit down and have a drink,' he suggested.

'I don't drink,' Jane told him.

He laughed, disbelievingly. 'Come on, girl, I know you – you like a drop of the hard stuff as much as I do.'

'Not anymore. I haven't had a drink for months.'

'Come on,' he cajoled her, 'what's a celebration without a drink?'

'What would we be celebrating?'

'The two of us getting back together again.'

'Do you mean it?' she asked.

'Course I mean it. Why wouldn't I mean it?'

'So you'll stay, and help me to bring up our baby?'

'Nothing could give me greater pleasure.'

She has already crossed him over the matter of the baby's money and seemed to have got away with it, but she knew him well enough to realize how dangerous it would be to cross him a second time.

'All right, then,' she agreed. 'I don't suppose one little drink can do any harm.'

They sat down on the sofa. One little drink soon turned into two, and then three, and four, and less than an hour after Archie had crossed the threshold, the bottle was empty.

'If we are going to start a new life together, I really need that money to pay off my debts,' Archie said.

Jane looked around her. The patterned wallpaper which she and Grace had painstakingly pasted up together was starting to waver, and both floor and ceiling were rolling back and forth, like the waves she had seen on her one childhood visit to the seaside.

She was drunk, she realized – as drunk as she had been when she had offered her body to the customers of the King's Head. But she wasn't drunk enough to give Archie what he wanted.

'It's baby's money, not mine,' she slurred.

The first blow to her face was expected, but she had forgotten how much it could hurt – had forgotten just how vicious Archie could be when he was angry or drunk (and now he was both).

He stood up, to get a better swing at her. His second punch was to her left breast, his third smashed into her stomach.

'Are you going to give me what I want?' he demanded.

'No,' she gasped.

He grabbed her by the shoulder, dragged her off the sofa and threw her onto the floor. As he started to kick her, she instinctively shielded her head with her arms, and twisted into a foetal position.

He kicked her on the spine once, twice, three times, then he stopped and said, 'Have you had enough?'

She'd had more than enough. She had been beaten many times before, but never as viciously and methodically – never as painfully – as this.

'I won't tell you where the money is,' she groaned.

And she was thinking, 'Grace would be proud of me! *I'm proud* of me! I'm proud of what she made me.'

She expected the kicking to start again, but it didn't.

So maybe he saw it was pointless.

Maybe he would just give up and go away.

And to think that just an hour earlier she had stood in the hallway and welcomed him back – had so wanted him to stay. But that had only been because she had slipped back into being the old Jane. The new Jane didn't need him or any other adult. She was strong enough to face whatever life threw at her – as long as she had the baby.

'Right,' Archie said, 'if hitting you hasn't done any good, I'll just have to start on the kid, won't I?'

'You wouldn't,' she moaned.

'Just watch me.'

'It's your own child.'

'That means nothing to me. I don't want to have my face slashed, and I'm willing to do anything to stop that happening.'

'Help me to my feet, and I'll show you where the money's hidden,' she said, defeated.

In later years, Grace would tell herself that she went to Bombay Terrace that day to seek comfort from her *kimpum* – and for no other reason. She would go on to argue that if she hadn't discovered just how terrible conditions were in Jane's house, she would never have acted as she did.

And when that argument no longer convinced her, she would say that it was a good job that she had gone when she had, because by doing so she had saved a life. So maybe it really had nothing to do with her at all – maybe it was what some greater power, beyond her comprehension, had always intended to happen.

But deep down she knew the truth, which was that even if Jane had been being a perfect mother, she herself was driven by so deep a desperation that she would always have acted the way she did.

As Grace opened the front door of Jane's house, a smell hit her which had been absent for months – the stench of cheap alcohol. She should have been distraught, because she had put her heart and soul into keeping her *kimpum* clean, and now it seemed as if it had all been for nothing.

She should have been distraught, but she wasn't – because despite herself, she felt a burst of happiness surge through her body.

She opened the door to the living room. Jane was lying on the sofa, eyes closed, mumbling incoherently to herself. The baby had clearly soiled herself and looked very uncomfortable and unhappy, but when she sensed Grace's presence, she looked up and gurgled.

It didn't seem fair that this baby, who was being so badly neglected, was still alive, while her own baby, who'd had all the care in the world lavished on her, was dead, Grace thought.

She reached into the cot and lifted the baby out. 'Hush, hush, sweet one,' she cooed. 'Hush, my little Julia. I'm your mummy now.'

Jane stirred on the couch, then looked blearily up.

Grace could see now that she'd been pretty badly beaten up, but that didn't sway her an inch, because if Jane had been beaten up, she'd probably done something to deserve it, and that was further evidence that she was not a suitable mother for this baby.

'What are you doing?' Jane slurred.

'It's very stuffy in here. I'm just taking the baby out for a breath of fresh air,' Grace said.

She was doing her best to sound innocent, but there was an edge to her words that warned Jane something was wrong.

Jane struggled to her feet. 'She's . . . she's my baby,' she said. 'If she needs taking outside, I'll take her.'

'Look at yourself,' Grace said, with a contempt that was ugly and self-justifying. 'You're in no state to handle her. You can't even manage to handle yourself.'

'She's my baby. Give her to me,' Jane insisted, lurching forward.

Grace cradled the baby on her right arm.

'I'm afraid you'll drop her,' she said. 'Why don't you sit down again, and then I'll hand her to you.'

'No,' Jane said. 'I want her now.'

She took a shaky step forward, and Grace punched her in the face with her left fist.

Jane tottered. There was a look of deep hurt on her face, but it was more the hurt of betrayal than it was of pain. She made one last attempt to maintain her balance, then toppled over backwards.

Grace looked down at her. She might die there, she thought – but that didn't matter. Only the baby mattered.

She rushed down the hallway, opened the front door, and stepped outside. She knew she had to get away before the madness in her faded and she was forced to recognize her duty to her *kimpum*.

She did not dare run too fast with the baby in her arms, but she made what progress she could, side stepping the rubble which had lain there since the dark days of 1940, choosing a clear path whenever one was available.

She had gone maybe three hundred yards when she heard the sound of the rocket engine. She looked up, and saw the V-1 approaching, then whirled around and saw Jane staggering groggily through the door of the house.

And then, suddenly, the flying bomb was making no noise at all.

When you can't hear it, that means you're as good as dead, she thought in a panic.

She was going to lose two babies in one day! And it wasn't fair!

There was a sudden loud explosion, and she felt the ground beneath her feet vibrate.

She looked back again. Bombay Terrace was enveloped in a huge cloud of dust. The slates from the roofs surfed through the air, like flat stones skimmed across a pond. Chunks of brickwork rose high above house level and then, (as if they were part of some aerial ballet) delicately arced before tumbling back to the ground.

There was no sign of Jane.

Grace clutched the baby tighter to her, and started running again.

# THIRTY-TWO

'How do you know it wasn't Jane's baby who died?' Derek Stockton asks, his voice carrying a hint of desperation which says – more accurately than the actual words ever could – that he is hoping for a miracle that will reverse what he secretly knows to be true. 'Why couldn't that be the baby that Grace pushed out into the river?'

'It wasn't,' I say bluntly – because it would be cruel to sugar the truth.

'You can't know that,' he persists.

'But I can,' I tell him. 'Annie Tobin was standing out on the landing outside Grace's flat that night . . .'

'Who is Annie Tobin?'

'She was Grace's babysitter. She was also, according to a teacher who was there at the time, Grace's favourite pupil, perhaps because Grace could see that she was very vulnerable and really needed a friend. Am I making sense here?'

Derek Stockton nods solemnly. 'Grace was always attracted to waifs and strays.'

'So she was on the landing, and she heard the baby crying,' I recap. 'She'd never heard her cry so loudly before, and she thought that must mean she was in real distress. But it wasn't that at all – the baby she heard was just stronger and older than Grace's baby – because that baby was Jane's.'

'As you said, this Annie Tobin heard all this through a door. It could just have been . . .'

'Grace liked Annie very much,' I say. 'She trusted her. So why did she turn on her? Why did Grace, who was positively spilling over with the milk of human kindness, viciously attack a vulnerable teenager?'

*It was as if . . . as if she really didn't want to be nasty to me, but she had no choice*, Annie had told me.

'She had to force herself to have an argument with Annie, because otherwise she would have had no excuse for refusing to let Annie see the baby for one last time,' I continue.

'Yes, yes, that makes sense,' Stockton says, lowering his head.

It's as if I've suddenly placed a great weight on his shoulders, and I wonder what I could have said to have caused such a reaction.

Then I understand! It's because I've closed off the avenue for miracles – because I've set free the truth he was trying to suppress.

'Grace told you that Julia wasn't yours, but you hoped she'd been lying to you for some strange, twisted reason of her own,' I say. 'Now you see that she wasn't lying at all.'

'That's right,' he admits.

'I think we both need that drink now,' I say, and when he makes a half-hearted attempt to rise from his slumped position, I add, 'don't go troubling yourself, I'll make them.'

I walk over to the drinks cabinet, which is rosewood, and so beautiful and delicate that I am almost envious.

'What can I get you, Dr Stockton?' I ask. 'A glass of whisky?'

'Brandy,' he mumbles.

# THIRTY-THREE

*13th April, 1972*

G race was drafting the article she had promised the *Anthropologist* when she heard the doorbell ring. She frowned, as she wondered who might be responsible for this interruption. The manor's location ensured that there were very few casual visitors – indeed, she couldn't remember the last one.

The doorbell rang again. It was clear that whoever was calling wasn't going to simply give up and go away.

With a sigh, Grace stood up and walked to the front door. When she opened the door, she was surprised to find herself looking at a woman with wild eyes who was wearing a red duffle coat.

'Can I help you?' she asked.

'Where's Ellen?' the woman demanded. 'I want to see my Ellen.'

'I'm sorry,' Grace confessed, 'but I have no idea what you're . . .'

'Don't you know who I am?' the woman demanded.

She did look vaguely familiar, Grace thought. In fact, if she were much skinnier and thirty years younger, she might . . .

It couldn't be!

It simply couldn't be!

'You're not . . . you're not Jane, are you?' Grace gasped.

'Where's my Ellen?' Jane said. 'Where's my baby?'

'I thought you were dead,' Grace said. 'Where have you been since 1944?'

'In a lunatic asylum,' Jane told her bitterly. 'Until the day before yesterday, I didn't even know who I was, but I know now, right enough.'

'Oh, you poor thing,' Grace said.

She sounded just like the old Grace, the good kind Grace who had taken pity on her as she stood outside the King's Head, Jane thought, and she discovered that the hatred which had been building up inside was draining away.

'Oh, you poor thing,' Grace repeated. 'Well, don't just stand there – come inside.'

Grace led Jane to the kitchen, and sat her down at the big wooden table.

'Would you like something to drink?' she asked. 'A glass of wine, perhaps, or a whisky and lemonade?'

'I don't drink,' said Jane, who was experiencing such a jumble of emotions that it almost paralysed her.

'Would you like a glass of water, then?' Grace asked, solicitously.

'Yes, please.'

Grace fetched the water, and Jane took a sip of it.

'I'm wearing my hair bracelet,' she said. 'I've always felt I *had to* wear it, but I didn't know why. Then I saw your picture in the paper, and I understood what it was supposed to mean.' She shook her head, almost in disbelief. 'I don't know why I'm still wearing it now that I remember what happened. It must be because, in spite of everything, I still love you.'

'And I still love you,' Grace said. 'You have to believe me, Jane, if I'd known where you were, I'd have got you out years ago.' She reached across the table and took the other woman's hands. Jane did not resist. 'But now you are out, everything will be wonderful. I've got a lot of money, and I'll look after you. I could buy you a little house in Spain, almost on the beach. Would you like that?'

'I want to see my daughter,' Jane said.

'But what would be the point of that, after all these years? She doesn't even know you exist.'

Jane pulled her hands away.

'I want to see Ellen,' she told Grace. 'I'm going to see her, whatever you say.'

'Have you thought of the damage it might do to her to learn that I'm not her mother?' Grace asked, and an icy edge was creeping into her voice. 'Have you considered how it would destroy my husband if he discovered he's not really her father?'

'I'm sorry for your husband – honestly I am,' Jane said. 'And I realize it will come as a bit of a shock to Ellen—'

'Julia,' Grace interrupted her. 'Her name's Julia.'

'But I'm the one who gave birth to her, and she's entitled to know that I'm her mother.'

Jane had been looking down at the table, as if she were ashamed, but hearing the words she had spoken herself, she felt a growing conviction that she was – beyond question – right.

She raised her head and looked Grace straight in the eye – and what she read there terrified her.

It was like looking into two dark pits of evil – two swirling whirlpools of malevolence.

She's mad! Jane thought, as fear settled icily in the pit of her stomach. I'm supposed to be the lunatic, but it's her! It's her!

Despite this chill in her gut, her hands were sweating.

And her heart?

That was pounding out a frenzied drum solo!

'Is something the matter, dear, dear Jane?' Grace asked, in a voice that hardly seemed human.

'It's . . . it's very hot in here. I have to go outside for a minute or two,' Jane croaked.

'That's a good idea,' the monster sitting opposite her agreed. 'A little fresh air will help you to see things much more clearly. Would you like me to come with you, dear?'

Jane shook her head violently. 'No, no, I'd be much better on my own.'

She rose from the table and stepped into the corridor. And all the time she was listening – more intently than she had ever listened before, it seemed to her – for the sound of Grace getting up to follow her. But there was not even the slightest creak of Grace's chair – not even a hint of it scraping along the floor – and when she reached the front door she was sure that the other woman had not moved.

She opened the front door and stepped out onto the forecourt. Looking around her, first to the left and then to the right, she saw – as she'd known she would – nothing but open fields.

It was at least half a mile to the nearest farm, and though there was nothing to stop her making a run for it, she knew she would never make it all the way.

She walked with an unsteady gait over to the ornamental fountain, and looked up at the three dolphins spouting water into the basin below. They seemed so serene – so at one with the world. It was hard to believe that anything could go wrong with these gentle creatures guarding her.

She trailed her hand in the water. It was cool and it was soothing, and the falling jets created a breeze which caressed her feverish forehead. It was probably because of the sound of the water that she did not hear the door open again, or the footsteps as Grace stealthily approached her.

It was all over in the blink of an eye. One moment, the back of Jane's neck was as white as a swan's, the next a deep red gash ran along it, and the next . . . the next, her head lurched forward, and – realizing there was no longer anything to restrain it – fell like a tossed coin into the fountain.

The trunk, *sans* head, stayed where it was for a second – the victim of inertia – and then the assassin's hands pushed it, and it, too, fell into the fountain.

The bright red blood became somewhat diluted as it spread through the basin, but it was still dark enough to be recognized for what it was when – recycled – it started to gush from the dolphins' mouths.

There were tears in Grace's eyes. She had not wanted to kill Jane. She'd loved Jane. But she had loved Julia more – had denied her affection only in order to protect her, just as she was protecting her now.

And Derek? She owed him *everything*, and if she had had to sacrifice her own life for him, rather than Jane's, she would have done it willingly.

# THIRTY-FOUR

I pour a brandy for Stockton in a large balloon glass, and make myself a strong gin and tonic. I like my G&Ts with lemon and ice, but I don't want to break the spell by going into the kitchen, and so I decide to put up with drinking it warm and citrus-less for once.

I take him his drink, and sit down myself.

'Your turn,' I say.

I am not more specific. I don't need to be.

'I lied when I said that I expected Grace to be there at the airport to pick me up,' he says. 'I knew she wouldn't, because I was deliberately arriving one day earlier than I'd told her I would be.'

'Why would you do that?' I ask.

'I wanted to catch her unawares.'

'Again, why?'

'Just before I left for the United States, I began to notice that Grace was behaving very oddly with Roger Quinn,' he says. 'He's the Professor of Ethics at St Luke's,' he amplifies.

'I know,' I tell him.

'Of course you do. What made it even worse was that Roger was my best friend, so it was a double betrayal.'

'You thought they were having an affair?' I say.

'Yes, I did. I'd catch them just looking at each other – exchanging secret glances. And once, I found them talking very conspiratorially in a corner. They stopped doing it the moment they saw me, but I knew what was going on, all right.'

*'Shortly before she was murdered, Grace and Roger Quinn, Derek's best friend, spent days and days organizing a surprise 55th birthday for Derek – a party which, sadly, never happened,'* Charlie had told me in the Eagle and Child.

'You were wrong,' I tell him.

'I know that now. But the longer I was in America, the more I became convinced it was true. So I flew home earlier, to see if I could catch them at it. I don't know what I'd have done if I had – I'd certainly never have been able to bring myself to hurt either of them – but by then I really wasn't thinking straight at all.'

'What did you find when you got home?'

'Grace was in the kitchen, working on something on the table, and from where I was standing, by the back door, it looked to me like a Halloween mask. Then she saw me there. "What are you doing here?" she said, but I didn't reply – I *couldn't* reply because now I understood what exactly it was, and there were simply no words to express the horror I was experiencing.'

I feel for him.

I really do.

I feel for *all of them.*

'Tell me the rest,' I say gently.

He does. The words pour out of his mouth in a torrent of passion. His eyes, swollen with sorrow, become a screen on which I can almost see the whole tragic scene being played out.

*'What are you doing here?' Grace asks.*

*And then, before he can collect himself enough to answer, she rushes across to him, and grabs him tightly by the lapels of his jacket.*

*'I killed her and buried her body in the bluebell wood,' she says – and she is sobbing now. 'I had to kill her. She left me no choice.'*

*'What do you mean?' he gasps.*

*She is still holding on to him tightly, and he doesn't know if it is begging or threatening.*

*Maybe it is both.*

*'If I'd let her live, she would have told Julia the truth,' she moans.*

*'What truth?' he asks. 'I don't know what you're talking about.'*

*She releases her grip on him, and takes a few steps backwards.*

*'I'm so very, very sorry,' she says.*

*'That's a start,' he says, clutching at the first straw to float his way.*

*'What is?' she asks.*

*'That you're sorry that you killed her.'*

*'Oh that,' she says dismissively. 'That doesn't matter. I'm sorry that I failed you as a wife.'*

*And insanely – with the shrunken head lying on the table only feet away from him – he wants to reassure her that she hasn't failed him at all, that she's what's given meaning to his life.*

*But before he can say this, she speaks again. 'Julia isn't our child' – she points to the shrunken head – 'she's hers.'*

*He can't comprehend what she's saying. He . . . just . . . can't . . . comprehend.*

*'But you were pregnant,' he says. 'You gave birth. I know you did. I've seen the birth certificate.'*

*'Our child died,' she tells him. 'I woke up one morning, and she was gone.'*

*'But where is she . . . where is she buried?'*

*'She isn't buried at all – I pushed her out onto the river on a burning boat.'*

'I think that's when I lost it,' Derek Stockton says to me. 'The other Julia – the dead Julia – had been my child, and Grace had denied her a Christian burial. How could she?'

'What happened next?' I ask.

'I told her I was leaving her,' he says.

*He exits the kitchen, crosses the living room, and heads towards the bedroom they have shared for thirty years.*

*She scuttles behind him. 'Why are you going to the bedroom?'*

*'To pack some clothes.'*

*'But I don't see why . . .'*

*'I'm leaving you, Grace.'*

*'You can't leave me!' she screams.*

*But he is already laying out shirts on the bed.*

*'I won't tell the police what you've done, but you have to,' he says.*

*'Why are you leaving?' she asks, as if she hasn't heard him.*

*'Don't you know?' he says, but he can tell from the puzzled look on her face that she probably doesn't, so he adds, 'You killed a woman,'*

*'But I've explained to you why I had to do that.'*

*'And you denied my poor dead baby the blessing of Almighty God.'*

*'Why should it matter if she joined the Trinka spirits instead of going to a Christian heaven?'*

*He says nothing, because he can't trust himself to reply.*

*'You can't leave me,' she sobs. 'I won't let you leave me! My life is nothing if you're gone. It's better that we both die.'*

*'I'm going,' he says firmly.*

*And that's when he sees the knife in her hand.*

Neither of them had handled it well, I think, but that was because they both held deep-seated beliefs, and – not for the first time – I thank God I'm an atheist.

'I only meant to disarm her,' Derek Stockton tells me, 'but I was a commando in the war, and we were trained to never give our opponents a second chance.'

'So your instincts took over, and before you knew what was happening, she was lying dead on the floor?'

'Yes.'

'You quickly worked out that if your wife went missing, the police would immediately suspect you,' I say.

'Yes.'

'But if she'd been murdered while you were in America, you couldn't be held responsible for it. Your biggest problem was that if the police learned you'd come back unexpectedly early, they'd start wondering why you hadn't informed your wife. And that would lead them to suspect that the reason you hadn't rung was that it would have been pointless – because you knew she was already dead. And it's only a small step from that to deducing that you'd hired the killer. In other words, they'd have reached the right conclusion – that you'd killed your wife – but by using the totally wrong logic.'

'No tragedy is ever without its irony,' he says sadly.

'So what you needed to do was to leave a message on the answerphone which told your wife of your change of plans. Where did you make that call from, by the way?'

'There's a public telephone box in the village. I drove to it, made the call, then returned home and rang the police.'

'But before you made that phone call, you rubbed out the last message on the answering machine, didn't you?' I ask.

'Yes,' he admits.

He'd had no choice about that, because the machine recorded the messages in the order they were received, and he couldn't leave one saying he was calling on Friday when there was already a message from Geoffrey Markham in which he must have said something like, 'Grace, it's Saturday morning, and you still haven't got back to me.'

It was a risk erasing the message, of course, but it was not a big one, as was demonstrated by the fact that the police didn't even notice it. And even when super PI Jennie Redhead spotted the discrepancy, I had no idea what it meant – and certainly didn't connect it to Derek Stockton – until I'd collected all the other evidence.

'Where did you hide Grace's body while the police were here?' I ask him.

'If you stop to think about it, you'll realize you already know,' he replies.

And he's quite right. The moment I put my mind to it, I do know.

'It was in the priest hole, wasn't it?' I ask him.

'Yes, it was.'

My sudden wave of anger takes me completely by surprise.

'Why did you show *me* the priest hole the first time I was here?' I demand. 'Did it give you some sort of sick kick to see me looking at it and never realizing what it had been used for? Did you congratulate yourself on having made a complete fool of me?'

'No,' he says, 'it wasn't like that at all.'

'Then why did you do it?'

'I don't know,' he admits sadly. 'Maybe I thought it would give you some clue as to what had happened. Maybe I wanted to get caught – I believe many murderers do.'

'And now you have been caught,' I say.

'Yes,' he agrees, 'now I have been caught.'

'What did you do with the body?'

'I took her onto Dartmoor – it's a place we often went hiking, and I knew she loved it. I couldn't leave a marker to show where the grave was, but I did the best that I could, burying her in accordance with Christian rites and practices.'

She wouldn't have wanted that, I thought. She would have liked to go in a burning boat. But there's no point in telling him that.

Besides, I don't want to rob him of what little comfort he has left.

'What happened to Jane's head?' I ask.

'I buried it with Grace's body,' he tells me.

'Why?'

'It's what she would have wanted. She needed the head close to her to protect her.'

It made absolutely no sense, of course. He had buried Grace's body in accordance with *his* beliefs, yet had buried Jane's head in accordance with *Grace's*. It was nothing less than an extreme form of cultural and religious schizophrenia, but I suppose that was only be expected from a man who had just killed the woman he loved.

'By the time you got back from Boston, Grace had already buried Jane in the Bluebell Wood,' I say, 'yet you were able to tell DS Hobson the colour of the dress Jane was wearing. How could you know it?'

'Oh, that,' he says, as if it's of no consequence, which I suppose – my curiosity aside – it isn't. 'I found a swatch of the dress next to the head. It must have been a part of the ritual.'

Ah, yes – I remember now that the police puzzled over why a piece of the dress was missing.

'It's entirely my fault that she died,' Derek Stockton says, and to my surprise – again – I feel the need to defend him.

'How is it your fault?' I ask. 'She was the one who attacked you. You'd never have killed her if she hadn't come at you with a knife.'

'But she shouldn't have needed to come at me with a knife,' he says. 'I profess to be a Christian. I should have forgiven her for the hurt she'd done to me, and persuaded her to accept responsibility for the hurt done to others.'

But you haven't exactly been quick to accept responsibility for what *you've* done, have you, I reflect silently.

'You think I should have given myself up the moment I killed her, don't you?' he asks, reading my mind.

'Well, yes,' I agree.

'You think I've played this whole elaborate game to avoid having to go to prison.'

'That's the logical inference. Is it wrong?'

'Yes, it is.'

'Then what's right?'

'I love my daughter, Julia,' Derek Stockton says. 'I'm not talking about the Julia who died – who I didn't even know existed until three years ago – though I do love her and mourn for her every day. I'm talking about the other Julia, who I've believed to be my daughter for over thirty years.'

'Understood,' I say.

'Since she's your client, you must have seen for yourself what an effect her mother's murder has had on her. How do you think she would feel if she learned that her real mother had been murdered by the woman she only thought was her mother, and that the man she thought was her father had killed the woman she thought was her mother.' He pauses. 'No, not the man she *thought* was her father,' he says, defiantly. 'I *am* her father.'

'I know you are,' I agree.

'I couldn't put her through it. I simply couldn't. I wanted to confess – wanted it so badly, because there can be no healing without confession, but for Julia's sake I decided that I would postpone the punishment I so richly deserve, until such time as I am judged by Almighty God.'

'I have no choice but to report this to the police, even if it does mean that Julia learns the truth,' I say softly. 'I wish there was some other way, but there simply isn't.'

'I could stop you, you know,' he says. There is a sudden hard edge to his voice, and his body has tensed as if ready to attack. I realize that in his mind he is back in the war – prepared to kill not because he wants to, but because he considers it necessary. 'I could decide that in order to save my daughter's life, I might have to rob you of yours.'

My heart is beating faster – it would be a miracle if it wasn't – but the truth is, I'm not the least bit frightened.

'Even though I'm trained in unarmed combat too, and I'm much younger than you, there's a good chance you could kill me if you really put your mind to it,' I say. 'But I'm as sure as I've ever been of anything that you won't even try.'

'How can you be so sure?' he asks.

'Because it isn't what Jesus would do. This is your Gethsemane moment – the moment when you're given the opportunity to show real courage.'

His body relaxes.

'You're right,' he says, 'I could never have done it.' He pauses. 'Would you just wait twenty-four hours before you turn me in, Miss Redhead?' he pleads.

'What good will that do?'

'It will give me time to prepare Julia for the future she will have to face alone. Just one day. That's all I need. I promise you, I won't make a run for it.'

I know he won't. What would be the point in running when he'd always be there, wherever he went?

He sees me to the door, and stands by the dolphin fountain as I drive away. Looking in my rear-view mirror, I see he has even managed a small, sad smile and half-hearted wave.

I can't condemn him, any more than I can condemn Grace. They are both victims of circumstances who have tried to do the best they can. He should never have fallen in love with her, and she should never have left the rainforest, which was her natural moral universe.

I reach the end of the track, and get out of the car to open the gate, drive the car through, and close the gate behind me.

I will never see Dr Derek Stockton again, I think. Nobody will. He has found the one course that will protect his daughter from the truth, and he is probably even now following it.

# PART SEVEN
## 23rd December, 1975

# THIRTY-FIVE

Bright flickering lights are festooned across the street, and rough-and-ready Christmas tree sellers (Christmas tree rustlers?) lurk on street corners, keeping one eye open for potential customers and the other for the police. Countless people bustle in and out of shops, carrying bags crammed with gifts with which they hope to enchant their loved ones the day after tomorrow. Yes, the Christmas spirit is in the air, and even the drunks around the Carfax Tower seem more festively paralytic than usual.

The students have gone – the poorer ones to earn a little cash by working as relief Christmas postmen, the more prosperous to luxuriate in the home comforts which their rooms in the ancient colleges lack. The dons and professors have gone off with their families – some sunning themselves on Caribbean islands, others racing down the ski slopes in France or Switzerland. And the tourists are gone, because this is the time of year to abandon the wanderlust and return to your own hearth. Even Charlie has gone, back to Wiltshire where, as lord of the manor, he will act as a sort of baronial Santa Claus for his tenant farmers and their families.

I, on the other hand, am still here. I have turned down Charlie's offer to accompany him to his ancestral home. I have also resisted suggestions from my mother (half-heartedly made, at best) that I should spend Christmas with her, so no doubt she will instead spend it with my cousin Enid, a parochial narrow-minded pea from the same pod.

I am standing in front of the St Thomas Aquinas Catholic church. I have been watching it for well over an hour, and so far, I'm pleased to report, it hasn't moved an inch.

I'm not really here to *watch* the church at all – what I'm actually doing is trying to pluck up the courage to go inside.

In the end, it is not my strength of character that forces me into the church – it is the cold. I push the heavy wooden door open, and it creaks in protest.

Surely, if God really was as omnipotent as they say, He'd keep it oiled, I think.

Stop it, Jennie, I tell myself. Stop trying to be a smart arse. Stop trying to turn the whole thing into a joke. You're here for a serious purpose.

And so I am, but it's not proving very easy. I'm uncomfortable enough in Protestant churches (God knows!), but Catholic churches – where the air is thick with incense, and the walls are hung with harrowingly anatomical crucifixions – really give me the creeps. Still, I force myself to walk down the aisle, and park my backside on a bench close to the confessional.

There is no queue, for which I am grateful, but I hear a low female mumble from inside the box, which indicates that some woman is already in there, baring her soul.

I used to think that time dragged while waiting for the pub to open its doors, but compared to this wait, it now seems to have positively flown by.

How *do* you fill the time if you're not all wrapped up in holy contemplation? I don't know.

Once or twice, I catch myself drumming my fingers on the bench, and immediately close my hands into fists, as if I were expecting a punch up.

Finally, an old woman in black leaves the confessional, and I quickly take her place.

'Look,' I say without preamble, 'I'm not here for myself. I want to make an appeal on someone else's behalf.'

'That's not so much unorthodox as truly bizarre,' says the voice from the other side of the grill.

I congratulate myself on choosing Father O'Brien for this encounter. Although I'm no expert on priests, I imagine that most of them would have been completely knocked off balance by my opening remark, but O'Brien – that famed swigger of Guinness – has taken it in his stride.

'Well, let's hear it, then,' he says.

'The person in question has committed suicide, which I understand is a mortal sin, for which he could burn in hellfire for all eternity unless he is forgiven,' I say. 'And the problem is, he can't ask for forgiveness now he's dead, so I was hoping you could intercede for him.'

'Anonymously?' Father O'Brien asks.

'Well, yes,' I agree, realizing as I speak how foolish that sounds.

'So I'm supposed to say something like, "Dear God, please forgive this man, Mr X, who I know absolutely nothing about." Is that it?'

I search around for a suitable response – and suddenly, I have it!

'God will know who you're talking about!' I say, triumphantly. 'He knows everything.'

'Clever,' he admits. 'But perhaps there's no need to call him Mr X. After all, we are talking about Derek Stockton, aren't we?'

'How did you know that?' I ask, before I can stop myself.

'There haven't been many suicides round here recently, so I don't really need to be a *detective* to work out who you're talking about.'

I don't like the emphasis he puts on the word 'detective' at all.

'All right, it's Dr Stockton,' I admit.

'The Church's teachings on suicide are not as black and white as you seem to think they are,' he tells me. 'Grave psychological disturbance can diminish the suicide's responsibility for the act. In addition, God provides the opportunity for salutary repentance in ways known only to Him. And the Church will always pray for suicides as a matter of course.'

'Thank you,' I say.

'What puzzles me is why you're here asking me to forgive Derek,' Father O'Brien says. 'I thought you were supposed to be an atheist, Jennie.'

'You called me Jennie!' I say.

'It's your name, isn't it?'

'Yes, but I thought this was supposed to be anonymous.'

Father O'Brien laughs. 'Oh, that old chestnut,' he says. 'A priest would have to be blind and deaf – and probably stupid – not to recognize the person on the other side of the grill, and we've certainly drunk together often enough for me to know your voice when I hear it. But you still haven't answered my question – why are you asking for forgiveness when you don't believe in it?'

'I don't really know,' I confess. 'Maybe it's because *he* believed in it. Maybe it's a question of backing all the horses in the race, just to make sure you have a winner.'

Maybe, even, it's because I'm only copying Derek Stockton, who didn't accept Trinka beliefs himself, but still buried Jane's head with Grace's body. Yes, maybe that is it – though even under the seal of the confessional, I don't feel able to tell Father Jim that.

And finally, maybe it's because I feel complicit in the suicide – since I knew what he was going to do, and I did nothing to stop him.

I go back to my office, but not in the hope that there will be a line of clients so long it reaches down the stairs, each one eagerly waiting to engage my services. That will definitely not happen, because between Christmas and the New Year, people's crises, questions and unresolved problems seem to be put on hold in favour of mince pies, crackers and family rows.

No, the reason I return to the office is because, having talked to Father O'Brien, I have decided I have a little tidying up to do. Specifically, since the truth that I've uncovered in my investigation cannot be revealed to the wider world without making Derek Stockton's sacrifice totally pointless, I need to set about destroying what notes I have on the case.

Most detectives, I suppose, would do this by feeding the notes into their shredder, but I can't afford a shredder. Instead, I set the notes on fire, page by page, and hold them over the metal waste-paper basket until everything but one corner is burnt, at which point (to spare my fingers) I let go of them, and watch the burning remnants glide into the bin. There is no danger of this setting off the smoke alarm – I can't afford one of those, either – but it is a time-consuming process.

It is a depressing process, too, since what I am destroying is the history of three people – none of them wicked – who tried to do their best, but were betrayed by their own weaknesses.

Once the task is completed, I step out onto the landing, because – to be honest – my office feels a little smoky, and while I am there, I hear the letter box click open, and the last post before Christmas land with a dull thud on the doormat.

I go down the stairs to the hallway. I know most of the mail will be for the merchandizer of erotic goods on the ground floor, but it is worth checking anyway.

It's always possible, I tell myself, that my fame has reached the ear of some jet-setting millionaire who has misplaced his grandson, and wants me to find him. Unfortunately, the work will involve a great deal of travel to exotic places (such a trial!) the letter will say, but in some attempt to compensate me for such inconvenience, the millionaire is prepared to pay me a fabulous fee and ensure I am only lodged in the very best hotels.

There is no such letter – surprise, surprise – but there is a postcard. On the front, there is the picture of a vast sandy beach, bathed in brilliant sunshine, on which any number of happy people frolic without a care in the world.

On the back, there is a message. It reads:

> Having a great time on this cruise. It's only the second day,
> but I've already met tons of fascinating people (men!)
> Thank you so much!
>     Annie Tobin

In the film *Casablanca*, Rick says, 'It doesn't take much to see that the problems of three little people don't amount to a hill of beans in this crazy world.'

And maybe the newly found happiness of one little person doesn't matter either, but it's enough to make me feel good about myself – at least for a while.

9 781780 297163